lucky
BALLER

NEW YORK TIMES BESTSELLING AUTHOR

KAYLEE RYAN

Previously published under the title, *"Lucky Bastard"* as a part of the Cocky Hero Club World.

Editor: Hot Tree Editing
Proofreading by: Virginia Tesi Carey, Deaton Author Services, & The Ryter's Proof
Photo Credit: Wander Aguiar
Model: Pat Tanski
Cover Design: Perfect Pear Creative Covers
Paperback Formatting: Champagne Book Design

lucky
BALLER

CHAPTER 1

Tessa

"I FEEL LIKE I'M CHEATING." LOOKING OVER AT MY BEST FRIEND, Autumn, I catch her smile and roll her eyes.

"Really, Tess?" She chuckles, bouncing her son, JJ, on her hip.

"What? I can't help it. I'm a Miami Mavericks fan for life."

"I know, so does everyone else here. I can't believe you wore a Mavericks T-shirt to the Cougars training camp."

"I'm here for moral support." I reach out and tickle JJ's side, making him laugh. "What kind of best friend would I be if I let you come to this on your own? Besides, you know nothing about the game. Someone has to explain it to you."

"All I need to know is that my husband is the new kicking coach, and with that comes my loyalty, and this little guy's." She smiles at her son.

"I admit, it's a good move on the Cougars' part in hiring the legendary

Jeremy Baldwin as their new kicking coach. Their kicking game needed some work."

"Right?" She laughs. "We can't live off him selling ass photographs forever. We all know my salary at the shelter isn't going to pay for our new house."

"I don't know," I tease, tapping my finger against my chin. "His ass is legendary."

"Stop." She pushes her shoulder into mine. "Don't let him hear you talking like that. His ego is big enough as it is."

I nod. She's right about that. Jeremy is confident, and yes, a little cocky. However, when it comes to his wife and son, he keeps it in check. They're his entire world, and he doesn't care who knows it. In fact, I think he enjoys showing them off to the world. Hence the reason we're here for training camp. It's family day and not open to the public.

"He has earned his nickname," I agree, returning my attention to the field. "You know, I might be a die-hard Mavericks fan, but I can still appreciate a man in football pants." My eyes take in the players on the field, and I come to the conclusion that football pants are a girl's best friend. Just saying.

"I'm not sure I ever realized the appeal until now, but, my friend, I think you're on to something," Autumn agrees.

"Hey, princess," Jeremy says, greeting his wife. We're standing on the sidelines. Since it's family day, it's pretty much open. "Come here, little man." Jeremy reaches for JJ, who happily holds his arms open for his daddy. "You ladies need anything?" he asks.

I'm tempted to tell him one of his players, but I bite my tongue. I talk a good game, but random hookups aren't my thing. Don't get me wrong, I commend those who can have sex with a stranger and walk away the next morning, satisfied, and never look back. I'm just not wired that way.

"We're all set," Autumn replies.

"I'm going to take him out on the field with me. Introduce him to some of the guys. Practice is almost over, then I'll introduce you." He leans in and presses his lips to her before walking away with JJ.

"You know," I muse, "if you weren't my best friend, I might be a little jealous of you."

"What?" She turns to look at me. "Why would you be jealous of me? I have unidentified bodily fluids on me from my son at all times, a husband who's cocky as hell and thinks he knows it all, and a mortgage for a house on Matthew Street that cuts into JJ's college fund."

"Oh, stop. You're living the dream and you know it."

"I'm not sure if it's *the* dream, but my dream, yes. I love the life Jeremy and I are building."

"Hence the jealousy."

"You'll find your happily ever after," she assures me, putting her arm around my shoulders. "He's everything I never knew I wanted."

"He's so good with him." I motion toward the field where Jeremy has JJ on his shoulders while he's talking to one of the players, and JJ, well, he's all smiles. At two, he has no idea the depth of where he is. Most kids never get to experience a professional football game, let alone be on the field with the players and coaching staff.

The whistle blows, and the players start motioning for the families to join them on the field. Autumn and I head toward Jeremy and JJ.

"Thomas Bourgeois, this is my wife, Autumn, and her best friend, Tessa. Princess, Tessa, Thomas is our starting kicker." Jeremy makes introductions.

"Ladies," Thomas says, giving us a charming smile. He glances at my chest, and I can't help but smirk. "Looks like we need to get you some Cougars gear." He winks.

"Nah, I'm good." I give Thomas, or number two, a smug smile.

He throws his hands to his chest over his heart as if he's wounded. "Come on now, don't be like that," he tosses out with a grin. I give him a look that tells him I'm not buying what he's selling. He throws his head back in laughter and stumbles back a step, bumping into a teammate.

"What's up, Bourgeois?" the very tall, very sexy number eighteen asks.

"This one." He points at me.

I feel my body heat as number eighteen rakes his eyes over me. Slowly, they catalog every inch of me. Finally, his eyes scan back to my chest and freeze there. "We need to do something about that." He nods to my chest.

It's a good thing I'm a solid C cup or I'd be offended they were talking about my actual chest size. However, I know it's the Miami Mavericks logo that sprawls across my chest that's offending them. "Eyes up here."

He smirks. "You'd look good in a number eighteen Cougars jersey. I can help you out of that one."

"Excuse me?"

"I said I can help you out with that. A Cougars jersey." He points to my chest.

"Bless your heart," I say, making my voice sugary sweet. "I'm sorry, but I'm a Mavs girl." I shrug, not taking my eyes off his. His eyes are the deepest sky blue. You know those tropical vacation videos you see on social media, the ones that promise relaxation and free drinks? His eyes look like the water in those videos. Vibrant blue.

"Oh, no, no, no, this won't do," he says, crossing his arms over his chest, planting his feet on the turf.

His arms are thick and toned with muscle, and he has those veins… You know, the sexy veins in a man's arms? The ones that tell you that he works hard at what he does, whether it's his job or in the gym? In this case, I'm sure it's both. I mean, he plays for the professional football league. He didn't get here by pure luck. I allow myself to indulge and take in this beautiful man before me.

"Like what you see?" he asks.

Thomas mutters, "Lucky bastard," at the same time.

"Actually, I was just sizing you up. Comparing you to number eight on the Mavs. You do know who A.J. Holland is, right?"

"Pfft," he scoffs. "I know A.J., but I promise you, sweetheart, I can make you feel better than him."

"What?" I stand a little taller. I should be offended, but if I'm honest with myself, I'm a little turned on.

"I said, I'm better than him." He grins.

I don't know if my mind and body are playing tricks on me, but damn, if this isn't the second time in a matter of minutes I've taken his words as a sexual innuendo. I need to squash this shit.

"Oh, that's cute. I'm sure one day you might get to his level," I fire back. There, back on a level playing field. However, the grin that tilts his lips and the dimple that peeks out from under his beard tell me my words don't affect him. *Damn it.*

He turns to look at Thomas. "She yours, Bourgeois?"

"Mine, actually," Jeremy speaks up. "Landon, this is my son JJ, my wife, Autumn, and her best friend, Tessa. They're mine," Jeremy announces with no room for discussion.

Once again, I'm reminded how lucky my best friend is—to have a man like Jeremy to navigate life with. He loves her and their son unconditionally. And because Autumn is my best friend, I get grouped with them. He's a good man, regardless of his cockiness at times.

Landon Barker raises his hands in the air, his number eighteen practice jersey rising to show the V where his gym shorts hang low. He might be a cocky player, but if he kept his mouth shut, he'd definitely be one to keep around to look at. Damn, I can't imagine the countless hours he has to spend in the gym and on the field to be ripped like that.

As if he can read my mind, he rips his practice jersey and the compression shirt he had on underneath over his head and wipes down his face. I tune out the conversation around me as I take him in. My eyes roam over his muscular chest as I work my way down to his abs. I count silently in my head. Eight. I lick my lips as I imagine what it would be like to run my hands over them, maybe trace them with my tongue.

"Hey." Autumn bumps her shoulder into mine, pulling me out of my fog where it was just me and number eighteen's abs.

"Sorry." I turn to face her.

"The food's set up. We're going to head over and eat." She points over my shoulder where, sure enough, the catering staff has brought an array of picnic-type foods to several tables on the field.

"Definitely." My eyes dance back to Landon, where I find him watching me. "I'm suddenly starving." I lick my lips for emphasis before turning back to Autumn. "Let me take JJ while you and Jeremy make your plates, then I'll make mine."

"Are you sure?"

"Positive." I reach my arms toward Jeremy to take JJ from him, and he practically jumps into my arms, laughing when I snuggle him close, then settle him on my hip. Having JJ in my arms will keep Landon at bay. At least, that's the hope. Not that I wouldn't have offered all the same, but it's an added bonus that he's now our buffer.

Jeremy and Autumn walk toward the tables, and I stare after them. "Did you have fun today?" I ask JJ.

"Daddy." He points to where Jeremy and Autumn are filling their plates.

"Look." I point up to the Jumbotron that has Jeremy's smiling mug on display, trying to distract him. He's daddy's boy through and through. Slowly, each member of the coaching staff gets their turn before it moves on to the players. Of course, the first player would be their starting quarterback, Landon Barker. His dark hair, those ocean blue eyes, and his cocky smirk are enlarged on the screen. I stare at him and take in his features. The hint of his dimple winking through his beard and the sparkle in his eyes. "Lucky Bastard," I mumble under my breath. He was born with good genes that I'm sure has panties dropping all over Los Angeles—hell, all over the world if I'm honest.

"Maybe you should pull out your phone and take a picture," a deep voice rumbles from over my shoulder. His hot breath dances across my skin.

Turning my head, I see Landon. "Nah, just comparing your stats to Holland's. You've got some work to do." I have no idea if what I just said is true. I love football, but I'm not one of those keep-all-the-stats kind of football fan. I'm more of a kick back, drink a beer, eat some wings, and yell at the TV kind of girl. Oh, and don't forget the pants. I like to think of myself as a connoisseur of football pants. Not just the pants, but the asses that fill them. Trust me, ladies, if this is not something you've witnessed, tune in on Sunday afternoon and see for yourself. I promise that you won't be disappointed.

"You're something else, you know that?" There's a smile playing on his lips, and part of me feels relieved I haven't offended him, and the other part is irritated that I didn't. It doesn't make any sense, and I can't believe I'm letting him have this kind of effect on me. "Why don't—" he starts, but I step away from him when Autumn turns to wave at me.

I don't stick around for whatever lewd comment I'm sure would have come out of his mouth. I'm not here to take part in a sparring match with the sexy quarterback. No, I'm here to support Jeremy and be the sidekick to my best friend. That's where my priorities lie today. One step after another, my feet carry me to Jeremy and Autumn.

"You hungry?" Autumn asks JJ as I set him in the chair beside her.

He doesn't answer her but reaches for a piece of fruit from the plate she placed in front of him. "I'm going to go grab a plate. You guys need anything?"

"Maybe a few extra napkins." Jeremy chuckles as he watches his son shove another handful of sticky fruit into his mouth.

"Got it." Making my way to the tables filled with food, I'm impressed.

I may be a Mavericks fan, but the Cougars obviously know how to go all out. Today has been fun. To see how the other side lives, bumping elbows with professional football players and their families. Sure, they're not my team, but I can accept this day for what it is, which is a once-in-a-lifetime experience.

"You know…" A deep, sexy voice appears beside me. "If I didn't know any better, I'd think you were trying to avoid me."

"Look at you, hitting the nail on the head," I say, dismissing him as I fill my plate. I'm not trying to be a bitch, not really. I just know what these guys are like. I see them in the tabloids with a different woman on their arm each time. I know they're just living their best lives—a new woman to fill their bed in every city. I'm not judging. To each their own and all that. It's just not me. I'm not about that. I don't do casual, even for the sexy football god that is Landon Barker.

"Right," he sniggers. "Look. I'm here for three more weeks, but maybe once training camp is over, we can have dinner."

"Dinner? Is that what all the cool kids are calling it these days?"

He smirks.

Fucking dimple.

"No, thanks."

"Come on, sweetheart, don't leave me hanging."

"First of all, my name is Tessa, and second, I don't date players." Not just football players, but men in general who look at dating as a sport. I'm not interested in all that or the STDs that come with it.

"Tessa." His voice is deep and husky, and it sends a shiver through me. My body needs to get on board with the no-players thing.

I take my time as I finish filling my plate and grab a large stack of napkins before I turn to face him. He has the same pose as earlier—legs spread apart, arms folded across his chest, and all the sexiness that he is on full display. "Go out with me."

"Thank you, but no." With that, I turn and walk away. There is a very big part of me that wants to turn around and yell "SIKE" and ask him when and where, but as I get closer to the table where my friends are sitting, I remember why I don't. Jeremy has JJ on his lap, and his head is bent as he places a kiss on Autumn's shoulder. I want what they have, and dating the sexy Landon Barker isn't going to get me any closer. I'm not naïve enough to think I can change him. A tiger doesn't change its stripes, and that's fine; I'm good with that. I just can't bend my will and date him when I know it's not going to go anywhere.

Taking my seat next to Autumn, I pass her the extra napkins. I focus on my food and my friends and try like hell to ignore my body's reaction to Landon. I ignore the way I have to wiggle in my seat to ward off the desire that my body craves. I won't deny he would be fun. Hell, I'm not even sure that fun describes what it would be like to be with Landon Barker. More like an out-of-body experience, and I'm sure it would be a moment I would never forget, but I also know me, and sex leads to feelings… and that would be tragic. As if my eyes are connected to him, they seek him out. I find him standing about fifteen feet away, laughing and cutting up with a few of the players, without a care in the world. He obviously isn't having the same struggle I am. He's not warring with himself over my rejection. He's not trying to cool his body's reaction to me.

Lucky Baller.

CHAPTER 2

Landon

IT'S BEEN A LONG THREE WEEKS OF CAMP, BUT WE'RE READY. Both rookies and veterans are on point, and I can feel it. This is going to be another great season. The final whistle blows, and a collective cheer goes up among us. Mostly because we're ready to get to our own beds, and for those who are married and have kids, home to their families. Me? I'm looking forward to my bed. It's pillow-soft and exactly what I would imagine it feels like to sleep on clouds, and it's calling my name. But first… "Baldwin, wait up," I call to our new kicking coach, Jeremy Baldwin.

He stops and turns to look for whoever happens to be calling his name. I jog up to him and grin. "Can I ask for a favor?" I've been thinking nonstop about Tessa, and it kind of pisses me off. No other woman has managed to keep me on the hook this long. Then again, I've been tied up at training camp. It might also have a little something to do with the fact that she turned me down. Cold. That's never happened to me. Not that I can remember. It's also a little her. She's a fucking knockout. Long, dark curly locks and green eyes I could get lost in. That's if I let myself. I can imagine the way they would heat as I pushed inside her. I shift my stance, my cock already on board with my imagination.

"Depends," he says with a laugh.

"Tessa," I say, throwing her name out there.

"What about her?" he asks, standing taller and squaring his shoulders.

"Can I get her number?"

"Did you ask her for it?"

"Yeah, she shot me down."

A slow grin tilts his lips. "Did she now?"

"Laugh it up," I say with a grin of my own. "Come on, Coach," I urge him.

"Look, Landon, you seem like a good guy. Tessa is my wife's best friend and a close friend of mine, as well. I'm not just going to hand her number over. You want her, you have to work for her." He stares me down, begging me to argue with him.

"How do you expect me to do that? I don't even know her last name. The only connection I have to her is you." I'm well aware I'm starting to sound desperate and, in a way, I am. I can't break my perfect record. She can't be the first woman to ever turn me down. That just won't do.

"Fine, I'll throw you a bone. Her name is Tessa Deaton." He slides his hands into the pockets of his shorts, and the bastard full-on grins at me. He's enjoying this way too much.

"Guy code and all that. Come on, man. You have to give me more than that."

"I don't have to do anything but love my wife and son. Well, and pay taxes." I give him a pleading look, and he sighs. "Fine, she works with my wife at the Safe Haven Animal Shelter. That's all you're getting, so don't ask for more from me. And"—he points his index finger at me—"don't make me regret telling you."

"Scout's honor," I say, holding up three fingers.

"Right. Like I believe you were ever a Scout," he scoffs.

"Okay, so maybe I was never a Boy Scout, but I can promise you I'm not some kind of crazy stalker."

"Yeah, yeah. Like I said, don't make me regret it, and we're good."

It's not like he's my actual coach; he's the kicking coach. He can't torture me on the field. "Done." I jog off to the locker room to shower and head to the hotel to get my shit and go home.

"Where's the fire?" Case Riley, our center, asks as I'm tossing my shit in my bag.

"No fire. Just ready to get home."

"We hitting up Henry's tonight?"

Henry's is a small bar close to the stadium. I'm not sure when or how it got started, but he has a side entrance with a key code. The players enter there into a private room. We have our own bartender, music, big-screen TVs, the whole nine yards. If we want to just slip away out of the limelight but still feel normal, Henry's is the place to go. The place stays packed, both for its location to the stadium and for the players who decide to venture out into the public area of the bar. Cleat chasers make it their stomping grounds.

"Maybe." I'm not committing until I talk to her. I might have better options. And if not, tonight, I'm going to stay hidden, no matter how hard Case tries to convince me otherwise. A couple of beers and then my big, comfy bed. That is the exciting life of a professional quarterback.

"Eight," he calls after me. I've already got my bag thrown over my shoulder and am heading toward the door. I have a phone call to make.

X X
O O

Walking into my condo, I drop my bags by the door. Three long weeks away, but we're ready. The team is meshing, and I see good things in our future. I also see my ass sleeping in my ultra-soft bed for the next twenty-four hours. Walking down the hall to my room, I flop back onto the bed. Damn, it's good to be home.

Pulling my phone out of my pocket, I hold it in the air over my face and pull up my search engine. I type in *Safe Haven Animal Shelter* and wait for the results. Clicking on their website, I see Jeremy's wife, Autumn, and Tessa smiling back at me. I skim through the main page until I get to the bottom and find *Contact Us*. Clicking that, the number pops up, and my phone asks me if I want to call.

Hell yes, I do.

"Safe Haven Animal Shelter, this is Tessa." Her sweet voice greets me.

"Hey, Tessa, it's Landon."

"I'm sorry, who?" I can hear the confusion in her voice, which is like a kick in the balls.

"Landon Barker." I wait, letting my name sink in.

"Number eighteen?" she questions.

"Yeah. How have you been?"

"I'm sorry, were you calling in regard to the shelter?"

"No. I called for you. To talk to you."

"I'm afraid I'm on company time. Thanks for calling," she says, and the line goes dead.

I stare at the screen of my phone with the alert telling me the call was ended. What the actual fuck was that? She hung up on me. Hitting the green *Call Back* button, the line rings twice before she picks up.

"Safe Haven Animal Shelter, this is Tessa."

"Did you really just hang up on me?" I ask.

"Landon." She sighs, and the sound, although not meant to be sexual, goes straight to my dick.

"Give me two minutes."

"Fine. What can I do for you, Number Eighteen?"

Normally, a woman calling me by my number is a turnoff. That's what cleat chasers do. They just want to bag a player and hopefully be the one who gets to ride along on their coattails. However, I don't get that vibe from Tessa. In fact, she's irritated as hell right now. "Have dinner with me." It's more of a demand than a question.

"No."

No hesitation in her voice. "One dinner. We can get to know each other." That's what women like her want, right? The good girls who you would take home to your mother. They want to be wined and dined. That's not my MO, but there's a first time for everything. Don't get me wrong. I've had dinner with women, but it's usually at a charity event or is team sponsored. I've not been keen on the actual act of dating. Or the calling and asking thing. I think the last time that happened, it was senior prom. *Great, now I'm my seventeen-year-old self.*

"Look, Landon, I'm sure you're a great guy, but I'm just not interested."

"Tessa—" I start, and she cuts me off.

"I really need to go." With that, the line goes dead.

"Well, shit." I huff, letting the phone drop to the bed next to me. What's it going to take to get to this girl? I'm tempted to call her back, but I already know what the outcome is going to be. She's going to hang up on me for the third time today. No thanks. I need to regroup and decide what my next step is going to be.

My phone rings, and I sit up, slapping the bed looking for it, a strange feeling filling my chest. The feeling that maybe it's her. I frown when I see Case's name on the screen.

"What's up, Riley?"

"Henry's at eight."

"I'll be there."

"Good. See you." He ends the call. Short and to the point, but really, what else is there to say? We just spent three solid weeks together.

Looking at the clock, I have three hours before I have to meet Case. A nap is in order. Kicking off my shoes, I swing around on the bed, resting my head on the pillow, and close my eyes. As soon as I do, she's who I see. The fire in those green eyes as she shot me down. I can only imagine that same fire is in her eyes right now. I smile at that. She's not going to know what hit her.

Game on, sweetheart.

Game on.

× × ♪
○ ○

At ten minutes till eight, I'm typing in the code to the back entrance of Henry's bar. The room is quiet, except for old man Henry himself wiping down the bar.

"Landon," he greets.

"Hey, Henry, how's it going?" Henry is in his late sixties. He opened this bar over thirty years ago and has gained the trust and respect of the Cougars during that time.

"I'm this side of the sod, so I can't complain." He chuckles. "How was training camp?"

"Team's looking good this year."

"Didn't expect to see you here tonight."

Henry knows me well. "Yeah, Case talked me into a drink."

"How are your folks?" he asks, wiping down the bar that I'm sure doesn't need to be wiped down at all. A habit he's picked up over the years.

"Good. Loving retired life."

"You're a good son," he tells me. "I'm sure they appreciate all you've done for them."

"They sacrificed a lot for me growing up. It's the least I could do. And keep that on the DL. You're going to ruin my street cred." I grin at him.

He throws his head back in laughter. His deep, husky voice from one too many cigarettes is comforting. Familiar. "Like you've got street cred," he counters.

"Damn, cuts like a knife," I say, holding my hand to my chest as we both laugh.

"What else is going on with you?"

"First night of freedom." I don't mention Tessa or how she continues to shoot my ass down. I need to wrap my head around it before I start getting any kind of outside influences.

He studies me. "And?"

"And nothing." I shake my head. Henry is like a damn therapist, always wanting to pull the juicy details out of you. Only he pries your soul open with booze, and before you know it, you've spilled your guts to him in the span of a couple of hours. I'm convinced he has some kind of bartender superpower or some shit.

"There he is." Henry looks over my shoulder to where Case saunters into the room.

When I say saunters, it's more of a glide, which is odd for a man his size. As the team's center, Case Riley stands at six foot five and weighs in at two hundred and ninety-five pounds. He's a big man, and the fact that he can stroll anywhere is a surprise to everyone. He's damn good on his feet despite his size.

"You missing me, Barker?" he asks, sliding into the seat next to me at the bar.

"You called me, remember?"

"Three weeks, Barker. Three weeks we're in lockdown, and you want to chill at home." He shakes his head as if he can't believe I would want to stay in for the night. If he'd ever slept on my Hastens mattress, he would understand. It's extravagant but so worth it. As football players, we need to take care of our bodies. That includes a good night's sleep. A man can't scrimp on his mattress, not in our profession.

"I missed my bed." I shrug.

"You and that damn bed." Case shakes his head. "How's the crowd?" He motions his head toward the main bar area as Henry slides a Corona in front of him.

"Busy, but then again, everyone knows that training camp is over. You know how they are. Any chance to catch a glimpse."

"You're a good man, Henry," Case tells him. "It's nice to be able to get out of the house, have a beer, and not be swarmed."

"What?" I turn on my stool to look at him. "You feeling all right, bud?" I ask. Lifting my hand, I place the back of it against his forehead, just like my mom used to do when I was a kid. "No fever." I smirk as he swats my hand away from his face.

"Fucker," he mumbles under his breath. "So…" He takes another long pull from his bottle of beer. "What's the latest?" he asks. I'm not sure if he's asking me or Henry, but I choose to think it's the latter and keep my trap shut about Tessa. I really don't feel like taking his shit tonight. My ego has been hit enough today.

"Same thing, different day." Henry chuckles.

"How's the missus?" I ask. I watch as a slow smile brightens his wrinkled face. It also helps to change the subject, and I hope that keeps Case from noticing I'm a little off tonight.

"She's mine." He grins. "Gets prettier every day."

"How long you been married?" Case asks.

"Forty years," Henry and I say at the same time.

"That's right." Henry nods. "Last month."

I know because he told me and I got them a gift. A weekend away at a local bed and breakfast. Henry works too much.

"I couldn't imagine the same pu— uh, woman for that many years." Case trips over his words, making both Henry and me laugh. A few beers and he forgets to censor his mouth. It's something we're used to. Hell, we all do it.

"You will," Henry assures him. "One day, you will."

"Nope." Case finishes off his beer and slides the empty toward Henry, who quickly replaces it with another.

"What about you, Landon?"

I shrug. "It's hard to find the real deal when you're in the spotlight. I'm not against it, but this job is a bitch to deal with for us as players, even harder for spouses and kids. Besides, there is something to say about variety." I give him an overzealous grin. That's what I'm supposed to say. That's the public persona that everyone knows. However, one day, I'd like to settle down. I want a wife and kids. I just don't see it happening for me anytime soon. Maybe after I stop playing. When I'm out of the limelight, the vultures will move on to my replacement. Maybe then I can find the real deal. Someone who wants me, not my title or my bank account.

Tessa flashes in my mind with her sparkling green eyes. She is definitely the type of girl you would choose for your forever. I barely know her, and that's as obvious as the sky is blue. I don't want her to change her last name for me, though; just a date will do.

One date.

I know, wishful thinking.

We spend the next hour talking about more random stuff. The season, Case's hate for laundry, and somehow, the conversation turns back to my bed. As bad as I didn't want to come out, I'm glad I did. It's good to just hang out and shoot the shit. Next time, we'll invite the guys, but I knew this night would go way beyond low-key if we did that. I make it home in twenty minutes. It's amazing how little traffic there is when there's not a game. After stripping out of my clothes, I slide under the sheets. With the super softness of my bed for the first time in weeks, other than my earlier nap, it doesn't take long for sleep to claim me.

CHAPTER 3

Tessa

I BARELY SLEPT LAST NIGHT. I BLAME NUMBER EIGHTEEN AND HIS blue eyes. I have no idea what Landon Barker is up to. What I do know is that whatever it may be, it doesn't involve me, no matter how persistent he is. Although it's admittedly thrilling to have his attention, it's for the wrong reasons. It's all about the chase, one I won't be surrendering to anytime soon.

"Good morning," Autumn says, joining me in our shared office space. She's the manager and I'm the assistant manager of the Safe Haven Animal Shelter. That's how we met, and we've been best friends ever since.

"Hey." I smile and go back to the volunteer schedule I've been working on.

"Any phone calls today?" she asks with a grin.

"Ugh." I groan, sitting back in my chair. "No. I'm hoping he got the

"You know, Jeremy said he asked him for your number yesterday before they all went home."

That has me sitting up a little straighter. "Please tell me he didn't give it to him."

"Nope, but he did tell him your last name and where you worked."

"Well, that solves that mystery." Yesterday, we both racked our brains as to how he figured it out. I should have known it was Jeremy. I was too flustered to even consider him.

"He told him if he wanted your number, he had to work for it."

"Great. That's all I need is Jeremy encouraging him. Tell him next time, he can tell Landon I'm not interested."

"He says he's staying out of it from now on. He gave him what he needed to find you. The rest is up to him."

"He'll get bored soon. I mean, he's Landon Barker after all. He can have any woman he wants, and he's not going to wait around on me."

"You never know. You could be the one to change him." Autumn shrugs like the words that just came out of her mouth are not the most unrealistic she's ever spoken.

"I don't want to change him. That never works. He is who he is, and that's not a bad thing. He's just not for me."

"How do you know who he is?" She raises her eyebrows.

"Fine. I don't know him. I have a perception of him, and it's not one I feel works well with who I am. How's that?"

"You're being judgey."

"Like you didn't judge Jeremy."

"Oh, I did. I admit that. You're forgetting something," she says, standing from her desk that faces mine.

"Tell me, ole wise one. What could I possibly be forgetting?" I ask, amused. I can only imagine what she's going to throw at me next.

"What you're forgetting, my dear Tess, is that yes, I judged Jeremy, but I also married him." She raises her left hand and wiggles her ring finger that houses her wedding band and engagement ring. Not that they're easy to miss.

"So you found your unicorn. Not all of us are that lucky. And you didn't change him. He changed because of you. To be better. There's a difference."

"I agree with you. But how do you know that Landon won't be the same way? How do you know he's not already a commitment guy? Because of a few tabloids? Come on, Tessa, you know better than to believe everything you read in those things or online. Hell, talk to Jeremy. He can give you his firsthand experiences."

I admit she has a point, but it's all too much. *He's* too much. He's this gorgeous, professional athlete, and I'm the girl next door who helps run an animal shelter. He might not be bored now because of the chase, but he will be. Eventually. I'm saving us both the drama and potential heartache that's surely inevitable.

"I don't," I say when I realize she's watching me still, waiting for an answer. "I have to go with my gut on this one, and my gut tells me that Landon Barker has heartbreak written all over him."

Autumn shakes her head. "Girl, I've been where you are. Sometimes you just have to take the risk."

"I've never been much of a risk-taker."

"Just promise you'll keep an open mind."

"Sure, whatever, but it's a moot point. I made it clear that day at the field, and both times he called yesterday, that I wasn't interested. I'm sure he's tucked his tail between his legs and moved on to the next willing and able woman. Lord knows there are plenty in line to volley for his attention."

No sooner than the words leave my mouth, the chime over the door alerts us to a visitor. Standing from my chair, I walk down the hall to the reception area. There I find a woman holding a planter of flowers. "Hi, I have a delivery for a Tessa Deaton."

No, he didn't. "I'm Tessa." I step closer and accept the planter, placing it on the reception desk.

"Sign here, please." She hands me a clipboard, and I scrawl my signature across the page. "Thank you. Have a nice one," she says, and is gone as fast as she arrived.

"Flowers?" Autumn asks, wearing a grin. "I wonder who they're from?" She's being coy; we both know damn well who they're from. No one sends me flowers. Ever. As in, I've never received flowers before in my entire life. Sure, a corsage for prom when I was in high school, but never like this. It's amazing what it does to brighten your mood. The quarterback is persistent, I'll give him that. He's good at the game, and although the flowers are a pleasant surprise, I'm not playing. Nope, my ass will remain on the bench. At least when it comes to him.

"They're for you." I make it a point to grin widely, exaggerating the look, which makes her laugh.

"Oh, really?" She reaches out for the card, but I'm faster, snatching it before she has a chance to.

I grip the small card in my hand as I lean in to smell the roses, literally. Not just roses but calla lilies, which are my favorite. The bouquet is gorgeous with the white roses and the pink lilies intertwined. Without even knowing, he chose the perfect arrangement. Then again, I'm sure he just called the flower shop and told them to pick. On second thought, he probably had an assistant order them. Guys like him, all rich and professional, can't be bothered with mundane acts such as ordering flowers. Suddenly, my happy feeling is deflated. I'm sure that's it. He wouldn't take time out of his day to send them himself.

"Are you going to read it? Or would you rather stand there staring at this stunning arrangement with a dopey look on your face the entire day?" Autumn grins, proud of herself for calling me out.

I stick my tongue out at her like the adult that I am. Turning the small envelope over in my hands, I slide my index finger under the seal and pull out the tiny card. It simply says *Call me*, with a phone number. It's signed, with an *L*, and that's it. His cocky ass just assumed he's the only man vying for my attention. Sure, he's right, but still. He can't even include his full name?

"Well?" Autumn asks, impatient as ever.

"From an *L*." I shrug, handing her the card.

She reads over it and laughs. "Looks like we've got another cocky player on our hands. Are we supposed to read his mind that he's *the* L.B. that sent these?" She stares at the card, then grins. "Did I ever tell you how I met Jeremy?"

"Yeah, something about a bobblehead?" I try to pull up the memory.

"Yeah, and his bike… it had the initials J.B. engraved. I couldn't help but think it stood for jerky baller," she laughs.

I nod. "I remember you telling me that."

"Yeah, well, looks like you got your own initials man."

"What? You're talking crazy."

"No, really. We need to give him a name for it."

"He has one. Landon Barker."

"No, no, not his real name. Where's the fun in that?" She thinks for a minute. "I've got it. Lucky Baller." She nods, proud of herself.

"And why is he so lucky?" I ask, knowing I'm going to regret it.

"He's got your attention. What more luck does he need?"

I shake my head at her. "And what's with this *we* stuff? We have another cocky player on our hands? What's up with that? You trading Jeremy in?" I tease, knowing damn well that's not even a possibility.

"We're a package deal," she says, not missing a beat. "He wants my bestie, he gets me, my man, and my son. He has to pass our approval."

"Too bad he's never going to get the chance to be under your microscope."

"We'll see," she says, waving the small card in the air at me.

"Give me that, crazy girl." I take the card from her and shove it into my back pocket. I'll toss it later.

× × ♪
○ ○

I don't think there has ever been a day longer than this one. It was a quiet day at the shelter. Autumn had to leave at lunch to take JJ to his annual checkup, which left me and the animals. We had two volunteers on the schedule for today, but they were gone by one. The entire afternoon was just me, the animals, and my thoughts. Oh, and that pesky small white envelope that still resides in my back pocket.

Autumn lectured me before she left that the right thing to do to was text him and tell him thank you. Sure, it was a nice gesture, but he knows I'm not interested. Still, I can't stop thinking about the fact that it's in my back pocket. Once I've pulled into my driveway, I grab my things and head inside. As I walk up the front steps, I take in my home. It's not much, just a small two-bedroom, one-bathroom house, with a little patch of grass that is supposed to be my yard. With the California sun, it's more of an ugly brown patch. It's not much, but it's all mine. Well, mine and the landlord's, but one day, I'll have a place of my own. Despite the brown yard and close neighbors, it still beats apartment living.

Placing my bag on the kitchen counter, I set my keys and phone beside it. The first thing I do every day after getting home is strip down and shower. I love the animals, obviously, but they don't always smell the greatest, and after cleaning out kennels, I always feel gross when I get home. Kicking off my shoes, I head down the small hallway to my bedroom. I make quick work of stripping out of my clothes and tossing them into a clothes basket, then grab some shorts, a T-shirt, panties, and decide to forego a bra. It's just me after all, and I'm not expecting company. I turn from my dresser and spot the small white envelope on the floor.

Landon.

It must have fallen out of my pocket. Bending, I pick it up and toss it in the small trash can in my room. There. Done. I don't have to worry about its existence any longer. Pretending that the card no longer exists, I proceed out of my room and to the bathroom to take a long, hot shower.

Showered, with my wet hair piled on top of my head, sans bra, I head to the kitchen to decide what to have for dinner. I love to cook, but cooking for one? Not so much. Reaching into the freezer, I grab one of the many Healthy Choice microwave dinners. Not exactly what I would call a feast, but it's dinner tonight all the same. While the microwave does its thing, I grab a fork, rip a paper towel off the roll, and retrieve a bottle of water from the refrigerator. The microwave beeps. Careful not to burn myself, I remove the thin plastic covering and dump my meal into a bowl. It's some kind of chicken and rice meal. I toss the trash away, and voila, dinner is served. With my hands full, I manage to grab my phone and make it to the living room without spilling everything. I settle in on the couch for a night of mindless TV. At least that's the plan until my phone rings. I can't help but release a heavy sigh when I see it's Autumn. I know why she's calling.

"Hey," I greet, setting my now-empty bowl on the coffee table.

"Did you text him? Wait, no, please tell me you called him?"

"Nope," I say, popping the p.

"Tesssaaaa." She drags out my name.

"Autummmnnn," I mock her.

"What am I going to do with you?"

"Not badger me to call him?" I offer up the suggestion, knowing damn well she's not going to take it.

"Stop it." She laughs. "I'm being serious. You could be missing out on something amazing."

"I want more than just amazing sex, Autumn."

"Who said anything about sex?" I can hear the amusement in her voice.

Damn it. "You know what I mean."

"Actually, I do. I have my own cocky player, and let me tell you—" she starts, but I stop her.

"No. Just no. I love you, but the last time you told me about you and Jeremy, I couldn't look at him for a week. Keep that shit locked up, Baldwin," I tease.

"Oh, whatever." She giggles. "Just text him. Tell him thank you."

"No. Then he'll have my number, and he obviously doesn't understand the meaning of the word no. Why would I give him full access to me all the time? Not happening."

"Chicken," she goads.

"Cluck cluck," I reply, barely able to contain my own laughter. "Look, he's going to get the hint eventually. If I text him, that opens things up for a conversation that doesn't need to happen. We've said what needs to be said. He asked. I said no. End of story."

"Jeremy is still at the field. When he gets home, I'm going to get the dirt on Mr. Quarterback. I'll have a full report for you tomorrow."

"You don't have to do that. It's not going to change my mind." I refuse to admit that learning more about him, straight from the source, or at least from someone who actually knows him, is appealing.

"Hey, what happened to keeping an open mind?"

"Did I agree to that?" I ask, pretending to be confused.

"What's that? You want to know all the things? Done. I'll get Jeremy on the job."

I don't argue with her. I know she's going to ask Jeremy regardless. "Goodnight, Autumn," I sing into the phone.

"Not so fast, missy."

"Ugh," I groan.

"Send me a picture of the flowers. Where did you put them? In the living room?"

"No. I left them at the shelter."

"What? Why on earth would you do that? They're beautiful."

"We can enjoy them at the office."

"Tessa, they're yours. You should be enjoying them at your place."

"Yeah, yeah. I'll see you tomorrow, when we can both enjoy the flowers."

She sighs heavily, as if I'm her greatest disappointment. "Bye, Tess." She hangs up, and I can imagine her rushing Jeremy as soon as he walks through the door, ambushing him for details about Landon. I should be worried because she can talk that man into anything. Case in point, their pet pig, Pinky. Some of the stories she's told me about how Pinky came about are hilarious. I've never known anyone to have a pet pig, especially one that stays in the house, but somehow, he fits them.

Cleaning up my mess, I wash the few dishes and lock up. I'm just ready for this very long day to be over. Climbing into bed, I stare up at the shadows on the ceiling. The house is quiet, except for the whirl of the small fan I keep on the nightstand. There's nothing else to distract me from my thoughts. Thoughts that are consumed with a little white envelope sitting in the bottom of my small trash can. I can't help but wonder what his motivation is. It has to be the chase. I can't for the life of me figure out what else it could be. Glancing at the clock, I see that over an hour has passed. I need to get some sleep. Slinging the covers off, I stomp to the trash can and, under the glow of the moonlight, retrieve the small envelope. Opening the top dresser drawer, I toss it in and quickly close it back. There. Now, if by chance I change my mind at any time, I'll have no regrets that I tossed his number. I climb back into bed and can finally feel myself relax. As I drift off to sleep, I can't help but think that Autumn is going to have a field day with this new information.

CHAPTER 4

Landon

I T'S BEEN THREE DAYS SINCE I SENT HER FLOWERS. THREE DAYS of checking my phone obsessively. She's not going to call, I know that, but I had hoped.

I should wash my hands of the situation and just move on, but something tells me not to give up. Something deep in my gut, and I always trust my gut. Sure, it's probably just the nagging feeling that she's the first to turn me down, but it feels like something... more. Whatever it is, it's driving me crazy.

"Barker."

I turn to see Jeremy Baldwin standing next to me. "Hey, Coach. Bourgeois is looking good." I nod to the field where Thomas is kicking field goals.

"He is." He nods. "He's got talent."

"Big praise from the soccer star."

He laughs. "We all have room to grow. Trust me. I know that all too well. Anyway, I thought you should know you've been a hot topic at my house this week."

Interesting. "Really?"

"Like you didn't already know." He shakes his head, an amused smile tilting his lips.

"She's a tough nut to crack," I say. I don't bother telling him I'm talking about Tessa. He already knows.

"Not so much."

"Are we talking about the same person? Tessa Deaton?" I counter.

"That's her." His grin grows wider. "You've somehow managed to get my wife on your side."

"What does that mean?"

"It means the flowers were a good move, and now Autumn wants to know everything about you."

"Autumn, right." Is that disappointment I feel?

"Yep. I've been instructed to gather all the dirty details and report back."

"And what would your wife think about you telling me that?"

He throws his head back and laughs. "My wife, Autumn, is an attorney. She's not currently practicing, but she still has the... shall we say, 'special talent.' You're lucky it's me asking and not her."

"Maybe she can work on Tessa," I mutter under my breath.

"I need to bring some nugget of information home to my wife. So, tell me this, Barker. Why Tessa? From what I know of you, this isn't your MO."

I can appreciate his forwardness. "It's not. I've dated mostly for charity events or team events, things like that. Nothing... like this," I confess.

"Again, why Tessa?"

I shrug. "She turned me down."

He tilts his head to the side and studies me. "That's it? She turned you down, so you're sending flowers and obsessing over your phone, moping around here like you've lost your best friend because she turned you down?"

"Who's moping?" I ask, because the other two are facts.

"You are. You've been distracted all week, and your game shows it."

"Wait just a minute. My game is fine. Kaden and I are connecting, making the plays," I say, referring to me and our starting running back, Kaden Hahn.

"You're making plays, but your head's not in it. You're on autopilot. Your arm is lax, and your throw's timid compared to what you're capable of." He pauses, letting this new revelation sink in. "Look, for some reason, my wife is rooting for you. She thinks you'd be good for Tess. But she's family to us. She's not a game." With that, he turns and walks away.

I should yell out to him. Stop him from walking away, but I'm frozen, my feet unable to lift from the turf as if I'm standing in quicksand. The last three days float through my mind, and although I hate to admit it, he's right. I've been going through the motions. I've got to get this girl out of my head, but I'm too far in to turn back now. I need to at least take her to dinner or for drinks. Fuck me, *something* to get her out of my head. I'd like to think dinner and some time in my bed would be the perfect ending to this little… whatever this is, but if I can't get her to call me after sending her flowers, I know damn sure my dick isn't getting anywhere near her. No matter how bad we both want it. And she does want it. I can see it in her eyes every time she looks at me. I see it as her breathing changes anytime I'm near her. She's fighting this pull between us, and I don't know why.

Pushing Tessa out of my mind, I get back on the field. I finish practice, being more present than I have been all week. In the locker room, I'm quiet as I rush through a shower and head out with nothing but a couple of waves and nods to the guys.

Twenty minutes later, I remove the keys from the ignition and stare at the shelter in front of me. I didn't plan to come here, but this is where

I ended up. I don't rush to get out as I try to form what I'm going to say. More than that, I try to work out what the hell I'm doing and why this woman is getting to me.

Ten minutes later, I still have no answers and realize that I'm a creeper who's sitting in the parking lot of an animal shelter. Reaching for the handle, I start to climb out of my SUV, but I freeze when I see her. Her long dark hair is braided and thrown over her shoulder. She's wearing a tank top with the shelter's logo and a pair of tight pants, leggings—a man's best friend.

I can't take my eyes off her. She's leading a horse my way. She turns her head to talk to him, and I see her stumble. My hand jerks open the door, and my legs rush to carry me to her, but it's too late. She stumbles and falls to the ground. The horse gets spooked and rushes past me. I don't try and stop it as I rush to her, falling on my knees beside her.

"Tessa," I say with a pant.

"Ow." Her voice is soft and constricted with pain.

"Hey, let me look at you."

She lifts her head, and the pain in her eyes twists my gut. "L-Landon?" she asks, confused.

"Yeah." I swipe her bangs out of her eyes. "You okay?"

"What are you doing here?" She moves to sit up and winces.

"Let me help you." She doesn't fight me as I stand and place my hands under her arms and lift her. She tries to step out of my hold and ends up falling into my arms as she cries out in pain. I don't think, I just swing her into my arms bridal-style and carry her to the front door. "Can you turn the knob?" I ask. She's able to turn the knob, and I kick the door open with my foot. I bypass the receptionist desk and move down the hall. "This your office?" I ask her.

"Yeah." She nods, her face still scrunched up in pain.

I don't ask which desk is hers; the bouquet of lilies and roses tells me. I hide my smile, but something inside me lifts knowing that she kept them. Carefully, I set her in the chair. "Let me take a look." I run my hands down her leg, all toned muscle, and stop when I reach her ankle.

"It's fine, or it will be. I just landed on it wrong." She tries to pull her leg out of my hands, but I'm not having it. "You never told me what you're doing here."

"I came to see you."

"Me?" she asks, confused.

"Yeah, it's been too long since I've seen those green eyes." I'm staring at her, our faces close as I kneel before her. I have the sudden urge to pull her into a kiss.

"Come on, Landon. Why are you here?"

I didn't know it was the truth until the words left my lips the first time, so I repeat, "To see you." Gently, my fingers trace over her ankle, which is already starting to swell. "I'm sorry I didn't get to you in time. I saw you stumble. I tried."

"Not your fault or your responsibility."

"Maybe not, but I'm still sorry all the same. Looks like a sprain."

"Great," she mutters.

"Are you the only one here?"

She nods, her eyes glassy. "Yes. We had a volunteer scheduled, but they were a no-show. JJ's daycare called, and he's got pink eye, or so they think. Autumn left to pick him up and take him to the doctor."

"Okay. Well, I think if you ice it and keep it elevated, it should be okay. Where can I get some ice?"

"I can manage. You should go."

Unable to resist, I reach up and cradle her cheek in the palm of my hand. "I'm here, and I'm going to help you." Her green eyes regard me. They truly are a unique color, so much so, my breath hitches as she stares at me. Blinking hard, I scan her face, and that's when I see a soft dusting of freckles on either cheek. I didn't notice them before, but I like them. They suit her. Makes her more… human, I guess. She's not like the women I'm used to. Dressed to the nines, more makeup coated on their faces than the department store can carry, and always with a mission: bed a player. Tessa is a breath of fresh air, one that I didn't realize I needed until this very moment.

"Thank you," she whispers.

"Where can I get some ice?"

"We have a storage cabinet in the bathroom across the hall. There's a first aid kit. There should be some ice packs in it."

"Okay. I'll be right back." I fight the urge to press my lips to hers or even to taste her freckles. Instead, I stand, give her arm a gentle squeeze, and leave to find the ice packs.

"Here." A few moments later, I hand her a bottle of water that I found in the breakroom. She takes it, and I tear open a small packet of Ibuprofen. "Take these. It will help with the pain and inflammation." She doesn't argue as she holds out her hand to accept the pills before tossing them back, drinking half the bottle of water.

"Thank you."

I nod. Grabbing what I assume is Autumn's chair, I roll it over to prop her leg up on and then squeeze the ice pack to activate it. I squish it around in my hands for a couple of minutes, getting it mixed up before placing it on her ankle. She winces but otherwise doesn't say anything.

"You good here?"

"Yeah, I'll be fine."

"Good. Now, tell me what I need to do to get the horse back in the pasture."

"Shit, I forgot about Buckwheat."

"Buckwheat? Do all the animals have names?"

"Most of them. I can call Autumn or Jeremy when he gets home."

"No need. I'm here. Just tell me what to do."

"Landon—" I hear the argument forming in that one word, so I place my finger to her lips to shut her up. *Have her lips always been that full and… kissable?*

"I'm helping you. Now tell me what I need to do."

"He's a big baby," she relents. "But if you get some feed in a bucket and give him some time, he'll come to you."

"Okay. Where's the food?"

"Out in the barn. I can show you." She moves to get up.

"No." My voice is firm. "You're staying put. Here." I hand her my phone. "Call your number on my phone."

"What?"

"I said call yourself from my phone. That way, you can talk me through it, and you won't be tempted to get up to see what I'm doing. When we're done, you can delete the call so I don't have your number."

"That's crazy. Why would you want me to delete my number?"

I shrug. "I want to earn it, Tess. Now call yourself." I don't know what I'm doing. This is the perfect opportunity to get her number, but I meant what I said. I want to earn it. There's something to be said for having to work for her affection. It's not something I knew I wanted or even needed in my life until I saw her fall to the ground. I can't explain it. I was worried about her. Not just "oh no, I hope she's okay," but worried. I don't understand what's happening here. I barely know this girl, but she consumes me. One small interaction of banter and her not throwing herself at me is apparently all it takes to have me hooked. Who knew?

I see a slight tremble in her hand as she takes my phone. Her fingers slowly press against the screen as she dials her phone. It's sitting on her desk, so I grab it, lifting it to my ear. "Tessa's phone." I grin. To my surprise, she grins back. "I'm going to get Buckwheat. Keep your ass in that chair." I point to the chair as I speak into her phone, talking to her. I'm staring her down when she shakes her head, and a slow smile crosses her face. It hits me in the gut and has me puffing out my chest at the same time. I did that. I put that smile there, and I can't wait to do it again.

"Go." She points toward the door, and I salute her. Her chuckle follows me all the way down the hall.

Outside, I'm not exactly sure what I'm going to be up against. I spot Buckwheat over by the barn. "He's by the barn," I tell Tessa.

"Good. Horses are smart. He knows where he's fed, and it's feeding time."

"I can do that. How much?"

"He gets one scoop, a chunk of hay, and his water needs to be filled."

"Got it." I reach the horse. "Hey, buddy." I hold my hand out to let him smell me. "Can horses smell fear?" I ask Tessa.

"Yeah, all animals can. Are you scared, Landon?" Her voice is teasing, and I love it.

"No, but he looks scared."

"He probably is. Poor baby."

Buckwheat turns his head, bringing himself closer to me. "Hey, bud. Let's get you back in the field, okay?" He snorts, and I take that as a yes. Stepping away, I open the gate, hoping he'll just walk right in. He doesn't. "Gotta be stubborn, huh? You get that from Tessa?" I ask.

"Hey." She laughs.

"You know it's true," I tease. "Okay, so the feed's in the barn?" I ask, even though she already told me.

"Yes. We keep it in a barrel to keep rodents and other animals out of it. There's a scoop inside."

I make my way into the barn, and sure enough, there's a large blue plastic barrel with a *Horse Feed* label written on the side. Twisting off the top, the scoop is there just as she said.

"Did you find it?" she asks.

"Yeah, he gets one scoop, right? Heaped or even?"

"What?"

"A heaped scoop or an even scoop? These things make a difference, Tessa."

She laughs again, and I love the sound. "Heaped is fine."

"Noted." With my heaped scoop in one hand and the cell phone held to my ear with the other, I make my way back outside to Buckwheat. His head rises, and I swear his eyes grow wide when he sees the scoop of feed in my hands. "This is for you, buddy," I tell him. "Come on." I hold it out, letting him get a whiff, and he sticks his tongue out, trying to take a bite, but I pull the scoop away. A little of the feed falls from the scoop to the ground, so he bends to try and devour it. "Come on, Buckwheat, this way." I hold up the scoop and slowly walk into the field. I'm glad that I left the gate open earlier.

"Is he following you?" Tessa asks.

I turn to look over my shoulder. "He's thinking about it. Where do I feed him?"

"Just on the ground is fine. There's a bare spot next to the water trough. You see it?"

"Yes."

"That's where we usually feed him."

I dump the scoop of feed onto the ground and hear galloping feet. I turn in time to see Buckwheat come to a halt and begin to eat. "He's in," I tell Tessa.

"Oh, good." I can hear the relief in her voice. "Now, some hay."

"Right." I make sure the gate is secure and head back to the barn to return the scoop and make sure the lid is sealed tight on the drum. "The bale of hay lying beside the feed?" I check.

"Yeah, just a chunk."

"How big is a chunk?"

"I don't know, about a four-inch piece. He gets grass, but we still like to give him hay because that's what he's used to."

"Okay. And where do I toss this?"

"Next to his food."

"Easy enough." I toss the hay over, but Buckwheat doesn't seem to notice as he's still hoovering the feed that's spread out on the ground. I don't have to ask where the water is, as there is a spout that hangs over the trough. I pull the handle and lean against the fence as it fills. "How's the ankle?" I ask.

"It hurts, but I'll be fine. I'll go home and rest it tonight, and she'll be good as new."

"It's your right foot."

"Yeah."

"You can't drive."

"Autumn will come and get me."

"Or I could take you home. Maybe we can grab some dinner on the way there."

"Landon, we've talked about this."

"No, you said no to dinner, not a ride home."

"No." She says the words, but it's not with the same conviction as before.

"Come on, Tess. You know who I am. It's not like I'm some mass murderer."

"That's comforting," she says dryly.

"Let me finish up whatever you need doing here. We'll hit a drive-thru or order pizza, and I'll take you home. Easy."

"I'll need my car."

"Who says you can drive tomorrow? I have to be at the field at nine. I can swing by and pick you up." *Or I could stay,* I think, but keep that thought to myself.

"Autumn can pick me up."

I want to argue, but even I know when to stop. Besides, what's she going to do when I show up at her place in the morning? "What else needs to be done?"

"Just the night check. I need to make sure all the animals have water and that the cages are secure. Everything else that I had on my list today can wait. The animals are what's important."

"You sure?" I ask as I shut off the water and head back toward the building.

"Yes. If you don't mind?"

"I told you I didn't. I'm on my way back inside now." As bad as I hate to end the call, I lock the screen instead of snooping to get to know her better. Working for her attention has merit, and that smile she gave me earlier… I'm definitely going to work for more of those. I'm not sure what that means, or if I want it to mean anything. For the time being, I'm just going to go with what feels right, and we can figure out the rest as we go.

CHAPTER 5

Tessa

L ANDON ENDS THE CALL, AND I LOOK DOWN AT HIS PHONE IN my hands. He said I could delete the number. My fingers hover over my number, but I can't do it. I'm curious if he'll check, and if he does, if he'll use it. I'm not sure that he will. Not after him telling me to remove it, that he wanted me to be the one to give him my number. In a way, not deleting the call is me giving him my number, right?

"You need anything?" Landon asks from the doorway.

I place his phone on my desk and shake my head. "Thank you for your help, Landon."

"You're welcome." He flashes me his dimples. Surely, he knows the power of those things.

"So, point me where to go next."

"Down the hall, there are two rooms. We just have cats and dogs and Buckwheat right now. There's a utility sink, and next to it is a hose that's hooked up to the water. Just make sure each bowl is full. You shouldn't have to open the cages."

"Got it. Anything else?"

"No."

"I'll be quick." He winks and disappears down the hall.

Tilting my head back against the seat, I close my eyes. I can't believe this is happening. That I fell, and he was the one there to pick up the pieces for me. Why did it have to be him? I know I'm crazy. Any woman would be thrilled to have Landon Barker at their beck and call, but he's... too much. Too sexy, too confident, too... everything.

"Hey." His deep voice pulls me from my thoughts.

Opening my eyes, I see him kneeling next to the chair, a concerned expression on his face. "You okay?"

"Oh, you mean other than the sprained ankle—by the way, thanks for the diagnosis, Doc—and the fact that you have to do my job and take care of me? Sure, I'm just peachy."

"Come on, Miss Independent. Let's get you home." He stands to his full height and begins to remove the ice pack from my ankle.

"Thank you so much for all your help, but I can call Autumn. If we could just switch phones," I say, grabbing his from the desk and handing it to him. I should have already called her, but I haven't. I don't want to analyze why that is. I'm just going to blame it on the pain, and maybe it has a little to do with the sexiness of the quarterback who's been tending to my needs. I mean, my ankle.

My phone rings, and he grins as he pulls it out of his pocket and looks at the screen. He turns it to show me, and it's Autumn. "See, perfect timing." I hold my hand out for the phone, but instead of handing it to me, he flashes those damn dimples and swipes at the screen.

"Hello." He pauses. "This is Landon." He goes on to explain why he has my phone and what happened. "I'm going to grab her some dinner and take her home." Another pause. "I can pick her up in the morning."

"Let me talk to her," I say loudly, holding my hand out for the phone.

"No, she's not okay with it." He laughs. "But I'm doing it anyway."

"Landon," I say, my voice stern.

"She wants to talk to you." He winks as he hands me my phone and takes his, sliding it into his back pocket.

"Hey, Autumn."

"Sounds like you've had an eventful day. How's the ankle?"

"It's swollen and hurts to stand. I should be fine resting it tonight."

"He's taking you home, huh?"

"I thought maybe—" I don't say more because I know she knows what I'm getting at.

"Yeah, I would have, but he's there, and he really wants to help you."

"What if he's some psycho killer or something?" I ask, sneaking a look at Landon. He's leaning against the edge of my desk, legs crossed at the ankles, arms crossed over his chest, and a cocky smirk on his face. Like the adult that I am, I stick my tongue out at him, causing him to laugh.

"He's not."

"You don't know that."

"Jeremy, is Landon Barker a serial killer?" I hear her ask her husband, and I roll my eyes. I hear him chuckle and say no. "See," she tells me.

"Fine. Can you pick me up in the morning?"

"You have a ride."

"Autuuuuuumn," I whine.

An evil laugh comes through the line. "I'll see you tomorrow. Take care of that ankle." The line goes dead, and I'm tempted to toss my phone at Landon's smug face.

"Do you have what you need?" Landon asks.

I point to my purse and my lunch bag on the corner of my desk. He picks them up and hands them to me. "Ready?" Before I have a chance to answer, he's bending and lifting me into his arms.

I squeal a little, which causes a low chuckle to come from deep in his chest. "You know, it feels better. I'm sure I can drive." My attempt to convince him falls on deaf ears.

He continues to push through the door and carry me to his SUV. "Can you open the door?" he asks.

I hesitate as I think about arguing, but I'm sure he'll just figure out a way to do it on his own. Besides, being this close to him, being in his arms, wrapped in all that muscle with his scent surrounding me, it's doing things to me that it shouldn't. I don't want to be attracted to him, but I am. I need distance, so I reach out and pull open the door. He moves it over with his leg and carefully places me in the passenger seat.

"I'm going to go lock up." He jogs back to the door, makes sure it's locked, and then jogs back to his SUV. He easily slides behind the wheel and looks over at me. "All right, what are we thinking for dinner?"

"I have food at my house. For me," I add as an afterthought. "I can eat there."

"I'm sure you can, but you need to stay off that ankle. Come on, let me buy you dinner."

My stomach growls. *Traitor.* I don't look at him because I know he heard it, as well. "Fine, a drive-thru. Thank you," I murmur the last part. What I don't say is that I was taking a late lunch. I wasn't hungry, so I had planned to walk Buckwheat and then eat before checking on everything and closing for the day.

"You pick."

"Anything. I'm not picky."

"Really? So, what if I said I wanted a juicy burger and fries?"

My stomach growls again, and my mouth waters. "I'd say add a large sweet tea and you've got a deal." I can feel his eyes on me as we pull up to the *Stop* sign. I don't dare look at him. I don't want to know what he's thinking right now.

He reaches for his phone, taps on the screen, and places it to his ear. "Hey, Henry. I need a to-go order, please." He rattles off three cheeseburger deluxes, two orders of fries, and two large sweet teas. "Yeah, I know, but this is a special occasion." He listens, then says, "Thanks, Henry," before ending the call.

We drive in silence for the next fifteen minutes, nothing but the low hum of the tires on the road filling the cab. I don't know who Henry is or where he's taking us, so when we pull up to the back entrance of a small bar not far from the stadium, my interest is piqued.

"I'll be right back."

I watch him as he goes to a back door, enters a code, and disappears inside. Where are we, and why does he have the code to get in? Not that it's any of my business, but if this is some shady place of business, I should know, right? He did bring me here, after all.

A few minutes later, he's back and hands me a white paper bag that smells like heaven. "What is this place?" I ask, setting the bag on my lap.

"A bar. The owner, Henry, is a fan of the Cougars. He has a back room, kind of an extension of the main bar area, for the players. Only we have access. It's a place we can go to kick back, have a beer, and not worry about the fans. Don't get me wrong, we love our fans, but sometimes you just want to chill. I just want to be Landon Barker, not Landon, the Cougars QB. Henry makes that happen."

"That's... nice of him."

"Yeah, he's done it for years. I take full advantage of it, and his food is melt-in-your-mouth good. This will be the best burger you've ever eaten."

"I don't know. I've had some pretty good burgers in my day. My dad is a machine when it comes to the grill."

"I'm telling you. The best," he says, pulling out of the parking lot. "So, where are we headed?" he asks at the *Stop* sign.

"Make a left." He does, and just like that, we're headed to my place. We don't talk unless it's me giving him directions. Twenty minutes later, he's pulling into my drive.

"Nice place," he says, removing his keys from the ignition.

"It's not much, but it's mine," I say defensively.

"Hey." He reaches over and places his hand on my arm. "I wasn't being rude or sarcastic. I meant it." I hate that my defense is up with him. He's just a regular guy who happens to get paid a lot of money for doing something he loves and, I must admit, is damn good at. I love my home, and I'm not embarrassed by it. I need to chill. I'm letting his career, his fame, cloud my judgment for the man that he is. The man who's taking such good care of me. I nod and reach for the door handle, pushing the door open. "Stay put," he says, climbing out of his SUV and rushing to my side. "I'll come back for this." He takes the bag from my hands and places it on the floorboard. "You got your keys?"

I fumble around in my purse, praying that they're in there and not on my desk back at the shelter. Finally, I feel them and pull them out, holding them up for him. "Got 'em."

"Okay. I'm going to go unlock the door and prop it open. You stay here. I'll be right back to get you."

"I can try and walk," I counter, and he gives me a look that tells me to stay put. I go through my mind, trying to remember if my house is a mess. I'm pretty sure everything is tidy, no bras lying around or anything like that. Don't judge. I like to set the girls free once I'm in for the night. I often do that before I shower so I can get dinner started. That is, if I'm cooking. Anyway, I'm good. I think.

"Ready?" he asks, appearing before me. I nod reluctantly and take his hand, letting him help me from the SUV. Once I'm out, I hold my leg in the air because the thought of putting pressure on my ankle hurts to even think about. I nod, and with very little effort, he's got me in his arms and carries me inside. "The couch okay?" he asks.

"Yes. Thank you." He sets me down and grabs a pillow from the other end. I watch as he reclines my section and then places the pillow under my ankle. It's odd to have him here in my home, in my space, taking care of me. He could have very easily just dropped me off, but instead, he's making sure I'm comfortable. I'm not sure how I feel about that.

"I'll be right back." He disappears outside, closing the door behind him. He's barely gone when he's pushing back through the front door. My purse, lunch bag, our drinks, and our food are in his hands. "Okay to just set these here?" he asks, pointing to the coffee table.

"Yes. Thank you."

"Here." He hands me a tea. "It's the best sweet tea you will ever drink."

"I doubt that. I'm from Georgia. Nobody makes tea like they do in the South."

"Just try it," he urges.

Wanting to see what the fuss is all about and to prove him wrong, I place my straw in the cup and take a hefty drink. It's good. "It's good, but not Georgia good," I tell him.

"How about it's the best sweet tea on the West Coast?" He smirks.

"Whatever helps you sleep at night," I joke, and he grins. "Now, what about this burger you raved about?"

"This one is yours, and here are your fries."

"Thank you." I place them on my lap, unwrap the burger, and take a big bite. My hand covers my mouth while I chew because I literally bit off more than I could chew, and he doesn't need to see all that. "Oh my God," I say when I finally swallow. "That's incredible."

"Told you. Want to know what else is incredible?" He doesn't wait for my reply as he continues. "That you eat real food."

"As opposed to eating fake food?" I ask, taking another bite.

He grins. "No, as opposed to 'oh, just a salad for me,'" he says, pitching his voice to be more feminine.

"Umm… was that supposed to be me?"

"No, but that's what I'm used to. Explain that to me. Why do women not eat in front of men? You have to eat to live, so… what gives?"

"I can only assume they're nervous or trying to impress you. Me, on the other hand, I'm neither," I say, taking another bite. If I thought he was being real about this "let me take you to dinner" thing, that it was more than just the chase, I might be nervous, too. However, he's not, and this is the only dinner he's getting. I've seen the women on his arm, the models, the actresses. I'm nowhere in their league. That's not a dig at myself, just stating the facts. He plays on and off the field, from what I've read, and I turned him down. I'm probably the only woman in America to do that. I've stunned his ego, so now he has to prove he can get me to say yes.

"Maybe that's what it is," he mutters.

"What?"

"I'm sure that's what it is. You're right."

We finish our burgers, his two to my one, and start on our fries. "Can you hand me my purse?" I ask. He does as I ask and places it next to me on the couch. Pulling out my wallet, I grab a ten-dollar bill from my wallet and hand it to him.

"What's that?" He looks at the ten-dollar bill as if it offended him.

"For dinner."

"I'm not taking your money, Tessa."

"Please." I try to bat my eyelashes to see if he'll cave. No such luck.

"No. Put that away." His voice is stone serious, which is not something I'm used to seeing with him, so I nod and put the ten back in my wallet.

"Thank you for dinner. Thank you for bringing me home, taking care of things at the shelter, all of it. Thank you, Landon."

"Was that so hard?" he asks.

"And to think I was starting to believe you might not be that bad."

"Hey, I have a reputation to uphold."

"Oh, yeah, and what reputation is that?"

"With the ladies." He bounces his eyebrows up and down, and I try my best not to laugh, but I can't hold it in.

"Laugh it up. Your boy's got skills."

"No. Just no," I sputter with laughter. When I finally stop laughing, I finish off my fries and throw my trash in the bag. "That hit the spot, thank you."

"You're welcome." He gathers all his trash, shoves it into the bag, and stands.

"Where are you going?" I ask, craning my neck to watch him as he walks into the kitchen.

"Looking for the trash can," he calls back. A few minutes later, he's back sans bag of trash, but holding an ice pack from the freezer and a towel from the drawer beside the stove. He places the towel over my ankle and the ice pack on top of it. "That okay?" He peers up at me.

"Thank you." I'll admit, I never expected this side of him. I had him labeled as rich and pretentious, not soft and caring. It's a definite contrast to how I had him categorized in my mind. His taking care of me makes him more… endearing. It's dangerous. I need to keep my wits about me. I can't let one afternoon of being nice allow me to fall in line with the masses that fall at his feet.

He nods, steps over my legs with his long-ass ones, and takes his seat on the couch. "Now what?"

"Um, I'm not sure what you're asking."

"Want to watch a movie?"

"Don't you have places to go and people to see or do?" I ask.

"Yes. I have to be here, and I have to see—" He pauses and glances down at my chest, before his eyes come back to my face. "Or do you." He grins.

"You've been here, we had dinner, I let you pay, and I appreciate your help, but I've got it from here."

"Come on, just one movie. It's still early." He reaches for the remote on the coffee table and turns on the TV. He makes himself at home, pulling up Netflix and searching through the movies. "What do you feel like watching?"

"Landon." He turns his head to look at me. "Go home."

"I'm good." He turns back to the screen and pulls up a movie. It's a romantic comedy, which surprises me.

"This is what you pick?"

"Yeah, don't women like these things? The romance movies?"

"Yeah, but that doesn't explain why you picked it."

"Don't worry, Deaton. I know this date doesn't end with that kind of happy ending," he jests.

"Date?" I ask, incredulous.

"I picked you up, literally." He smirks. "We had dinner, and now we're watching a movie. I qualify that as a date."

"Nope. No. Not happening, Barker. Get your ass out of my house."

"Fine." He raises his hands in the air. "It's not a date. We're just two gorgeous people spending time together. How's that?"

"Gah. You are so full of it."

"Thank you."

I roll my eyes and settle back on the couch to watch the movie. What choice do I have? He's taken care of me and bought me dinner... I guess it's the least that I can do. Blocking him out, which is so damn hard to do, I focus on the TV and get lost in the movie. It's one I've seen before, but I'm easily engrossed in the story regardless.

Halfway through the movie, my bladder is screaming. Reaching out, I remove the ice pack and lower the leg of the couch.

"What are you doing?" he asks, pausing the movie.

"I have to pee."

"Let me help you." He stands and reaches for me.

"I think I can walk on it." His hands grip my arms as I take a tentative step. It's painful, but not anything I can't handle. "See."

"I see, but I also know from experience..." He points to his chest.

"Professional athlete, remember? Anyway, I also know from experience that the more you rest and ice it, the faster it will heal." With that, he bends and lifts me into his arms. "Where are we going?"

"Down the hall. The door at the end of the hallway." My heart rate kicks up a notch. Being in his arms does something to me. When you look past the cocky and the career, and you strip him down to the man, all that's left is his caring nature he's shown me today and his pure sex appeal. It's kind of hard to forget that when his strong arms are carrying me.

He walks us down the hall and stops just outside the bathroom door. "I'll stay right here and wait for you." He pushes on the door and holds it open for me. Carefully, he sets me on my feet, keeping his hands on my waist to make sure I don't fall.

"I'm good, Landon."

He nods and releases his hold on me. I hop through the door, lean against the bathroom counter, shut the door, and twist the lock. I take what feels like the first breath since the moment I fell. Landon is pushy and intense and so damn stubborn. He's also caring, and that's not something I expected from him. He's also the sexiest man I've ever seen, and it's taking willpower I didn't know I possessed to sit next to him. If I were the adventurous type, I'd crawl into his lap and let him have his way with me. I have no doubt it would be one for the history books, but that's not me. I know if I let that happen, I would regret it the next day. With sex comes feelings, and I just can't separate the two.

"Tessa, you okay in there?" Landon calls through the door.

Shit. "Yeah, just a second." I scramble to the toilet, work my leggings down, and somehow manage to sit without falling over. It takes me a minute to go, even though my bladder is full, knowing he's standing right outside the door, listening. Finally able to do my business, I manage to stand and hobble to the counter to pull up my leggings and wash my hands.

When I open the door, he's there. Without a word, he picks me up yet again like I'm nothing but air and carries me to my spot on the couch. "Do you have any popcorn?" he asks.

"Yeah, it's in the pantry."

"I'm going to get you a fresh one of these." He picks up the ice pack from the table. "And I'll make us some. What do you want to drink?"

"I have some tea still."

He nods. "Be right back."

I must be in some kind of alternate universe. I don't understand why he's still here or why he's hell-bent on staying around. He knows he's not getting laid tonight, or at least he should.

"Here." He places a fresh towel and ice pack over my ankle. "It's too early for these, but I saw them in the cabinet and wanted to bring them to you so you didn't have to get up for them later." He sets a bottle of Advil and a bottle of water on the table beside me. Before I can thank him, he's back in the kitchen and returning with two more bottles of water and a huge bowl of popcorn.

That's how the rest of our night goes. We watch the rest of the movie, and he starts another. By the time it's over, I'm exhausted and ready for bed. "I'm going to clean up." He stands and picks up the bowl and the now-empty water bottles. "Then I'll help you to bed."

"I can manage."

"I'm sure you can, but you don't have to since I'm here." He walks off.

Who does he think he is? Yes, he did me a solid today, and I appreciate it, but I can manage just fine on my own. Standing, I begin to hop down the hall to the bathroom to wash my face and brush my teeth. I stop about halfway, even though my hallway is not all that long, to take a breather.

"What are you doing, Tess?" Strong hands grip my hips, and his hot breath caresses my ear.

"I'm getting ready for bed."

"Not without me," he says, and I swear he leans in just a little closer.

"I can manage. Thank you for everything. Will you please make sure the door is locked on your way out?" I ask, dismissing him.

"Right after I put you to bed." I squeal when he lifts me off my feet, just from his grip on my hips. "Which room is yours?" he asks from behind me.

"Put me down."

"I can do this all day, Tess. Which room is yours?"

"I need to brush my teeth." I give in. There is no use fighting with him.

"We can do that." He carries me to the end of the hall and doesn't put me on my feet until I'm standing in front of the sink. "Do your thing." He motions to the sink as he lowers the lid on the toilet and takes a seat.

"Are you kidding me right now?"

"Nope."

"Landon, just go. I'm fine. I don't need you here in my house, packing me around like I'm a toddler. I can handle it. I appreciate you wanting to help, but I can manage on my own."

"And I can stay until you're ready for bed."

"You're not going to be here in the middle of the night or in the morning when I'm getting ready. I'm a big girl, Number Eighteen. I can manage."

"Maybe I should stay," he muses.

"No! You are not staying here."

"Then do what you need to do, let me tuck you in, and you won't have to see me again until tomorrow morning."

"Gah! You are so damn frustrating."

He nods. "So I've been told."

Needing this day to be over, I rush through washing my face and brushing my teeth. I don't tell him I'm done. Instead, I turn and start to walk—well, hop out the bathroom door. He slides up to my side, places his arm around me, and lets me lean on him as we make our way to my bedroom.

"Which one is yours?"

"This one." I point to the door on the right side of the hallway. The door is open, and thankfully, my bed is made, and there is nothing in plain sight that shouldn't be, at least from a quick glance. We make it to the bed, and I sit down.

"Where are your pajamas?"

"I can get it, Landon," I say, exasperated.

"So can I. You can change while I go get the meds and a bottle of water. Then I'll go. Promise."

"Top drawer." I point to my dresser. Just as he opens the drawer, I remember that's where I put the card from the flowers. Silently, I cross my fingers, hoping it's slid to the bottom and he doesn't notice it.

I'm not that lucky.

"Aw, you kept it." He holds up the little white envelope between his fingers, and of course, those damn dimples appear.

"I don't know how that got in there." Lies.

He smirks. "You should use it, you know. My number."

"No, thanks. I'm trying to get rid of you, remember?"

"I'm not going to go away that easily. In fact, you should give me your number so I can check on you."

"You're still here." My voice is raised. I'm not yelling, but the irritation he's causing is definitely showing through.

"I'll leave, but I want your number. I want to be able to check on you. You live alone, and I feel bad leaving you like this."

Something about the look in his eyes tells me it's more than that. But I find myself relenting just to get rid of him. I need him out of my space. "Fine. It's in your phone. I didn't delete the call. Don't be blowing me up." I huff, and he grins. I hate that I like that he's concerned.

He pulls out some pajamas and makes a show of shoving the little white envelope back into the drawer. He tosses the clothes to me, where I sit on the bed, and leaves the room, shutting the door behind him. I glare at the handle, wishing there was a lock. I've never needed one before now. Hell, knowing his cocky ass, he'll just take the door off the damn hinges. Not wanting to be caught with my panties down, literally, I quickly slip out of my bra and slide the pajama shirt over my head. I leave my leggings on. I can slip those off after he leaves. I'm sliding under the covers when he knocks on the door.

"Ready or not, here I come," he sings-songs and slowly pushes the door open.

"Gimme, and go." I hold my hands out for the bottle of Advil and the water.

"So testy," he taunts.

"Landon," I growl. I actually growl. That's what this man has brought me to. Growling at him like some wild animal, and not from pleasure, I might add.

"Here." He shakes out two tablets, screws the lid off the water, and hands them to me. I toss them back and watch him as he plugs my cell phone into the charger and places it on the nightstand. "You need anything else?"

"No. Just go home."

"All right. I'll see you in the morning. You get to the shelter at nine, right?"

"How do you know that?"

He shrugs. "Autumn."

"Yes," I say through gritted teeth. She's on his side, so I know her coming to pick me up in the morning is a long shot. One more encounter with him and then I'm done. He's testing my patience and has me horny as hell all at the same time. My body and mind are at war with one another.

"I have to be at the field at nine, so I'll have to drop you off at eight-thirty. That all right with you?"

"Fine."

"Need anything?" he asks. This time, his voice is softer, and it reminds me of how he was treating me when I first fell today.

Kind.

Gentle.

"No. Goodnight, Landon."

My breath stalls in my chest when he leans over and kisses the top of my head. "Night, Tess. I'll lock up."

And just like that, he's gone. I listen as his heavy footfalls carry him to the front door, and I hear the door close. The handle jiggles as he tests the lock. Finally, I fall back onto my pillows just as my phone pings with a message.

Unknown: Night, Tess. Door's locked.

I save his number. I have a feeling I'll need to know who's calling or texting me in the future and reply.

Me: Thanks.

I don't want to give him the idea that we're going to be texting back and forth all the time. I've thanked him several times today and this evening. He knows I appreciate it. It's done. Time to let it go. Placing my phone back on the nightstand, I turn off the bedside lamp and surprisingly, fall right to sleep.

CHAPTER 6

Landon

I'M STARING AT THE ALARM CLOCK WHEN IT ROLLS OVER TO 6:29. One more minute and it will blare at me to wake up. Reaching over, I turn it off to prevent the annoying buzzer from sounding. I slept like shit last night. I kept replaying my day with Tessa in my mind. This thing between us started because she turned me down. And there is still part of me that wants that satisfaction of knowing I changed her mind. However, she's unlike any woman I've ever met.

I love the banter, but more than that, I love that I'm just Landon when I'm with her. She doesn't seem to care about my career or my bank account. Is she just putting on a show? I really don't think that she is, but I don't really know her well enough to form that kind of opinion. That's why I want to get to know her. Yes, I want her to agree to go out with me, one date, but at the same time, is she really who she presents her-

woman who loves animals and isn't afraid to eat a juicy burger no matter who's watching?

I want her to be real.

I want her to be that person.

My gut tells me she is. I'm usually not wrong on these things, but there's a first time for everything. If this isn't the real Tessa, she's one hell of an actress. From what I know about her so far, she's legit.

Climbing out of bed, I strip out of my boxer briefs and head to the shower. Normally, I would go for a run, but my ass is dragging from lack of sleep, and with a long practice ahead of me in the hot Californian sun, I know better than to push it. Maybe I'll grab a nap when I get home, then go for a run this evening after the sun goes down. I could also hop on the treadmill, but I prefer being outside. Running on the beach is my favorite.

After my shower, I catch up on a few emails and watch ESPN until it's time to leave. I hit the local bagel shop and grab us a couple of bagels with cream cheese and two large coffees. I don't know how she takes hers, and for some unexplained reason, that irks me. So, I have them add cream and sugar to the bag just in case.

I pull up to her house ten minutes before eight. I see the curtain move, and that small gesture inflates my chest. She's watching... waiting for me. I don't try to contain my smile as I grab the bag of bagels and the carrier that holds our two cups of coffee. Miss Tessa is about to share her second meal with me. Juggling it all in one hand, I knock on the door. I know she's close because she was just at the window, but it takes a long damn time to open.

The breath leaves my lungs as soon as the door opens. Tessa stands before me in a polo shirt that fits her nicely, showing off her slender frame and those incredible breasts, with the shelter's logo on the chest. She's in a pair of khaki shorts that are in no way sexy, but on her, they are. I can imagine those toned, tan legs of hers wrapped around me. Her hair is bunched up on top of her head, her curls wild, yet on her, they're perfect. Her face is void of any makeup, and just like last night, the soft dusting of freckles on her cheeks is on display. It was a war I waged with myself to not pull her into my arms last night and trace them with my tongue. That urge is still there today, stronger than ever.

"Landon?" she prompts, and I shake myself out of my mental fog.

"Morning, Freckles," I say, the nickname slipping past my lips before I can stop it. A frown appears as her forehead scrunches up. I fight the urge to reach out and smooth the lines with my thumb. "I brought breakfast," I say instead.

"Come on in." She steps back.

"How's the ankle?"

"Sore, but I can put weight on it today."

"Can you keep it propped up at your desk today?"

"For the most part. After cleaning cages, feedings, baths, things like that."

"How about I come by after practice and help with those things?"

"That's not necessary. I'll be fine. I can't baby it."

"You need to rest it. Give it time to heal."

"Oh, really. Tell me, Mr. QB, how many times have you played injured? How many times have you been out on that field when you wanted to be at home, propped up in bed? Or on the couch with a cold beer, nursing your wounds?"

"That's different. That's my job. I get paid a lot of money to be on that field."

"This is *my* job, Landon. I might not make millions, but it's my job. I love what I do, and I love those animals who depend on me."

"I'm sorry," I say, hearing the hurt in her voice. "I didn't mean to offend you." She turns to walk away. "Tess." I reach out and gently grip her elbow. She stops and turns to look at me. "I'm sorry."

She nods. "I need to finish getting ready." She pulls away, and I let her.

"Can you eat first?" She stops but doesn't turn around. "Please?" Her shoulders deflate, and I know that I have her. Who knew one simple word could have her agreeing so easily?

"Nothing fancy," I say, following her into the kitchen. "Just bagels and coffee. I didn't know how you took yours, so I had them add cream and sugar to the bag."

"Thank you." Her reply is polite and formal. I want the teasing Tessa back.

"So, how do you take it?" I ask when she doesn't volunteer the information.

"Black, two sugars."

I nod. "Good to know." I hand her a bagel and unwrap my own. We eat in silence, and it's not as uncomfortable as I thought it would be. I find that I just like being near her. Crumbling my wrapper and tossing it in the bag, I finish off my coffee.

"There's more in the pot if you need it," she says before taking another bite of her bagel. She wraps up the remaining half and stands.

"What are you doing?"

"I don't want to make you late for practice. Besides, I ate a piece of toast when I took Advil this morning."

"Well, take it with you. You can eat it later."

"Okay."

Just like that, she stands and hobbles down the hall to finish getting ready. I fight the urge to follow her. Instead, I call out to her. "Hey, Tessa."

"Yeah?"

"You need help?"

"I'm good."

Damn, is that disappointment that she doesn't need my help? I take care of my trash, and although another cup would be nice to make up for my lack of sleep, I forgo another and instead grab a bottle of water from the fridge.

"Ready," she says.

She's got makeup on now, covering her freckles, and I hate that she's covering them up. "Why'd you cover them?" I ask, pointing to her face.

"What are you talking about?" She pretends like she doesn't understand the question, but by the set of her shoulders, I know she does.

My feet carry me to stand in front of her. My hand rises as if it has a mind of its own, and my thumb lightly skims across her cheek. "Your freckles, why did you cover them?"

"I'd prefer not to look like sixteen-year-old me." Her green eyes stare up at me.

"Sixteen-year-old you must have been gorgeous because, you now... with freckles exposed... you're the most beautiful woman I've ever seen." I didn't mean to lay that out there, but I'll be damned if she thinks of herself as anything but a knockout.

A blush coats her cheeks. Even under the makeup, I can see it. "We should go." She steps back, and the connection, the moment, is lost.

"Right. Where are your bags? I'll carry them out to the car."

"I can get it."

"I'm sure you can, but I'm doing it anyway."

She sighs. "On the couch."

I hold my elbow out for her, and after a few seconds of hesitation, she links arms with me. We stop by the couch, and I grab her bags, then guide her outside. I wait while she locks up and then help her to the passenger side of my SUV.

Once we're on the road, the quiet starts to get to me. Time to break the ice. "So, did you think of me last night?" I glance over to catch her rolling her eyes. Perfect. I want a reaction out of her.

"How did you know? Did you hear me call out your name?"

She gasps and places her hand to her chest as if she's offended or embarrassed.

The problem with that is, she may be teasing me, but the thought of her touching herself while thinking about me is making things very tight down below. My cock twitches, and I have to shift in my seat. That makes her giggle.

"You okay, Number Eighteen?"

"Minx." Her laughter fills the car, and I don't hate it.

"How long is practice today?" she asks.

"Five hours. Three on the field and two watching tapes, going over plays, special teams, that kind of thing."

"Have you always loved football?"

"Yeah. I guess from the time I was little, I would sit on my dad's lap and we'd watch it for hours. The only time I ever sat still, to hear my parents tell it." I glance over at her, and she has a soft smile playing on her lips. "Anyway, the school district we lived in didn't offer football, so my parents went with open enrollment when it was time for me to start kindergarten in the town next to ours. I started full-contact football at the age of five and never looked back."

"That's kind of amazing, to think how your love for the game started that early, and look at you now."

"My parents are the best. I owe them my success. All the times they took me to practice, five nights a week, and games on the weekends until I turned sixteen and got my license. They always made sure I had the best gear, going as far as buying my helmet each year to make sure that it was safe."

"They sound pretty great."

"They are." I nod. "What about you? Why the animal shelter?"

"I love animals." I can hear the truth in her words. "I came to Los Angeles for vet school, but I didn't love it. School, that is, or the thought of being in school for so many more years, so I changed my major to veterinary technician. Two years later, I was done. I applied to the shelter and was hired on the spot. Autumn had just taken over, and we hit it off. We've been best friends ever since."

"It makes a difference when you can do what you love. Makes it feel like less of a job."

"Exactly. Not once in the time that I've worked at Safe Haven have I dreaded coming to work."

"I get to play a sport for a living." I chuckle. "It doesn't get any better than that."

"I don't know, you saw the puppies, right?" she asks.

"You clearly win. I get to spend my day with smelly, sweaty men, while you get adorable puppies and horses that just like to eat."

"Hmmm, when you put it that way, you might be getting the better deal, minus the smelly part."

"Hey now." I reach over and tap her thigh. "I've already called dibs; those other Neanderthals need to find their own Tessa," I say, pulling into the lot of the shelter. A small smile tilts her lips, but she's quick to hide it.

"Thanks for the ride, and for your help last night." She grabs her bags from the floorboard between her feet and opens her door.

"I'll walk you in."

"No. You don't have to do that. Have a great practice." She slides out of the car and shuts the door with her hip.

I scramble to exit the car, as well; she's not too far ahead of me with that limp of hers. I rush ahead of her and pull open the door. She shakes her head but doesn't comment as she walks inside, with me following along behind.

"Morning, sunshine. How was last night? Or… and this morning," Autumn says, appearing from around the corner. "Oh, hi, Landon." Her grin is blinding. "Looks like I got my answer."

"Autumn," I greet. "It's nice to see you again." I then turn my attention to Tessa. "You got everything?"

She holds up her lunch bag and her purse. "Thanks for the ride."

Why do I have the sudden urge to pull her into a hug and press my lips to hers? Instead, I lean in close and whisper, but still keep my voice loud enough that Autumn can hear what I'm saying, "Thanks for the second date."

"W-What?" she sputters. "No. No dates."

"Come on, Freckles. We had dinner and watched not one but two movies last night before I took you to bed, and this morning, we had breakfast together. That was our second date."

"You did not take me to bed," she manages to say through gritted teeth.

"No? I didn't help you into your room and make sure you were settled before I headed home?" I ask with a smirk.

"Go." She pushes on my chest. "You're going to be late for practice."

I look over at Autumn. "I'll be here after practice to do whatever needs to be done today. Keep her off that ankle. She needs to elevate it and ice it."

"Yes, sir." Autumn salutes me, tossing out a wink.

Glad to know she's Team Landon. "I'll be here after practice. Take it easy today." With one step, I'm standing close to her again, invading her space. For some reason, this moment feels monumental with Autumn here watching us. Hell, even if she weren't here, it would feel that way. It's Tessa. There's just something about her. Leaning in, my lips connect with her temple. "Have a good day." The words are softly whispered just for her. This isn't a part of the show. This is me not wanting to leave her here.

What the fuck is wrong with me?

From the look on her face, she's wondering the same thing. I wink, turn on my heel, and walk out the door. If I stay any longer, I'm going to be late for practice, and Coach Neil will have my ass. Running sprints with a hefty monetary fine is not something I plan on taking on today.

"You're on fire out there today," Case says, joining me on the sidelines for a drink of water.

I grin and take another swig from the Gatorade bottle. "You're putting the ball in my hands and blocking the D-line."

"It's more than that. You get laid or something? Damn it, Barker. Did you hit up Henry's without me?" He gives me a look that tells me if that were the case, he'd be pissed.

"Nope." The rest of the team filters over, and we start talking about practice and our first preseason game in a few weeks.

"Hey, man, how's Luna?" I ask Trent Caudill. He's our starting right tackle, a beast of a man at six feet eight inches and weighing in at three-hundred-and-fifty-nine pounds.

"She's perfect. Pregnancy looks good on her," he says of his wife.

"When's the little crumb snatcher coming?" Jack Fields, our starting left tackle, asks. He's close to Trent in size, at six-six and two-hundred-and-ninety-eight pounds.

They're both blocking machines, and I know that when they're out on the field with me, I'm protected. To say that they're good at their jobs is an understatement.

"The week of Thanksgiving. I'm hoping we're home when it happens. Or we have a bye the following week. If she could hold off a few days, that would be ideal."

"Gentlemen, is this little hen meeting over? We have some tapes to watch." Coach Neil walks past us, and I see the smirk on his face.

He likes to give us shit, no matter if we're on the field or not. Not needing to be told twice, we head to the locker room for quick showers so we can file into the media room to watch film.

With my phone on my lap, I sit at the back of the room, and it takes Herculean effort to stay awake. I debate texting Tessa to see how her ankle is, but I'll see her soon enough. I don't know if she believed me or not when I told her and Autumn I would be back today, but I meant it. Somehow, she's become more than just the chase and someone I want to get to know. Regardless of whether or not she ever accepts my offer for a proper date, Tessa's cool, and my gut tells me that knowing her, that having her in my life, could only mean good things.

Two hours later, we're all blinking as our eyes adjust to the overhead lights that someone just turned on. "Class dismissed." Coach titters, obviously amused with himself. We hear that line often, and it's always followed by a laugh. He's a hardass on the field and about the game, but he's a damn good coach because of it. He's also a pretty chill guy when he's not ripping your ass while you're on the field or pointing out a mistake in a game while going over film.

"Henry's?" Kaden suggests.

"Can't."

"What do you got going on?" Case gives me a curious look.

"I have plans." I'm being vague, and we all know it.

"What kind of plans?"

"Just plans."

"Uh-huh." Thomas laughs. "He's getting laid."

I'm never going to hear the end of this. "I'm going to the animal shelter." I'd much rather tell them the truth and take their ribbing than for them to get the wrong idea about Tessa when they find out that's where I went. I've never really cared about their opinions of the women I've spent time with in the past. Mostly because outside of a hook-up or a date to a function, there haven't been any. Not since high school.

"You getting a dog?" Case asks.

"No. Tessa fell and hurt her ankle, so I'm going to go help."

"Tessa, is she the hot-as-hell chick that was with Coach Baldwin's wife?" Thomas asks.

"That would be her."

"Nice." Jack holds his fist out for me.

"Lucky Bastard," Kaden mumbles. "Why you gotta take all the prime pussy, QB?"

I ignore the fact that he just referred to Tessa as pussy and push forward. It's how we talk, we've all done it, but it suddenly feels wrong when we're talking about *her*. "Look, she hurt her ankle, and the volunteers are random at best, according to Tessa, so I'm just helping out. Feeding some dogs and whatever else needs to be done. No big deal."

"Maybe we should come with you," Jack offers. "You know, lend our brawn." He flexes his arms as if to show off his muscles.

"Nah, it's good. Thanks, though."

"Oh, I see," Kaden announces. "You're afraid she'll drop you and go for the real Cougar stud." He puffs out his chest, and we laugh at his display.

"It's no big deal. I'm just being nice. That's all."

"Okay." Trent grins. "If that's how you want to play it. Boys, I'm going home to my wife. I'll see your ugly mugs on Monday."

With a wave of goodbyes, we all go our separate ways, at least Trent and I do. I don't stick around to see if the guys are meeting up at Henry's now or later, for that matter. I have somewhere I need to be. After all, I never break a promise.

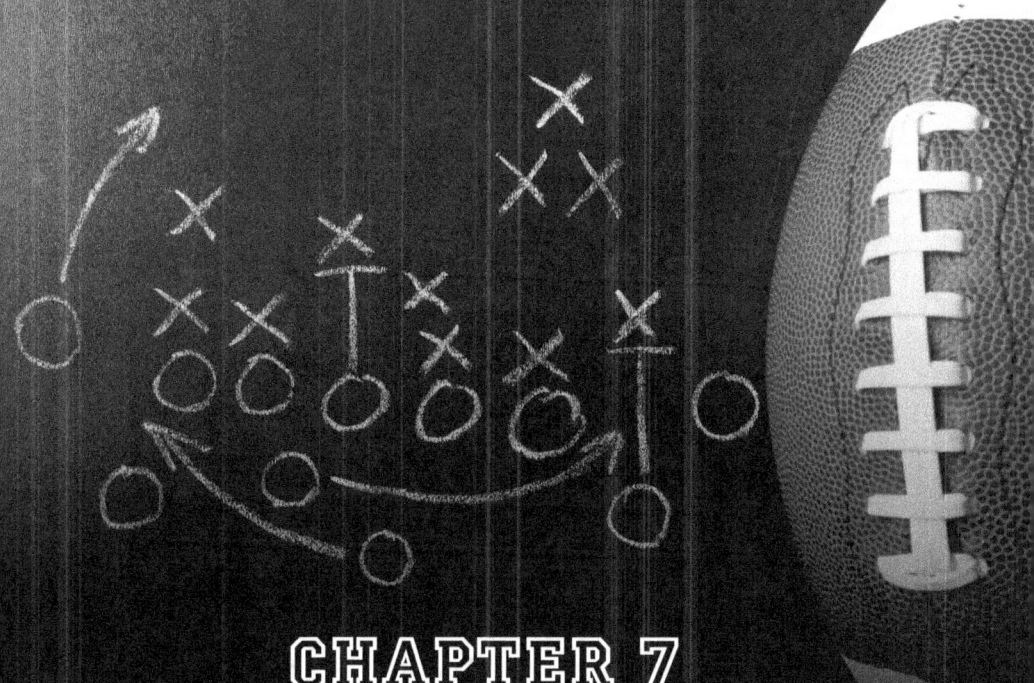

CHAPTER 7

Tessa

I T'S SATURDAY AFTERNOON, AND I'VE BEEN LOUNGING AROUND the house all day. My ankle still hurts, and I figure two days of rest and I should be good as new for work next week. Autumn is on call this weekend for the shelter, so I don't have to worry about following up to make sure the volunteers show up. We've talked about hiring another part-time person. Someone to staff the weekends, but it's hard to find someone willing to work both weekend days. The hours could be flexible, as long as the animals are fed and watered, the cages are cleaned, and the dogs get to stretch their legs. They could do that in a couple of hours each day. It's something I should bring up again and see what she says.

My house is clean, the laundry is washed, folded, and put away, and I have a chicken casserole in the Crock-Pot. It's way too much food for just me, so that will be my meals for the weekend, and I'll take the rest to work and send it home with Autumn for her and Jeremy on Monday.

When I do cook, that's usually what I end up doing with it. They don't seem to mind, and I hate the thought of food going to waste.

I'm scrolling through Netflix, trying to find a new series to binge-watch, when my phone pings with a message.

Number 18: How's your day going?

Me: Just hanging around the house. Yours?

I hesitate before hitting send. Replying like this opens up an all-new category of texting. Do I want that? I have to admit, Landon has surprised me. He came back to the shelter yesterday and, in no time, had everything on my to-do list completed. Of course, it helped that Autumn was like a mother hen, not letting me get out of my chair. Needless to say, with his help, I got caught up on all of my busy work that there never seems to be enough time in the day to complete. Hence, the reason I'm bored. I normally bring it home with me to work on during the weekend. I don't mind it, and I know Autumn appreciates me doing so as she does the same thing. I try to take on that role as she has a husband and a little boy at home. I'm just me. My mom is back home in Georgia, and my dating life is nonexistent at the moment.

Number 18: Same. How about some dinner?

Me: Already in the Crock-Pot.

I'm glad that this is the truth and I don't have to lie or just blatantly shut him down again. I would have thought he would have given up by now.

Number 18: Perfect. What time should I be there?

Me: …

Number 18: Come on, Tess. A man's gotta eat.

His text is followed by a picture of the inside of what I assume is his refrigerator. It's empty except for a carton of eggs, a gallon of milk, a few bottles of water, a couple of cans of White Claw, and a few bottles of Gatorade.

Me: I'm thinking you need to go grocery shopping.

Number 18: Will you go with me?

Me: No.

Number 18: I didn't think so. I'll be there in an hour. Do I need to bring anything?

Me: You're not invited.

I type the words, but I admit, he's not the worst company I've ever had. I was looking forward to a few days just to relax, but it's kind of lonely here all alone all weekend.

Number 18: I've got dessert covered.

Me: Landon!

Number 18: Gotta go. See ya soon.

I don't bother to text him back. I know he won't reply. I also know he's going to be at my door in an hour, possibly less, if our previous interactions and his tendency to be early is his usual MO.

I look down at the leggings I have on. They have little puppy golden retrievers on them, and the puppies are wearing Christmas hats. Sure, it's summertime in California, but my mom bought them for me two Christmases ago. They're super soft and comfy, and they remind me of home. My shirt is a simple black tank top that shows the straps of my sports bra. My hair is a knotted mess of curls on top of my head, my feet are bare, as is my face, since I didn't bother with makeup. I start to freak out, then decide this is a good thing. He's going to see me slumming it in my loungewear and run far, far away. I refuse to be anyone but myself, even for the sexy quarterback.

Sure enough, forty-five minutes later, there's a knock at the door. I stand from my nest on the couch, and I say nest because of all the blankets and pillows—I take lounging very seriously. Pulling open the door, I take in the sight before me. Landon is wearing basketball shorts, a skin-tight T-shirt, and slides. In his hand is a box from a local bakery and a bouquet of flowers.

"Are you going to invite me in, Tessa?" His husky voice is laced with amusement.

"I told you that you weren't invited." I try to sound stern, but it's hard when the man brings dessert and flowers. Oh, and let's not forget he looks good enough to eat.

"Come on now." He grins, and those damn dimples wink at me.

I was always going to let him in. I just had to make him think it was an inconvenience. Stepping back, I give him ample space to enter the house before closing the door behind him.

"Is that dinner I smell?" he asks, making his way to the kitchen to deposit the bakery box. He turns to face me. "Do you have a vase?"

"Yes, and I do." Reaching under the kitchen sink, I pull out a vase and add some water. I place it on the counter, and Landon carefully unwraps the flowers and slides them into the vase. I watch him and his big hands, and those strong arms as he arranges the flowers until he's satisfied. They're beautiful, and my heart tips over in my chest when I think about what it means when a man brings a woman flowers. Sure, it can be a kind, friendly gesture, but in most cases, that's not it. They want more— romantically. He's making it increasingly difficult to remember that he's in this for the chase. Or is he?

"There. Where do you want them?"

"The table is fine." I point to the center of the kitchen table and then rush to move the bowl of apples and oranges that are currently taking up that space, relocating them to the counter by the stove.

"So, what's for dinner?" he asks.

"Chicken casserole."

"It smells delicious."

"Thanks. It won't be done for another hour or so." I glance at the clock and see it's a few minutes after four.

"Perfect, let's get you off that ankle." He places his hand on the small of my back and guides us back to the living room.

The heat from his hand sears through my shirt and warms my skin. It makes me wonder what his calloused hands would feel like as they roam over my body. *No, don't go there, Tessa.* I take a seat and gather my nest, sliding under the cover and holding the pillows to my chest.

"What's up with all that?" He points to my lap.

I shrug. "It's more of a comfort thing. I like to cuddle, and well, when you're single and live alone, that's not possible, so this is the next best thing."

"I've never been much of a cuddler."

"Have you ever tried it?"

"Not really, no."

"There you go. Don't knock it until you try it." He nods and reaches for the pillows in my arms. "Hey, what are you doing? Get your own." I point to the loveseat that houses two more pillows just like mine.

"You said don't knock it until I try it," he reminds me.

"Fine." I concede and hand him the pillows. I expect him to hold them to his chest like I just did, but instead, he tosses them on the floor and then pulls the blanket off me. I don't fight him and let him pull it from my lap. My eyes dart to the blanket on the back of the loveseat, so I stand to grab it. In fact, I think I'll just start over with my nest there; he can have the couch. He is a lot taller than me.

Carefully, I begin to step over the pillows he tossed on the floor.

That's all I need is to reinjure my ankle, or worse, injure the other one. However, before I have the chance, his hands are on my hips as he pulls me into his lap. "Ahh!" I scream, not expecting this turn of events. "What in the hell are you doing?" I ask, trying to sit up so I can stand.

"I'm trying it out."

"Trying what out?"

"Cuddling."

"Not with me. With the blankets and pillows."

"You said they were second best. I need to try the real thing to know if I'm a cuddler, right?"

"Not with me." I try again to stand, but his hold is tight.

"Only with you" is his deep whispered reply. His lips next to my ear cause goose bumps to break out across my skin. "Just let me try it." His thumb slides under my tank top, and he begins to trace the skin just above my leggings.

I open my mouth to tell him no, but instead, it closes on its own, and I nod. It's been way too long since I've cuddled with a man or had a man's hands on me. His are big and warm, and if the pad of his thumb is any indication, surprisingly soft for a man who spends hours a day on the football field.

"How do we do this, Tess?"

"W-We uh, should lie down." I can't believe I'm encouraging him, but the thought of snuggling up with him is far too tempting. He taps my hip and, this time, allows me to stand. I could make a mad dash for the loveseat, or hell, I could kick him out, but I do neither. Instead, I stand and watch him arrange the pillows. He grabs the throw and tosses it over the back of the couch, and then reaches for the remote. Once he has what he thinks we'll need, he stretches out on my couch, lying on his side, and pats the small space in front of him.

I hesitate. Am I really going to do this? I mean, sure, it's just cuddling, but what if he thinks that means I'm willing to have sex with him?

Well, I mean, I am willing, but I won't do it. You know, catching feelings and all that.

"Come here, Freckles." His voice is soft, almost soothing, as his eyes capture mine. Taking a deep breath, I lie down in front of him, my body stiff, trying not to melt into his warmth. I really should turn up the thermostat. It's so hot outside, so I like to keep it cool in here.

Landon pulls the throw blanket from the back of the couch and drapes it over me. Then, to my surprise, he wraps his arms around me and pulls me close. "You good?" he asks, and his hot breath ghosts across my ear.

"Y-Yeah."

"What are we watching?" he asks, turning on the TV. He doesn't seem the least bit fazed that we're lying together so intimately on my couch.

"Anything." I should have known better than to agree to this. In a way, this is more intimate than having sex. The connection of our bodies, the warmth we share. It's overwhelming, and I can't help but wonder what it would be like if there was an us. If I was more than just the chase. If this thing between us was more than just the fact that I turned him down. Would this be our thing? Relaxing and cuddling on the couch?

He flips through the channels and stops on a movie channel that's playing *Sweet Home Alabama*. I love this movie. I am from the South, after all. "This okay?"

"Yes. But you can watch whatever." Satisfied with my reply, he sets the remote on the floor, tucking his hand behind his head.

My body is stiff as I fight the urge to relax into his embrace. We're lying on our sides, and his hand is resting on my belly, holding me to him. "Relax, Freckles." It's as if my body needed his words as permission to do just that. I feel my shoulders relax, and my body sinks further into the couch.

He mumbles something that sounds like "That's my girl," and I feel his lips press to the back of my head. This is way too much. It's wrong to be here with him like this, when we're nothing to each other. Nothing more than acquaintances, yet here I am, letting him into my home. Again. Giving in to his demands. Letting him hold me. Okay, maybe it wasn't a demand, but all the same, I shouldn't be doing this. I just can't seem to make myself pull away.

Drawing out of my thoughts, I turn my attention back to the movie. I let myself get lost in the love story. I've seen this one at least one hundred times, but it never gets old. I could repeat the lines by heart as if I played the role.

"So I can kiss you anytime I want," I whisper with Reese Witherspoon as she stands before her leading man in the pouring rain.

Landon's thumb traces small circles over my belly, and I endure it until the credits roll. Needing some distance, I sit up, pulling out of his embrace, and stand. "Dinner should be ready."

His eyes are bright blue and filled with something I can't quite name as he peers up at me. "Tess," he says softly, reaching out for me.

I step away from him. "I'm going to make us a salad. You eat salad, right?" My eyes travel to the eight-pack of abs clearly outlined beneath his form-fitting shirt.

"Yeah, I eat salad." He drops his hand and pulls his long form from the couch.

Turning on my heel, I make my way to the kitchen. I don't have to turn to see if he's behind me. I can feel him. I gather the bag of salad mix, a tomato, a bag of cheese, and the bottle of ranch and French dressing from the refrigerator. "I only have French or ranch." I hold up the bottles to show him.

"I'll eat either."

"Good. Tomatoes and cheese?" I ask.

"Yes." He comes to stand behind me, looking over my shoulder as I start to prepare our salads. "What can I do to help?"

"Uh… there's a bag of croutons in the cabinet there." I point to the cabinet by the fridge. I quickly avert my gaze back to the salad in front of me to keep from drooling over him. I am holding a knife, after all. I need to stay alert or I fear I could lose a digit.

"Plates?" he asks, taking the lid off the Crock-Pot and bending closer to inspect the contents or maybe smell it; I'm not really sure.

"Above your head. There's a spoon in the drawer in front of you." I can hear him messing around, and with a quick glance, I see he's plating each of us some of the chicken casserole.

"This smells fantastic. What's it in?"

"Just chicken breasts, cream of chicken soup, milk, salt and pepper, and some boxed stuffing."

"Easy enough."

"Do you cook?" I ask him.

"I know my way around the kitchen, but I don't do it often. Cooking for one isn't much fun. I always make breakfast. Hitting practice on an empty stomach is not fun. I eat a lot of takeout or at Henry's. What about you? From the looks of this, you know your way around a kitchen, too."

"I can cook. I just don't do it often. Like you said, cooking for one is not so fun. I had planned to eat this all weekend and then take the leftovers to work for Autumn, Jeremy, and JJ on Monday."

"I'm sure they appreciate that."

"They do. It happens pretty much every time I cook. I hate the idea of food going to waste."

"Yeah, me too. Eating out is easier."

"I eat a lot of frozen meals, which I know isn't exactly the healthiest option, but it works."

"Sounds like the two of us should share more meals together."

Deliberately ignoring his words, I turn to face him, saying, "Here you go." I hand him his bowl of salad. Grabbing my bowl and the two bottles of dressing, I place them on the table. Landon already has our plates with two forks, so there's nothing left to do but drinks. "What would you like to drink? I have water and lemonade, and I think I have a bottle of wine…." My voice trails off as I try to remember if I do, in fact, still have a bottle of wine.

"Water is fine. I'll grab it. Sit." He points to the seat next to his at the table, where he places my plate. It would be rude to move to the opposite end of the table to get some distance from him. He's so… big and commanding, and he makes my tiny house feel even smaller.

"So, your folks live in Georgia?" he asks, taking a bite of his salad once he's seated.

"My mom does. She loves it there."

"Good for her."

"What about you? Does your family live nearby?"

"They do, actually, about an hour from here. I still don't get to see them as much as I'd like. They make it to all of my home games, and we usually have dinner afterward. Sometimes Mom cooks at my place. She thinks that she still needs to take care of me."

"I can imagine that's a feeling, or need rather, that never goes away once you have kids."

"That's what she tells me." He takes a bite of his casserole, his salad bowl now empty. "Wow, this is really good."

"You doubted me?" I feign being shocked.

"Never." He takes another big bite. "You want kids?" he asks.

Luckily, I'm in between bites or I might have choked. "Yes. Do you?"

He nods. "Yeah, one day. At least two, if not more. It was lonely growing up as an only child."

"Right?" I say, nodding. "I was always allowed to have friends over, but it isn't the same. Not only that, but I'll never be an aunt, not by blood anyway. Well, I guess if my future husband has a sibling who has kids, I will. But for now, JJ is the closest thing to a nephew for me."

"You know, I never really thought about that."

I shrug. "I begged my mom for a sibling when I was little. It wasn't until I was older that I understood that she needed a man to make that happen. My dad never knew about me. I guess he was just passing through. They spent a magical week together, and then he was gone. She didn't know how to reach him, and when she finally found him, he was married. Mom just figured it was easier to let it go. I was eight at the time."

"That had to have been hard. Growing up without a dad."

"My mom is amazing, and except for the father-daughter dances, I didn't really notice much. It was me and Mom against the world."

"My parents said they didn't want more than one. That they couldn't imagine loving another like they did me." He grins and winks. I appreciate that he realized the conversation was getting heavy, and his attempt to lighten it is greatly appreciated. I don't really talk about my dad. I'm surprised I did just now. Something about Landon gets me to open up.

"Is that how the story goes?" I tease. "Would they tell the same version?"

"Okay, so maybe they said I was more than they could handle." He laughs, and the sound fills the kitchen and makes my house feel not so… lonely.

Landon helps himself to another serving while I finish my first. He polishes it off and stands, taking both of our plates to the sink. In no time at all, we have the kitchen cleaned up, and Landon pulls me by the hand back to the living room. This time, he sits down on the couch, his back propped up on the arm, and spreads his legs, patting the empty space between them for me to sit. "I don't think I've had enough experimenting to know if I really like this cuddling business." He smirks, and I roll my eyes.

"Come on, Freckles, humor me." He tugs gently on my hand, and I plop down on the couch. Rolling onto my side, I rest my head on his chest. He pulls the cover over me and begins to surf through the channels. He stops on some Sci-Fi movie. I hear the sound of the remote being placed on the end table and then feel his hand as he rests his large palm against my back.

We're both quiet for several minutes. He begins to rub his hand up and down my back, and my body relaxes further into him. I should fight it, but I don't have the power. For tonight, I'll let him win. We're just two friends hanging out and watching a movie. There will never be anything more than that, not between us.

"Not bad for date number three," he says softly, bending down so I can hear him better.

I peer up at him, and his blue eyes are soft as they take me in. "This wasn't a date."

"Oh, Tess, it was a date. I brought you flowers, we had dinner, and now I'm holding you. It's a pretty damn good one if I do say so myself."

"Landon—" I start, but he places his index finger up to my lips to stop me. "Just pretend with me. For tonight, let's just pretend that this is our normal."

It's a bad idea. A very freaking bad idea, and I know this, but I nod anyway. It's like I can't seem to control my reaction when I'm this close to him. He runs his thumb under my cheek, and for a brief moment, I think he's going to lean even closer and kiss me. He doesn't. He smiles softly, drops his hand, and turns his attention back to the TV. All the while, he never stops tracing the length of my back.

I'm in trouble.

I'm in so much trouble.

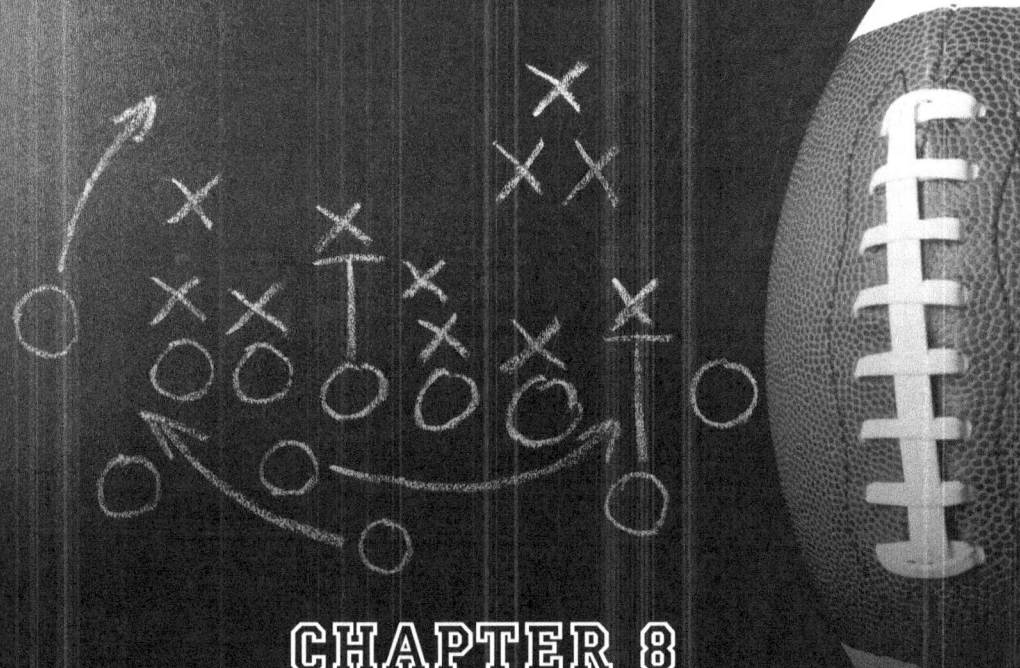

CHAPTER 8

Landon

I KNOW THE EXACT MINUTE THAT SHE FALLS ASLEEP. HER BODY fully relaxes into mine, and her breathing evens out. Slowly, I exhale as I try to decipher what's going on. As I try to wrap my head around what the fuck I'm doing. I'm surprising myself with this girl. I'm not acting like me at all, yet at the same time, it all feels... right.

The more I'm around her, the more I want to be. Is it the chase? No, surely not. Yeah, I want her to agree to go out with me without me having to trick her, but the funny thing is, it's not really about that now. Suddenly, it's just about spending time with her. Hearing her laugh, getting one of those beautiful smiles directed my way. It's watching her green eyes sparkle when she pretends to be irritated, or the way she trusts me to hold her here on her couch while she sleeps peacefully.

Life comes easy to me. Football was something I picked up on at a young age, and my skill has just grown from there. I've never really had to struggle or want for anything. Even in my professional football career, the scouts were coming to watch me play as a freshman. Yes, I work hard and give it all I've got, but it doesn't feel like work when it's something that you love.

Even women. I was the hot new QB on campus, and the girls flocked to me. Same way in high school. I've never had to find female companions, never had to pursue someone. Turns out, I like it. I like it a lot. In fact, I love that she doesn't seem to care that I'm a professional athlete. Hell, she's not even a fan of my team. I can't hide my smile when I think about her wearing the Mavericks T-shirt to training camp. She's her own person, knows her mind, and I really like that. More than I ever knew or thought I would.

My phone vibrates from its spot on the end table, and I wince, hoping like hell it doesn't wake Tess up. Reaching behind me, careful not to move her, I grab it, and the vibration against the wood silences. Glancing at the screen, I see Case's name. Letting the call go to voicemail, I fire off a text.

> Me: What's up?
>
> Case: Henry's?
>
> Me: Can't.
>
> Case: Dude, what's with you?
>
> Me: I'm on a date.
>
> Case: With who?
>
> Case: Wait. You don't date.

I do now.

> Me: I do now.

I can see the little bubbles bouncing, telling me he's writing back. I'm sure I've shocked him. I *know* I've shocked him. I don't date as it's hard to decipher the real from the fake. Who wants you for your fame and fortune and who wants you for you. I can say with 100 percent certainty that the woman in my arms couldn't care less about my career or my bank account. No way is this fake—the way she watches me or blushes when I call her Freckles. The way she continues to shoot me down, even when I can see in her eyes that telling me no is the last thing she wants to do.

Case: Prove it.

I hesitate before snapping a picture of her in my arms. My smile is wide and genuine as I hold her while she sleeps. I have to admit, this being my new normal sounds pretty fucking good. I could get on board with hanging out with her like this. Shaking out of my thoughts, I send him the picture.

Case: No shit.

Case: Are you boring her or what?

Me: Fuck off. Tell Henry I said hey.

Case: 10-4

I love how he easily lets me off the hook because he knows I'm with a woman, but if I had been sitting at home, enjoying the peace and quiet there, he would have been knocking on my door and dragging my ass to the bar. He's giving me peace for now, but I know as sure as I'm sitting here that the next time I talk to him, he's going to give me shit. Then he's going to want to know what's going on and what my intentions are. He doesn't know her, has only met her once, but he's still going to ask me.

Placing my phone back on the end table, I try to focus on the movie. I've missed over half of it, and it's unable to grab my attention, unlike the beautiful woman sleeping in my arms. She shifts, and now she's lying on top of me. I bring my other leg up on the couch and wrap both of my arms around her. Closing my eyes, I focus on memorizing how this feels.

I used to think guys like Trent were crazy for having a wife and kid while traveling all the time... to be away from them while we're on the road. It's not about the temptation. You can remove yourself from that easily enough. The guys who give in to temptation put themselves in the middle of it. I can't help but wonder what it would be like if she were mine. What would it be like coming home after being on the road to find her warm and snuggled in my bed? That image alone has my cock stirring to life, and we can't have that. Not with her body aligned with mine. I don't want to scare her off. No. In fact, I want to keep her with me as long as possible.

Holy fuck. I want her to be mine.

I let that thought take root, decipher what it would mean for me and for her, and then my mind goes to being with her like this all the time. No more random hookups. Instead, something meaningful and real.

Am I ready for that?

Am I ready for her?

Those are my last thoughts as I drift off to sleep.

$$\times \; \times \; \text{♪}$$
$$\circ \; \circ$$

Feeling as though I'm being watched, I peel my eyes open. Tessa is still on top of me, but now she's on her belly, her chin propped up on my chest by her hand. Her green eyes stare at me intently, and a slight blush coats her cheeks.

Busted.

"We fell asleep," she says before I have a chance to call her out on watching me.

"We did."

"I'm not sure how I feel about that."

Another thing that sets her apart from the others is that she's open and honest. Sure, sometimes I feel as though I have to pull it out of her, but we're just getting to know each other. I can only imagine that, over time, I'll never have to guess or pry it out of her. She'll just tell me like she did just now.

"Tell me what you're thinking."

"You first."

"I'm thinking we should make this a tradition, naps on Saturday afternoons."

"Pretty soon, the season will start, and you won't have Saturday afternoons available for naps."

"There's always the off-season." She closes her eyes, and I hate that we've lost that connection. "Tess." I brush some loose strands of hair away from her face while I wait for her to decide she's ready to face me again. When she does finally open her eyes, they're intense as they lock on mine.

"This isn't a game, Landon. I can't do this"—she indicates her head toward me—"kind of thing without catching feelings. I know me, and I know I can't do it. I won't pretend to say that I know you, because I don't. Do I think you're a good guy? Yeah, I do. Do I think that this is really what you want? No, I don't. It gets to you that I told you no, so you're pulling out all the stops for me to say yes. What happens when I do? What happens then?"

I don't have an answer for her, at least not one that she wants to hear. Instead, I answer honestly. "I'm not sure what this is. I'm not sure what it means that I'm perfectly content to hold you in my arms on a Saturday night when I could be… anywhere else." Hurt flashes in her eyes, and I rush to explain. "I didn't mean it the way that it sounded. I just mean that this is where I chose to be. Here, with you. Why do we have to name it?"

"Because I want the fairy tale."

I nod. I don't know what to say to that. She deserves the fairy tale, but I'm not sure that I'm the one who can give her that. We're at an impasse.

I want to spend more time with her, I want more moments like this, but I don't know if I can give her what she wants or what she deserves.

I guess only time will tell.

"You ready to watch another movie?" I ask instead. Her entire demeanor seems to deflate as if she was holding out hope that I would be her prince charming and sweep her off her feet. I wish I could be that guy for her. Right now, I don't know if I am. I have so many emotions running through me. Elation that this beautiful woman would even consider letting me be a part of her life. Fear that she wants it to be more. Worry that these feelings swarming me are just because of the chase, because she turned me down. That's how this started. I don't know what any of it means. I need some time to work it out.

What I do know is that I will never regret any amount of time that I get to spend with her.

"Sure," she says, and gingerly climbs off me.

I miss her heat instantly. "Want some leftovers?" I ask.

"No, thanks. Help yourself." She disappears down the hall to, I assume, the bathroom.

Standing from the couch, I stretch, then reach down and adjust my cock. I'm a man who just had the body of a beautiful woman aligned with mine; I can't be held accountable for my actions. I know she felt it, but she didn't say a word.

Making my way to the kitchen, I open the cabinets until I find a bowl and make another big serving of her chicken casserole. This shit is amazing, and I'm going to have to ask again how she made it. Grabbing two bottles of water, I head back to the living room. Tessa is there, curled up in the corner of the couch with the blanket thrown over her legs.

Is that disappointment I feel? "Got you a water." I hand her one of the bottles and take a seat on the opposite end of the couch. I fucking hate the distance that one cushion keeps between us, but it's what she wants. Until I know what I want, what all this shit bouncing around in my head means, I owe her that.

"I'm glad to see that's getting eaten." She nods toward the heaped bowl in my hands.

"It's so good. Can you send me the recipe? This is something I could make for myself and eat it for a few days."

"Sure. I'll text it to you." She reaches for her phone, her fingers flying across the screen, and then my phone vibrates on the table. "Sent."

"Thanks." I toss her the remote. "Your turn to choose."

She snags the remote from where it lands beside her on the couch and begins to scroll through the stations. "I really don't care what we watch." She settles on the Hallmark channel, and I can't even find it in me to be irritated. Normally, I would be, but this... two chick flicks in one night and no chance of getting laid, it's nothing. I don't care even the slightest because I'm with Tessa. That's gotta mean something, right?

Two hours later, I feel like I need to beat on my chest and fart or some shit just to prove my manhood. I'll never admit it out loud, but the movie was good. PG, but there's nothing wrong with that. I glance over at Tessa to catch her yawning. Looking at the time, I see it's after midnight, and even though I hate it, it's time for me to go.

"Thanks for dinner." I stand and gather my phone. I washed my dish during a commercial break.

"You're welcome. It was nice to have the company." She smiles up at me.

I want to kiss her.

I can't kiss her.

"Date number three in the books," I say to get my mind off her full, kissable lips, and because I know it's going to get her sparring with me. I love that side of her. The side that doesn't let my bullshit slide.

She rolls those big green eyes, but a smile plays on her lips. "You're something else, Number Eighteen." She stands and walks with me to the door. "Drive safe."

Unable to help myself, I wrap my arms around her in a hug and hold on a little longer than I should. Pulling back, I drop a quick kiss to her temple. "Always." With that, I force my feet to carry me out the door and to my SUV. As soon as I start my car, the porch light goes off, and just like that, I'm back to being an outsider. Just a man who craves being able to share a small piece of her world with her. I don't know exactly what this all means, but I know that one thing's for sure.

I'm in trouble.

I'm in so much trouble.

CHAPTER 9

Tessa

I SPENT ALL DAY YESTERDAY SHOPPING. MY ANKLE IS TENDER BUT feels much better. I couldn't sit in my house a minute longer. Not when it's surrounded by Landon. I can still smell him. Is that normal? I think not. I Febreezed my couch, but it didn't work. Maybe it's not in the fabric, and it's just me. I remember his scent. I remember him. All of him. He was obviously turned on, and I get it—he's a man, he had a woman lying on him. I don't blame him. Well, in a way, I do. He wasn't the only one worked up. However, neither one of us acted on that attraction that pulsed between us.

I ruined that.

It had to be that way. We're better off not crossing that bridge. Hell, I don't want to go near it. After all, I am afraid of heights.

"Good morning." Autumn's chipper voice greets me. "How was your weekend?"

"Good. Nothing out of the ordinary."

"Oh, really? How about we try that again, little miss too quick to blow me off? How was your weekend?"

I exhale loudly and then blurt it out. "Landon came over for dinner."

"Landon, huh?" She grins. "What prompted the lucky player to come over for a visit?"

"He asked me to dinner, I told him I already had dinner made, and he said he would be over in an hour. He showed up. We ate."

"Uh-huh. What else did you do?"

"Nothing. Watched a couple of movies and then he went home."

"Tess," she says, her tone warning.

"Autumn," I fire back.

"Spill it."

"Fine. We might have cuddled a little on the couch before falling asleep. Nothing happened. I told him I want more. I'm not looking for any kind of benefits that don't come with a relationship. That's just not me. He didn't confirm or deny that he's not willing to give it to me. We watched another movie on separate ends of the couch and then he went home."

"Goodnight kiss?"

"Does a hug and a kiss to my temple count?"

She nods vigorously. "That definitely counts."

Yeah, I agree with her. They both count, but I don't know how I feel about that. I'm already missing him, and that's bad, so terribly bad. Landon Barker is a heartbreaker, and I need to remember that. He's never been serious with anyone. Why would that change with me?

"Enough about me. What's on the agenda for today?" I ask, getting back into work mode. I need to push my impromptu weekend with the sexy quarterback out of my mind.

"We have a full line-up of volunteers today, so I'm thinking a deep scrub of the cages and kennels while we have the help."

"Sounds good to me. I'm going to go out and start working on Buckwheat's stall."

"I'll send help when it arrives." She waves as I push open the door and walk outside into the warm California sun.

I'm just getting Buckwheat turned loose in the round pen so that I can muck his stall, when my phone vibrates in my pocket. Pulling it out, I see *Number 18* and don't even read the message before swiping the screen. I'm that eager to hear from him. I refuse to think about what that means.

> Number 18: Morning, Freckles. Need my help today?
>
> Me: Nope. We have a full roster of volunteers today.
>
> Number 18: Maybe I should stop by just to make sure.
>
> Me: Why? You don't trust me now?
>
> Number 18: What? I can't stop to check on you?
>
> Me: You don't need to check on me.
>
> Number 18: Practice is getting ready to start. I'll text you later, if I don't stop by.

His message is followed by another with a winking emoji. It fits him perfectly. Sliding my phone back into my pocket, I get to work on Buckwheat's stall. Instead of clearing my mind, his messages bring him to the surface, and all I can think about is Saturday and what it all means. Does he really want me to give in to him so bad that he's willing to play nice and hang out at my place on Saturday night? He's the freaking starting quarterback for the Los Angeles Cougars. He could have had his pick of women for the night and a guaranteed happy ending to the evening. What's his game?

"Tessa," Autumn calls out to me. I stop and turn to face her. There's a man with her, a very handsome man. "This is Tony. He's volunteering today. I'm putting him with you."

"Hi." I hold my hand out to him. "I'm Tessa."

"Tony." He nods toward Autumn. "But you already know that." He laughs and claps his hands together. His *very* large hands.

I take a minute to take him in. He's tall. If I had to guess, about six feet, so shorter than Landon. He has blond hair and dark brown eyes. He's Landon's complete opposite, but still sexy in his own surfer kind of way. Gah! I need to stop comparing him to Landon. Maybe Tony is the exact distraction I need today.

"Where do you want me?" He smiles and runs his fingers through his curly blond locks.

"Grab a pitchfork. You can help me with the stall." I point to the wall where two more pitchforks are hanging.

"How about I take this one?" He tugs the pitchfork from my hand. "You can start on what you need to do next."

"All right, I'll be outside if you need me. Once this is done, we need to spray it out, and then I can bring him back in."

"Him?" He raises his eyebrows.

"Oh." I laugh. "Buckwheat the horse." I point over my shoulder toward the outside round pen.

"Got ya. I'll come find you when I'm ready."

"Thanks, Tony."

"Anytime." He winks.

I make my way outside and busy myself with brushing Buckwheat. It's not really a necessity, but it's a luxury he doesn't get often, as we're usually short on staff. I'm going to take some time today to pamper him, just like his previous owner would if she were able to still care for him.

About fifteen minutes later, Tony appears beside me. His shirt is off and tucked into his back pocket, and his chest is glistening with sweat. I make a mental note to thank Autumn for giving me the hottie for the day. "What's next, boss?" he asks.

I can't hide my amusement. "Well, we can leave this guy outside a little longer and let him enjoy the sunshine. Let's go see what the others are working on."

"Sounds good," he says, falling in step beside me. "You worked here long?" he asks.

"A little over two years."

"Cool."

"If you don't mind me asking, what brings you in to volunteer today?"

"Do you want the honest answer or the one I practiced?" He grins.

"Honest. Always honest."

He shrugs. "I was hoping to get to meet Jeremy Baldwin. I'm a huge soccer fan."

"You do know Jeremy is a coach for the Cougars now, right?"

"Yeah, but I also know his wife runs the place, so I was hoping to run into him."

"Huh. Well, he's at practice today. Sometimes he drops in after. I guess you're just going to have to stick around to find out."

"Now that I'm here, I might have another motive."

"Oh, yeah? What's that?" I ask, not bothering to turn to look at him.

"A date."

I stop and turn to face him. "A date?"

He nods. "I didn't expect my boss or mentor or advisor or whatever I'm supposed to call you, would be hot. Maybe I can get a date *and* an autograph."

I throw my head back and laugh. "Come on, Casanova, let's see what's next." I don't bother to reply. He's not my type, and I'm hoping he drops it. That's all I need is to add another man into my life to drive me insane. How is it that my dating life has been null and void the last few months and now, all of a sudden, I'm the popular girl?

I tell Tony to wait for me in the lobby while I go in search of Autumn.

I find her in our office. "Hey, we're done with the barn. Where should we go next? Cats or dogs?"

"Dogs. I have the two teenage girls in with the cats. Not to mention, the dogs are more work. You can use his muscles."

"He told me he was volunteering with the hopes of meeting Jeremy." I leave out the part about the date. No need to get that seed planted in her head.

"Aw, I'll text him and have him stop by after practice." Her fingers are already flying across her screen. "They have an early day today, so it should be around lunchtime."

"Great. We're going to get started." My stomach does a little flip at the thought that I could see Landon soon, but then I remember I told him I didn't need any help. Damn man has got me all over the place with my emotions.

"Okay, looks like you and I are going to tackle the dog room, as we call it. We have kennels to clean, so we'll start taking the dogs to the outdoor kennel so we can hose it all down."

"I'm your man." He winks.

He reminds me a little of Landon, but he's most definitely not him. He's too short, his hair way too light, and his eyes aren't the ocean blue I've become accustomed to. He's confident, though; I'll give him that.

Two by two, we move the dogs to the outdoor kennel. I don't rush the process as we play with them and give them treats. This is yet another luxury we don't always have. An hour later, we're in the dog room, and Tony is spraying everything down with the water hose while I start behind him with a brush on a long stick and a bucket of soapy water.

"Let me do that," he says, trying to hand me the hose.

"I'm good. This is something I do on a regular basis."

"Exactly why you should let me do it." He tries to take the broom, and I move quickly out of his reach, but lose my footing. He reaches out to catch me, and we both end up falling to the floor. He lands on top of me, but is quick to lift himself, holding his weight on his arms as he stares down at me as the soapy water seeps into my clothes. "Oops." He grins, and I can't help but smile back at him.

"What's going on here?" a deep, booming voice asks.

I know that voice.

I push up, and Tony takes his sweet time, removing his body from where he was suspended over the top of me. I start to climb to my feet only to slip again on the wet floor. Tony is there to catch me this time, and his strong arms lift me to my feet and make sure I'm steady before he lets go.

"Tessa?" Landon asks.

"Hey, we were just cleaning, and the buckets spilled, and well… you see the outcome." I laugh nervously. Why am I nervous? Oh, yeah, because Landon and his baby blues are assessing me, and I know this looks bad. Even though I've done nothing wrong and he has no claim to me, I still feel a little guilty.

Landon's eyes go to Tony's hand that's still holding on to my arm. "You can let go," he tells him.

"Holy shit. You're… you're Landon Barker," Tony says, his hand still holding my arm.

Landon nods. "I am." His voice is not his friendly banter that I'm used to.

"Dude, I was hoping to meet Jeremy. I never dreamed I'd get to meet a Cougar, let alone Landon Barker. Can I have your autograph?" he asks, sounding like an excited little boy that I think lives inside all men.

"Sure, as soon as you get your hand off my girl." Landon's eyes are laser-focused as he stares Tony down.

"Landon," I start, but he ignores me.

"Shit," Tony mumbles. "I didn't know she was yours." He turns his accusing eyes to mine. "You didn't tell me when I mentioned a date that you were with Landon freaking Barker." He drops his hand as if he's been burned.

"I'm not with him."

Landon nods now that Tony's no longer touching me. "Let's go find something I can write on." He turns on his heel and disappears from the room.

He's pissed, but now, so am I. How dare he come in here, telling the volunteers I'm his girl? I'm not his girl. I'm not his anything. We're acquaintances at best. Okay, maybe a little more than that, but I'm not his. I'm mine, and he has no right to come in here demanding things of anyone. I'm fuming mad. I want to march out there and tell him to leave, but I don't. Instead, I put my anger into cleaning up the mess Tony and I made, wet clothes and all. I'm on a mission, and it takes me no time to get the cages cleaned and the room sparkling. I put away the cleaning supplies and head to my office to grab a change of clothes. Autumn and I both keep spare clothes here because things like this happen when you work at an animal shelter. It's not the first time. Although usually, it's a rambunctious animal, not two grown men acting like toddlers.

Closing the office door, I strip out of my wet clothes. I slide into my clean, dry shorts and am just getting ready to pull my new shirt over my head when the door opens. I glance up, expecting to see Autumn, but it's not her. It's Landon.

"Shit." I rush to hold the shirt to my chest.

His eyes are heated as they rake over my body. "Tess."

"Turn around, Landon!" I screech. He does as I ask, and I pull my shirt over my head as fast as I can.

CHAPTER 10

Landon

I'M TURNED AROUND, FACING THE DOOR, AND MY HEART FEELS as though it's about to beat out of my chest. Tessa and all her creamy skin. My cock throbs in my shorts, and I suck in a deep breath. She's fucking gorgeous. This I already knew, but now... How will I ever get that image out of my head?

"You can turn around."

Slowly, I turn to face her. "Tess," I whisper, and reach a hand out to her.

"Don't." Her words are final.

My hand drops to my side. "Are you okay? Your ankle?" I ask.

"I'm fine, Landon."

I'm suddenly in new territory. I've never cared enough to step in or get... jealous. It's not an emotion I'm used to feeling, but I'm a smart man. I know that's what it was. When I saw him hovering over her, the way they were laughing and she was peering up at him, I hated it. Every single second of their connection. It took everything in me not to rip him off her. Lucky for him, he seemed more interested in me than he did her. That is, until he mentioned the date.

She can't date that guy.

"I'm not your girl, Landon. We're barely even what I would call friends, more like two strangers who have shared a couple of meals. You can't just go around spouting off that kind of shit." She's seething, and her green eyes are lit with fire. My cock doesn't understand that she's mad at us as he begs for her attention.

I shift on my feet to alleviate what she's doing to me. "I'm sorry." Two words I don't say often, but I can admit when I'm wrong. "I saw the two of you, and I just… I'm sorry." Those two words are easier to say than the truth. That I'm falling for her. I don't know what to do with that.

"Okay."

That's it?

"You can't do that. I'm not your concern, and what are you even doing here? I told you that we had plenty of help today."

"Practice was shorter than normal. I brought you lunch." I point to the bag on her desk that I'm sure she missed in her haste to change her clothes. Maybe she missed it due to her anger at me. Either way, it's there in front of her. "Turkey club and chips," I tell her. "It's not much, but…" I shrug. I don't know what to say.

"Thank you." She looks over to her desk, where the bag filled with our lunch sits. "That's very nice of you." She pauses to turn and look at me. "Are you hungry?"

"Yeah, I… uh… got some for you, me, Autumn, and Jeremy. I wasn't sure if he'd be here." I shrug.

"Have a seat. Let me go tell Autumn and grab us a couple of waters."

She moves to walk past me, and I hold my arm out, stopping her. My arm hits at her waist, and I pull her into me, wrapping my arms around her in a hug. "I'm sorry, Tess."

"I know. It's fine." She pulls out of my hold and moves around me to grab Autumn's and our drinks.

It can't be that easy. Is she really not going to make a big deal out of this? Is she not going to make me grovel?

"Here you go." She hands me a bottle of water a few moments later. "Autumn said Jeremy is on his way. He went to pick up JJ at daycare. We can go ahead and eat without them." I pull two sandwiches and two bags of chips out of the deli bag and hand her one of each. "Thanks. You can grab Autumn's chair or sit at her desk," she says, taking a seat in her chair.

Not willing to miss an opportunity to be near her, I grab the chair and roll it to her side of the desk. We both dig into our lunch, letting the quiet surround us. This quiet isn't comfortable. It's full of everything that goes unspoken between us. I need to tell her that I'm feeling things, things I've never felt.

"I appreciate you looking out for me. You were being a good friend. I can appreciate that. Just… pipe down on the 'my girl' stuff," she says, offering me a kind smile.

Friend-zoned.

"Sure," I say, swallowing my lunch, which now feels like cardboard in the throat. I guess if I can't commit to how I'm feeling, being friends with her is the next best thing. I can be near her, because a day not witnessing her smile or hearing her laugh is a day filled with gloom. She's magnetic.

"What can I do?" I ask as we clean up our empty wrappers.

"Nothing. We've got a good team here today. Thank you, though."

I nod. "Dinner tonight?" I know damn well she's going to turn me down.

"Landon—" She shakes her head with a grin.

"Hey." I hold my hands up in mock surrender. "Just asking a friend to have some dinner, share a meal, shoot the shit."

"Uh-huh." She's all-out grinning now, and I love every second of it.

"I guess I'm gonna go." While I say the words, I make no move to pull my ass out of this chair.

"Thanks for lunch. I'd offer to repay you, but I know better." She points to my face. "That look tells me I'm right."

"You're welcome, Tess." I force myself to stand and am surprised when she does, as well.

"I'll walk you out."

"Any new adoptions?" I ask as we walk toward the front door.

"Not this week. They come in spurts. We're actually due for another adoption fair. Autumn and I need to get on that," she says absentmindedly.

We reach the door, and I turn to face her. "I'll see you soon?"

"Yeah, see ya soon," she agrees and waves.

I want to hug her or kiss her or beg her to let me stay, but do none of them. Instead, I let my lead-filled feet carry me to my SUV.

"Where are you headed?" Jeremy asks, climbing out of his SUV as I reach mine.

"Home."

"I thought you brought lunch?" he asks, opening the back door and lifting his son out of his seat. "Can you say hi to Landon?" he asks his son.

The little boy waves, resting his head on his dad's shoulder. "Yeah, I did. Tess and I just ate."

"And you're leaving?" He raises an eyebrow.

"She said she doesn't need any help."

"And you took her word for it?"

"I made a scene, got all pissy when I walked in on a situation that wasn't what it looked like with a volunteer. I'm sure your wife will retell the story."

"What's your version?" he asks.

"Mommy!" JJ yells, holding his arms out.

"Hey, sweet boy," Autumn greets us. "Husband." She grins, going on tiptoes to press her lips to Jeremy's.

"Princess," he whispers, and even I can hear the love in his tone.

"See you inside," she tells him, then turns to look at me. "You got our girl all flustered."

"Yeah." I run my hands through my hair, not sure how much Tessa has told her.

"Good. She needs someone to keep her on her toes. You're a lucky man that you have her attention." She grins like she just won the lottery, and I have no idea what that's all about.

She doesn't give me the chance to comment before she's strolling off toward the building, her son telling her all about daycare this morning.

"Well?" Jeremy asks once his wife and son have finally disappeared from view.

"I guess they slipped on some spilled water. He was lying over the top of her, and I walked in just as it happened. He helped her up, had his fucking hands all over her. He recognized me and asked for an autograph."

"That doesn't sound so bad."

I wince. "I might have told him to get his hands off my girl and I would oblige him."

"Ouch. I know Tessa, and I'm sure that didn't go over well."

"She was pissed, but I apologized, and now she seems fine."

"And?"

"Is that normal? She just accepted the apology without another thought. I was expecting to have to grovel or something."

He laughs. "Maybe from a woman who wants to be the center of your attention. Not from a woman like Tessa. She's one of the good ones. She's not unreasonable. You gave her a sincere apology, and she accepted. Move on."

"She friend-zoned me."

He nods. "I'm guessing that wasn't your intention?"

"Fuck, I have no idea."

"You'd better figure it out." He points to where Tessa stands with

Tony, the guy who was all over her on the floor. Her head's tilted back as a laugh flows from her full, beautiful lips. My fists ball at my sides.

I want to go to them, to wrap my arms around her and show him that she's off-limits, but she's not. I force myself to climb into my SUV with a wave to Jeremy and drive away. He's wearing an amused smile as he watches me, and I ignore him.

What is this woman doing to me?

$$X \quad X \quad \int$$
$$o \quad o \quad \delta$$

It's just after seven, and I've already run five miles on my treadmill and ordered takeout. It was a Chinese food kind of night. Now here I am, pacing the living room floor. I eye my keys on the table, tempted to drive to her house to see her. That's pushy even for me, and besides, what am I going to say? I can't give you what you want or what you deserve, but I don't want anyone else to either?

My phone rings, and I fumble to grab it from the couch cushion, hoping it's her, but I should have known better. In a way, it's the next best thing. "Hey, Mom," I answer.

"Landon, how are you? It's been too long since we've talked."

"I know." Guilt washes over me. "Sorry, just been busy getting back into the groove of things this season."

"How's the team looking?" Dad asks. They have me on speaker, and I smile. These two are the epitome of two peas in a pod.

"Great. The rookies are meshing well with the veterans, and I see good things in our future."

"How about you give me your non-PR prompted speech?" Dad chuckles.

"This time it's the truth. Practices have been on point, and I think we can take it to the Super Bowl this year."

"What's wrong?" Mom asks.

"Nothing."

"Landon, don't make me come there," she warns in her mom's voice. I never could get anything past her.

"I met someone. At least, I think I did."

"What do you mean, you *think* you did?" Dad asks.

"She's unlike anyone I've ever met. She's one of those women who deserves everything."

"Oh, so she's not a cleat chaser?" Mom asks.

"No." I laugh. "She's not a cleat chaser."

"Good. Where did you meet her?"

"Through the new kicking coach. She's best friends with his wife." I go on to tell them about her wearing a Mavericks shirt to training camp.

"I like her already. When do we get to meet her?"

"Slow your roll, Momma Bear," I tease. "I don't know that you ever will."

"Why on earth not?" she asks.

"She friend-zoned me."

"Of course, she did," Mom agrees, like it's the most reasonable thing she's heard in her life.

"What's that supposed to mean?"

"Look, Landon, you're my son, and I love you more than anything, but I've seen you in action. Everything comes easy to you, even women. This one, I assume, isn't, and you don't know how to deal with that. You keep yourself closed off. I understand how hard it must be to know if someone is being genuine with your career, but, honey, how are you going to know unless you try?"

"I have tried. She keeps shooting me down."

"Son," Dad chimes in, "I think what your mother is trying to say is that you need to get to know her. For all the fear that you have of her taking you for a ride, or your bank account being her motivation, think about it from this girl's perspective. From what you've told us, she's not someone who has ever been in the spotlight. Having your attention has to be surreal to her."

"Exactly. You have to take your time, nurture the relationship. She might want to be friends now, but I can bet that's her way of protecting herself."

"She doesn't need protection from me," I scoff.

"We know that," Mom says soothingly. "But does she? Think about it, Landon. You're a professional athlete. Seen in the tabloids with a new woman on your arm at every event, and you're focusing your attention on her. I can only imagine she thinks this is a game to you."

"What?"

"Landon, do you like this girl?"

"More than I should," I grumble, and they both laugh. *Traitors.*

"Then nurture the relationship. Be her friend. Show her you're not the guy to hop from bed to bed. At least you better not be."

"Honey," Dad admonishes Mom. "He's a grown man."

"And I can still take him over my knee. All six foot four inches of him," she counters.

"Anyway," Dad moves on. "Your mother's right. You have to show her that you're not that guy. You have to show her that her heart is safe with yours."

"What if that's not what I want?"

"Then that's something you'll be able to figure out as you get to know her. You're either going to not be able to stop thinking about her, or she's going to become a friend that you value. Either way, it sounds like she's a good person, and you win."

"I can't stop thinking about her," I admit, and Mom squeals.

I groan, knowing I've opened a huge can of worms. Mom has been asking me when I'm going to settle down for years, and now that she has the hint that I might be thinking about it, she's never going to leave me alone about it.

"Take the time to figure it out, but, son, you can tell her all day long. You have to show her," Dad advises.

"Thanks. I need to go. I'll talk to you all soon."

"We'll be there for the season opener," Dad assures me.

"Love you," I tell them.

"Love you, too," they say in unison, and the call goes dead.

Nurture.

Show her.

Quickly, I type out a text.

> Me: How was your day?
>
> Tessa: Good. Thank you again for lunch.
>
> Me: You're welcome.

I stare at my phone, not knowing what to say. That's not like me. I'm never short for conversation, but with Tessa, I find myself not so lucky after all. Tessa saves me when she sends another text. It's a picture. Opening it up, I see a picture of the throw from her couch covering her legs.

> Tessa: Just relaxing.
>
> Me: Me, too. I have a long practice day tomorrow.
>
> Tessa: How's the season going?

I'm taken aback by her question. I've never had a woman other than my mother or maybe a mom or wife of one of the guys ask that question.

> Me: I'm positive about this year. The team is looking good.
>
> Tessa: I looked at the schedule. You play the Mavericks in week one at home.

Me: You coming to the game?

Tessa: Always.

Me: Wait a minute. You've seen me play?

She's taking too long to reply, so I hit *Send* on her name, and it rings twice before she answers. Her laughter rings through the line. "Landon," she sputters.

"Tess," I say, trying to be stern but failing. "Have you seen me play?"

"Of course, I have. I never miss a Mavs game."

"Fucking Mavericks," I mumble, making her laugh even harder.

"I'm going to convert you to a Cougars fan yet."

"Diehard Mavs, baby," she cheers.

"What did you have for dinner?" I ask her, changing the subject. Just the thought of her cheering for A.J. Holland pisses me off.

"Meh, nothing too exciting. I had the rest of the chicken casserole. You?"

"I ordered Chinese."

"I love Chinese," she says over a yawn. "I'm sorry. I'm so tired."

"Yeah, I ran five miles when I got home. I'm beat, too."

"Sheesh, no wonder you're in such good shape."

My chest puffs out a little at her compliment. "We have the season opener in a few weeks. Will you be there?"

"Nah, but I have my tickets for when you play the Mavs."

"On me. You can sit with Autumn. I'm sure she'd love it if you were there with her." I'm holding my breath, waiting for her to agree. Doesn't matter that I'm getting her tickets regardless.

"Let me talk to Autumn. I don't want to intrude."

"You won't be. You'll be my guest."

"I'll talk to her and let you know," she says, ignoring my comment.

"Fine," I agree as I hear her yawn again. "I'll let you go. Goodnight, Freckles."

She chuckles. "Goodnight, Number Eighteen."

Finally, I'm able to chill the fuck out, and exhaustion catches up with me. After locking up, I plug my phone in by the bed and climb under the covers.

CHAPTER 11

Tessa

I'M LATE. NOT THAT KIND OF LATE, LATE FOR THE DAY. MY ALARM didn't go off, and now I'm rushing around, trying to get ready. To top it off, I'm out of K-Cups, which means no coffee. I need coffee. Slipping into my gym shoes, I grab my purse, make sure I have my phone, and rush out the door. Only to turn back to make sure that I locked it.

Have I mentioned I hate being late?

Sliding behind the wheel of my Jeep Wrangler, I place my phone in the cup holder, sling my purse on the passenger seat, and pull out of the drive. I'm lucky that my job doesn't require me to be all snazzed up. Case in point: I have on a pair of leggings, a T-shirt with my work's logo, and gym shoes. I tied my mass of dark curls on top of my head and didn't bother with makeup. I hardly see anyone during the day anyway, just my boss, most of the time her husband, and their son. I have no one to impress.

Checking the clock on the dash, I calculate that I have just enough time to stop at the Cup of Joe Café for my morning coffee, and because I'm going to be there already, I might as well grab one of their famous cinnamon coffee cake muffins. They are life! If they didn't go straight to my hips, I'd stop by every morning. Alas, they do, so I stick with indulging about once a month as a treat. This month, I'm splurging twice.

It's just a Cup of Joe Café kind of day.

I wonder if Autumn wants anything. I hit the phone icon on my steering wheel. "Call Autumn," I announce, and dutifully, my beloved Jeep dials for me. The way my day has started, I can't chance taking my eyes off the road.

"Morning, sunshine." Her chipper voice blasts throughout the car.

"Hey, I woke up late."

She laughs. "There goes your mood for the day."

"Har har, and to think I called to see if you wanted anything from the Cup of Joe Café. I'm out of coffee at home, so I might be a few minutes late."

"Definitely stop. We all know how you are without your coffee," she teases.

"Harsh," I say, barely containing my own laughter.

"Banana nut muffin, please, and I've already had two cups of coffee."

"You sure?"

"Yes. I'll be bouncing off the walls. Besides, I'm trying to cut back on my caffeine, you know, in case we decide to have another baby. Going cold turkey is hell."

"What? Are you trying?"

"Nah, but we've talked about it. We want more, so it's only a matter of time. We're settled into the new house, so yeah… I wanted to get a head start."

"I'm so excited for you. All right, I'm almost there. We'll talk more when I get to work."

"Take your time," she says before saying goodbye. I hit the button on the steering wheel to end the call as I turn the corner.

The place is packed as usual this time of day, and I have to park at the end of the block and walk. I'm pressed for time, but my mouth is already watering for that cinnamon coffee cake muffin and coffee. I must have coffee.

As I push open the door, the smell of baked goods and yummy coffee surrounds me. There are so many different scents, I can't name a single one. The only way I can describe it is delicious. My stomach grumbles as I take my place in line. All the small tables are taken except for one, in the back corner of the café. Now, if I were staying to eat, that's the table I would choose. I'm not antisocial, but I like to people watch, fly under the radar, so to speak. A small corner table to devour cinnamon goodness would suit me just fine.

Speaking of people watching, I can't help but notice the man standing in front of me. My eyes rake over him in appreciation. Sure, it's just the backside, but impressive all the same. He's wearing one of those compression shirts. It's a royal blue color and forms quite nicely to his muscles. A pair of black basketball shorts hang from his hips, and I can only imagine he's one of those with the V—you know, where the shorts or, holy hell, even sweatpants hang just right. The thought has me licking my lips, for more than just a cinnamon coffee cake muffin.

The line moves forward, and so do I. My feet move on their own accord as I stare at his ass. What is it they say? So firm you can bounce a quarter off it? Yeah, this guy fits the bill for sure. I take another step forward, only this time, the line's not moving. "Umpf." My hands fly out and press against his back to keep myself from falling. "Shit." I immediately remove my hands from his toned, muscular back, but I can still feel the heat of his body on my palms. He turns to look at me over his shoulder, and I gasp.

Landon.

A slow smile crosses his face as he turns sideways. His eyes start at my crazy mop of hair on top of my head, before skimming over my body. Heat courses through me, both in embarrassment and well... a little bit turned on, if I'm being honest. Landon is sexy as sin, and to have his attention on me... well, I'm only human. What makes it worse is that I know what it feels like to have his arms around me.

Danger. Danger. Danger. I keep repeating the words over and over in my head. Landon Barker is dangerous. Not in an illegal kind of way, but in a he-can-break-your-heart kind of way.

Suddenly, I remember that not only is my hair in a messy knot, but I also have zero makeup on, and I'm in a T-shirt and yoga pants. Isn't that just my luck? I literally run into the sexiest man on earth and I look like a hot mess. Not to mention, said sexy man has been... pursuing me? Is that what he's been doing?

Damn alarm clock!

"You okay, Freckles?" he asks in his deep, masculine voice.

"I-I'm so sorry." I manage to squeak the words. Why am I suddenly nervous around him? This is Landon, and I'm not trying to impress him. Not really, but I'd still like to be presentable.

"Happens all the time." He smirks.

I'm sure it does. His eyes alone are enough to have panties dropping everywhere. Add in his thick, dark locks and his body, and it's obvious he's not just being a conceited jerk; he's speaking the truth. "I should have been paying attention," I say when I realize he's still looking at me.

"It's all good." He nods. His eyes are doing another lazy stroll of my body, making me feel self-conscious.

"I woke up late. It's been one of those mornings." I laugh humorlessly. You know what I'm talking about, those laughs that make everyone within earshot uncomfortable. Yeah, that's me. *Fuck my life.*

"Uh-huh," he says, a smile tilting his gorgeous full lips. "Something keeping you up at night, Tess?"

Why does his voice suddenly sound like sex? "So, uh, you come here often?" As soon as the words are out of my mouth, I want to force them back in. Landon has managed to turn me into a bumbling, lame, small-talking idiot.

"No, first time, actually." He doesn't give me more than that. My eyes rake over him, taking him in from head to toe. Why am I acting this way this morning? I think it's the eyes. Then again, maybe it's the muscles or that beard. Hmm, I do love me a beard. Either way, I need to snap out of it. This is Landon. The player, not just on the field, if my in-ternet research is accurate. We're friends, nothing more.

"Hello." He waves his hand in front of my face to get my attention. Not that it's possible, but if it were, my face would be even redder from embarrassment. "You okay?" He raises his eyebrows like he's not really sure. Is that concern on his face?

Great, I've officially presented myself as the crazy, messy, stare-off-into-space, laugh-at-the-wrong-time girl. Just the icing on this shit-tastic day. "Yeah, sorry, just thinking about what I'm going to get." Lies.

"I'm not sure either." He rubs his hand over his chin, over his beard.

"Cinnamon coffee cake muffin," I blurt out—my favorite. "You can't go wrong." I'm nodding like a crazy person. I blame all of this on my damn alarm clock. Waking up late puts me off-kilter every damn time. I hate it. I make a mental note to get a backup for the future. No more days like today. I don't think I'd survive them, and the day's just started.

"Next!" the barista calls out.

Just like that, he turns to place his order, and I'm once again faced with his strong,

muscular back and that ass. Realizing I'm standing here staring at said ass, I avert my gaze to anywhere but his ass. I settle on a poster advertising an upcoming craft fair at the local convention center. Maybe I'll see if Autumn wants to go. He turns to me. "What do you want, Tess?"

"Nothing, I have a list, so you go ahead." I wave him off.

"Tessa."

"Landon." I match his tone. "Really, I'm good. Next time."

"I'm holding you to that," he says, and turns back to pay for his order.

Closing my eyes, I take a cleansing breath. I need to get my head in the game. I'm not some teenager who can't talk to guys, and this is Landon. He's not a stranger. Sure, we're not BFFs, but we've spent some time together, so the way I'm acting is ridiculous.

"Ma'am," I hear an irritated barista call out. Opening my eyes and snapping my head to face forward, I see it's my turn. I'm holding up the line, and Landon is gone.

"I'm sorry. It's been one of those mornings," I say with yet another awkward laugh.

"Can I take your order?" she asks, giving me a small tilt of her lips that tells me she's not amused, but her job depends on her being friendly.

"Yes, I'll take a large black coffee with two sugars, one banana nut muffin, and one cinnamon coffee cake muffin."

"Sorry, the guy before you took the last cinnamon coffee cake. What else can I get you?"

My shoulders sag. Of course, he did. "Just two banana nuts," I say, defeated. Today is just not my day. Pulling my debit card out of my purse, I hand it over and try to give her a kind smile. It's not her fault. Hell, it's mine. I never should have suggested my favorite. If I hadn't been fumbling around like an idiot, I might not have. "Thank you," I say, taking my card back and sliding it into my wallet. She hands me my coffee and a small bag containing two muffins. Although the banana nut is delicious, I'm not nearly as excited as I was when I walked through the door.

"Have a nice day," I say politely, turning toward the door. I notice that everyone seems to be looking at the back corner of the room, and that's when I see him. Landon. The lucky player got my muffin. I take a step toward the door and stop. Everyone's staring at him; no wonder he thinks he's God's gift to women. Sure, he's easy on the eyes, but the bastard took my muffin. I take another step, keeping my eyes on him and the bag holding his delicious muffin, which sits on the table untouched. He's drinking what I assume is coffee and scrolling through his phone. He's not even eating it. Come on, when you have a Cup of Joe Café cinnamon coffee cake muffin within your reach, you don't ignore it for social media. Before I know what's happening, my feet are carrying me to him.

Obviously, this little adventure of mine wasn't planned out. Hence the reason I'm standing next to his table, holding my coffee and small bag, staring at his bag, knowing what's inside.

"What's up, Tess?" He smirks, setting his phone on the table as he stares up at me. Damn, those eyes.

"So, um, you got the last cinnamon muffin, and I kind of had my heart set on it. I thought maybe I could trade you or we could split it, and I could give you one of my banana nuts?" The words spew from my mouth.

He holds my stare. Those deep cerulean blue eyes seem to be penetrating my soul. I fidget from one foot to the next. I need to get to work, but dammit, I really wanted that muffin.

A slow grin spreads over his face as he raises his hands and motions for me to sit with him. He slides the bag containing all the goodness that is the Cup of Joe Café's cinnamon coffee cake muffin.

"Here." I shove my bag at him. "One of those is for Autumn," I tell him.

He pushes it back toward me. "I already ate breakfast. I just stopped for coffee on my way to practice."

"Then why did you buy the muffin?"

"Truth?"

"Always."

"I didn't plan to. You said it was your favorite. I was going to bring it to you today after practice. I didn't realize I'd bought the last one." He nods toward the bag. "Eat up, Tess."

Not needing to be told twice, I pull open the bag and lift the muffin, taking a huge bite. So far, this is the best part of this terrible day.

"Why are you grinning?" I ask him after swallowing.

"Date number four." He smirks.

"What?" I ask, just about to take another large bite.

"This is our fourth meal together."

"You're not eating. It doesn't count." I feel smug. Taking another big bite, I close my eyes to savor the muffin. When I open them again, Landon's eyes are watching me intently. He reaches for my bag, pulls out a muffin, and takes a big bite.

His eyes never leave mine as he chews and swallows. His dimples appear. "Date number four, Tess."

"Are you going to be late for practice?" I ask him, changing the subject.

"Are you going to be late for work?" he counters.

"Yeah, but Autumn knows, and besides, she gets a muffin out of the deal."

"Fair enough." He pops the last piece of his muffin into his mouth and glances at the time on his phone. "I should get going." He stands and gathers his trash, as do I. I can finish my muffin on the way to work. I walk toward the door and feel his hand on the small of my back. Reaching around me, he opens the door for me, and we exit the café.

"Have a great practice, Number Eighteen." I'm already feeling more like myself.

"Have a good day, Tessa. I'll call you later?"

I find myself nodding. He grins and turns, jogging off to his SUV. How is it that I've been in this town since college and have never run into him, and now, here we are, immersed in each other's lives at what feels like every turn? I point my Jeep toward the shelter and think about what to tell Autumn. I can already hear her telling me it's fate.

Is it fate?

Do I believe in fate?

Only time will tell.

CHAPTER 12

Landon

I T'S BEEN OVER THREE WEEKS SINCE TESSA AND I HAD OUR FIRST date. Well, not technically a date. I'm still working on that. However, I like to tease her about it. Every time we share a meal, I chalk it up to another date. It used to irritate her, and now she's asking me for a tally, making sure I'm still keeping track.

We're on date number fifteen, unofficially, of course. Each one is better than the last. Most of them are me stopping by the shelter after practice, but there have been a few weekends thrown into the mix, as well. Nothing like the night when we first cuddled, and to be honest, I'm disappointed. I was sure I would lose interest in her, in the way she makes me feel—breathless, like I'm ten feet tall, and sappy as fuck. No such luck. If anything, those feelings have intensified beyond what I could ever have imagined.

I want her. Hell, I knew then and should have owned up to it, but what my parents said had merit. I needed to show her the kind of man I am, not tell her. She needed to see it with her own eyes, and all I've done the last few weeks is try to show her that I'm falling. Fast and hard, if how much time I spend thinking about her is any indication.

I scan the stands and don't see her. Tonight is our first preseason game, and Tessa and Autumn are coming. They both passed on a private suite and opted to sit in the stands. JJ is staying with the babysitter, so in a way, it's girls' night. Glancing at the clock, I see there are twenty minutes until game time and no sign of them. I jog down the sidelines to where Jeremy is standing with Thomas.

"Hey, you heard from them?" I ask him, not giving a single fuck that he and Thomas are in the middle of a conversation.

Jeremy glances over at me, and his eyes are dancing with laughter. "They're on their way."

"What?" Thomas asks. "Is this the infamous Tessa you won't stop talking about?"

Yeah, so I might talk about her a little. Okay, a lot. "She's coming to the game."

"You nail that down?" he asks me.

"Not yet."

"What are you waiting on?"

To show her? "Just giving her time to process it. Going from a small-town girl to the girlfriend of a professional athlete is a big deal."

"Girlfriend?" Jeremy asks, surprised. "Does she know about this?"

"No, and you two are going to keep your traps shut. All in due time," I say, scanning the crowd again, and that's when I spot her. I wave, getting her attention, and a beautiful smile crosses her face as she waves back. She's wearing the Cougars jersey I dropped off at her place last night. At least I think it's the one I gave her. She turns to high-five a fan behind her, and that's when I see it. My name is across her shoulders. She's wearing my name and number, and that does something to me. I know how big a Mavericks fan she is, and even last night, she acted like I'd given her a bottle of poison as a gift. I was hoping it was an act from the smile playing on her lips. Now, here she is, wearing it with a smile. Fuck me, but I want nothing more than to peel it off her.

"He's a goner, boys," Thomas boasts. I don't even bother to try and shut him up. He's not wrong, and it's time to do something about it. I need to move us out of the friend zone.

"Lucky Bastard," Kaden mumbles. "You're always getting the prime pu—" I hold up my hand, giving him a warning glare to shut his mouth. He grins but doesn't finish what he was going to say.

"Not her," I say, my voice stern. We've had this conversation, and I don't want to have it again. If she were mine, he wouldn't be talking about her like some cleat chaser. I need to do something about that.

Keeping my head in the game while knowing she's here is harder than I expected it to be. I glance up at her often, and every time I do, our eyes meet. She's here for me. Not for the game or to cheer on either of the teams. Me. I want nothing more than to kiss the hell out of her, to show her my appreciation, of course. Shaking out of my thoughts, I get my head back in the game. First game of the season with my girl and my parents in the stands. I've got this.

$$\times \ \times \ \int$$
$$\circ \ \circ \ \delta$$

The clock hits zero, and just like that, it's halftime. We're up by fourteen, and the team is on fire. I glance up to the stands and catch her gaze before making my way to the locker room.

"Yo, Barker, you're hot." Kaden slaps me on the back. "Every damn time, you lay it right here." He opens his hand and points to his palm.

I shrug. "We're all killing it out there."

"Yeah, but there's something else going on. You're laser-focused," Jack chimes in.

"Except when he's looking up in the stands," Case ribs. "You trying to keep an eye on your girl, make sure her eyes aren't straying to a real man?" he jokes, doing some crazy move that makes him look like he's trying to fuck thin air.

"Don't ever do that again." I laugh.

"What? You don't think she'd want this? I'm two hundred and ninety-five pounds of steel and sex appeal, baby." He runs his hands up the side of his body, trying to channel his inner Vanna White.

"Fuck off." I push at his shoulder good-naturedly.

"All right, listen up." Coach Neil goes on to give us his halftime locker room speech. It's not all sunshine and rainbows just because we're up at the half. We may be on fire, but he wants to keep that fire lit to bring home the win. I want that, too. With Tessa here watching, I want to bring this one home. Oh, and my parents, too, but they've seen me play a thousand times. Tessa's seen me, too, but this time is different. This time she's here to see me. That's a game-changer.

Taking the field, my eyes instantly go to her. Expecting to find her watching for me, I'm surprised when I see Case's brother, Corey, chatting with her and Autumn. He's sitting in front of them and holding her attention. I try not to get annoyed, but it's hard. The whistle blows, and we take the field for the second half. Defense takes the field first, which means I'm on the sidelines watching in between glances at Tessa. Tessa, who's still talking to Corey. I want to toss the football and knock his ass out. I could do it, but then it would be on national television, and I'm sure it would not only piss off Coach but the higher-ups, as well. Not to mention, it would look bad on me and the team.

Maybe they'd understand when I tell them that some man, a guy I've met and had a beer with multiple times, is moving in on my girl. Then it hits me like a ton of bricks. She's not mine.

Not yet, but she will be.

It feels like we're fourth and goal and down by two. It's time for me to do what I do best and pull off a win. Not on the field, but with her. No more waiting. No more watching from the sidelines.

The second half of the game was a blur for me. I kept glancing up in the stands to see Tessa, chatting with Corey like she was there for him. With him. Lucky for me, football is like second nature, like breathing in a sense, and I was able to keep the game moving. By the time the clock hits zero at the end of the fourth quarter, we've won by three touchdowns.

The locker room is hyped with the guys cheering and laughing. It's a big boost for morale to win the preseason game. Stopping at my locker, I waste no time stripping out of my gear, grabbing a towel, and hitting the showers. The guys pull me into the celebration conversation as they recount a play I can't remember. I bullshit my way through it, like I did the second half of the game. This isn't like me, and I can't keep letting it happen. Next time, I might not be so lucky.

My hair is still dripping wet when I leave the locker room, my bag thrown over my shoulder.

"Where's the fire?" Case asks, catching up with me.

"No fire. Just excited to see my girl."

"Wow, that's different."

"Yeah, lots of changes," I say as I spot Tessa and Autumn, and with them is his brother, Corey. My feet carry me faster, my long strides burning up the space between us.

"I'll call you," Corey tells Tessa. My eyes zero in on where his hand is on her arm. He drops it when he sees us. "Good game, brother." He pats Case on the shoulder.

"Hey, Tess." I place my focus on Tessa. I have to or I might punch Corey, and he's a good guy. He's chill, and we've hung out a lot, but all I can see is his hand on her arm and him telling her that he's going to call her. My attention is better focused on her.

"Good game, Number Eighteen." She smiles up at me.

"You ready?" I offer her my arm.

"Ready? Where are we going?"

"Date number sixteen."

She throws her head back and laughs. "What am I going to do with you, Barker?"

"Keep me?" I bat my eyelashes all innocently. She's not buying it, which makes us both laugh.

"Where are you guys headed?" Autumn asks.

Tessa looks up at me to answer. She's not fighting this, and that gives me hope. "Whatever you want, babe." Her eyes widen at the endearment, but she looks to Autumn and answers.

"Henry's. The burgers are amazing. You have to try them." She looks back up at me. "I've been telling her about the burger we got there for weeks. Is that okay with you?"

"Yeah. Henry's sounds good."

"We'll meet you there," Case says as he and Corey walk away. Not before Corey waves at Tessa over his shoulder.

With Tessa on my arm, we make our way out to my SUV. "Did you drive?" I ask her.

"No, Autumn picked me up. She's going to take me home."

"I'll take you."

"I'm sure you're tired after the game. It's fine."

I open the door for her and wait for her to get settled before closing the door and racing around to my side. On instinct, I place my hand on her thigh as soon as we're out of the parking lot. "I'm never too tired for you, Tess." I've not really been this open with her. I've been reserved these past few weeks, just spending time with her. Showing her it's not a different woman every night. Just her. But no more keeping things in. I'm making my move. I don't care how long it takes to convince her that I'm in this for her.

"Aw, Number Eighteen, you getting soft on me after the big win?" she teases.

"Nah." I glance over at her. "I've always been soft on you." She's quiet, so another quick glance shows me she's staring out the window, and her reflection shows me a smile on her kissable lips.

Pulling into the back entrance of Henry's, I park next to Case, as Jeremy pulls in next to me. I rush to open Tessa's door, but she beats me to it. "I was going to get that."

"I know you're counting this as number sixteen, but it's not a date, Landon."

I stop and reach out, catching her arm, which causes her to stop, as well. She turns to face me, and I step closer. My hands cup her cheeks as I stare into her big green eyes. "Tessa Deaton, will you have dinner with me?" I ask her.

She swallows hard, and the green in her eyes grows even more vibrant. She blinks, and the connection is lost. "We're already here, you goof." Her tone is teasing, but I can see it. The insecurity. I don't know how to show her that she's all I see. I guess I'm going to have to try harder. "Come on." She pulls away from my arm and begins to move toward the door. I follow her because, well, I'll follow Tessa anywhere. Punching in the code, I hold the door open for her, Jeremy, and Autumn.

"The infamous Henry's," Jeremy says, taking in the place.

"Remind me to give you the code," I tell him. "Henry's cool, and this is team only in this back area and entrance. No fans, no cleat chasers. Just a place for us to hang and feel normal after practice or a game, even during the off-season."

"That's amazing," Autumn speaks up.

"I've never been inside, but the food we had a couple of weeks ago was so good," Tessa declares.

"Henry's getting a couple of pitchers of beer going," Case says as we reach the table he snagged us in the back.

Case sits on one end of the table, and Corey sits next to him on the side. Tessa takes the seat next to Corey, leaving the other end for me, and Jeremy and Autumn take the seats across from Tessa and Corey. I'm next to her, but so is he, and he's sitting closer. I hate this feeling, the one that tells me I could lose her. I've spent so much time trying to show her who I am that I could have waited too long and lost her. The thought has fire coursing through my veins. Anger at myself and, although wrong, at Corey for moving in on her. Can't he see she's mine? Surely, Case has told him to back off. Henry drops off the beer, and I pour a glass, draining half of it at once.

"You okay?" Tessa leans toward my end of the table.

"Yeah." I give her a reassuring smile. "What are my chances of converting you to a Cougars fan?" I tease.

"I don't know." She pretends to ponder the question. "I feel like I'm a traitor as it is. What if A.J. hears that I'm wearing a Landon Barker jersey?"

"Fuck A.J.," I say with absolutely no venom in my voice because it makes her smile.

"He's been my leading man since he was drafted to the Mavs four years ago."

"Ah, there's the difference."

"The difference in what?" she asks, confused.

"He's just your leading man. I'm more than that."

"Oh, yeah, and what exactly does 'more' stand for?" She's joking. This is what we do, but things are about to get real.

I lean in close. Her eyes are dancing with humor, I'm sure ready to laugh at whatever it is she thinks I might be about to say. I put joking aside and give her the real. "I want to be more than just your leading man, Tessa. I want to be your everything." She sucks in a breath, her eyes locked on mine, so I keep going. "I want to be your leading man, your favorite quarterback, your shoulder to cry on, the first person you call when you've had a good or bad day. I want to be your cuddle buddy. I want to be the man to give you all of life's pleasures." Her eyes heat, and my cock twitches. "And I want to be there for all the pain, too. Everything, Tessa. I want everything."

"You folks ready to order?" Henry asks from beside me.

"What are you getting, Tess?" Autumn asks from her spot across the table. She has no idea we just had a moment.

"Uh, Landon, whatever you got me last time is fine," she says softly.

"This the girl you made stay in the car?" Henry jokes.

"I didn't want you to steal my girl, Old Man," I tease. "Henry, this is my Tessa. Tessa, this is Henry, the man who makes this place happen for us."

"It's nice to meet you." Tessa smiles at him.

"A cheeseburger deluxe and fries, and the same for me. Add an extra burger," I tell him. He nods as he scratches down our order. "Oh, and add two waters to that." I look over at Tessa. "I know you like water with your meals." It's something that I've picked up on. No matter where we are, she always has to have water when she's eating.

"You caught that, did you?" she asks. The playfulness is back in her voice, but the look in her eyes tells me that she's still reeling from my speech just a few moments ago.

I wink at her, and her cheeks turn just the slightest shade of pink. I'm bringing my A game, Tessa Deaton. I hope you're ready.

CHAPTER 13

Tessa

I DON'T KNOW WHAT'S HAPPENING. I HAVE WHAT FEELS LIKE A thousand butterflies fluttering around in my stomach, and then there's the ache between my thighs. Both feelings caused by one Landon Barker. He's sitting in his chair, sipping his beer, as if he didn't just tilt my world on its axis. He's not the least bit affected by his confession.

He doesn't have to sit here with our combined friends and pretend he's not swooning over a speech I just made, or that he wants to tear my clothes from my body. He's lucky all right, because I want to do just that. It's wrong. We're friends. But the way he looks at me... I can't seem to be able to control it.

"Excuse me," I say, standing. Our food should arrive soon, and I need a minute. Just a few hundred seconds of time to get myself in check. I need to regroup.

"You okay?" he asks, reaching out for me. His hand lands on my arm, and I have to shift my stance and rub my legs together to dull the ache he's causing inside me.

"Yeah, just need to run to the restroom."

"The hallway by the bar. It's private, just for this section of the bar, so no worries about lines or fans."

"Like fans are going to worry about little ole me," I say teasingly, trying to get us back to the fun, flirty banter that I've learned to handle and is what I expect between us. Something passes in his eyes, but he doesn't comment.

"I'll come with." Autumn stands, and even though I needed some time to myself, I'm grateful. Maybe she can shed some light on what this is? Maybe I'm just reading too much into all of this.

I don't wait for her as I make my way down the hall. Pushing open the women's bathroom door, I'm surprised to find it sparkling clean and sigh in relief as I slump against the sink, trying to catch my breath.

Why am I breathless?

"Whoa," Autumn says, coming into the bathroom. "What was that?" She fans herself with her hands as if she's burning up.

"What?" I play dumb, but even I can hear it in my voice that I know exactly what she's talking about.

"Did you hear him? He called you his Tessa!"

I nod. "Caught that, did you?"

"Mm-hmm." She grins. "You two looked awfully cozy with whispers over there. What was that about?"

"Autumn, I— I don't know," I tell her honestly. Then I recap as much as my jumbled mind can remember of what he told me.

"He's in love with you."

"What? That's absurd. We've known each other for a month. He's not in love with me."

"He's falling, then. Hard. I can see it in the way he looks at you. For the record, it's the same way he's always looked at you, just more... intense if I had to put a name to it."

"What am I going to do?"

"I'm not sure what the issue is here, Tessa."

"He's this famous athlete, and I'm me. Tessa, who helps run an animal shelter. He can have any woman that he wants, and he has had plenty."

"Maybe so, but how many has he been reported to have been with since you?"

"None."

"One," she says at the same time.

My head whips up. "Who?" Is that jealousy I feel?

"You." That's right. Date eight, I think it was. We picked up takeout and brought it back to his place. He convinced me he needed help with learning to use his air fryer. Turns out, he doesn't even own an air fryer. Anyway, I ran in to get the food to try and keep the fans at bay, and I was photographed getting into his SUV. They didn't get my face, and the media doesn't know who I am. At least not that we're aware of.

"Right," I say when I break out of my memories to find her standing there, staring at me with her hands on her hips.

"What are you afraid of?" Her voice is softer this time.

"He's going to break my heart."

"First of all, you don't know that. Second of all, when this"—she waves her hands wildly in the air—"whatever this is, might not ever end."

I nod. "But if I let myself fall, it's going to be so much worse."

"Oh, Tess." She comes to me and puts her arms around my shoulder, giving me a side hug. "You've already fallen. You just won't admit it. Look at me and my cocky player. He's famous, and I'm just me, running an animal shelter, and we make it work. He loves me. I love him. It's that simple. It's not about money or fame or anything else. It's about the heart."

I give up on any pretenses to hide it and nod. "I know."

"See, that wasn't so hard. Just let it happen. If it works out, great. If not, you won't have the what-ifs. Trust me. I had two years of what-ifs, and that's not something you want to do. I had what-ifs and a broken heart. I would have much rather just had one of those. Take the chance. Go out there and show that player how lucky he is to have your attention and see where it leads you."

"Yeah. I mean, I don't know if I'll do it tonight, or here for that matter, but yeah. I'm going to do it. Thanks, Autumn." I give her a hug. "Oh, Landon said he would give me a ride home."

"Perfect. You don't have to do it here. Do it in the car or at your place. Invite him in for a drink, or you know, invite him to stay." She waggles her eyebrows.

"Too soon." I laugh.

"Is it?" She grabs my hand and tugs me toward the door. "Come on, before they think we ran away." She leads us back to the table, dropping my hand just as we're back in sight. I take my seat and try to catch up on the conversation between the men.

Not a minute later, Henry is delivering our food, and I concentrate on that. These burgers are so damn good. I polish off my food in no time, just eating and listening to the conversations around me. I chime in where I see fit, all the while my mind is running through tonight. Do I ask him in? How do I tell him I'm ready for a real date? One I say yes to for no other reason than to just spend time with him.

The next hour passes in a blur for me. In my head, I'm deciphering every look, every touch, every moment we've shared. I take part as I can, trying to act as though my head isn't spinning and my heart isn't racing. To be honest, day one, I wanted him. I just wouldn't allow myself to voice it. I was so afraid of being just another notch in his belt that I held him at arm's length, and my arms are tired. I can't hold him back anymore, and I don't want to. Autumn is right. I would rather have a broken heart than what-ifs. Who knows, maybe some of his luck will rub off on me and the broken heart will never happen. Either way, I'm tired of pretending.

"Tessa," Corey says, getting my attention.

"Sorry," I say sheepishly.

"What do you think? You in?"

"Uh, sure," I say, realizing that everyone's attention is on me. I'm sure it's whatever plans they have after we leave here. Corey grins and nods like I just gave him a million dollars.

"Right, well, we're headed out. We have to pick up JJ." Autumn stands from the table. "Tess, you need a ride home?" She looks from me to Corey and then over to Landon.

"No, thanks. Landon said he would give me a ride." We just talked about this, so I don't know why she's asking.

"I can take you home," Corey pipes up from beside me.

"That's sweet, but Landon can take me." I turn to look at Landon, and his jaw is clenched. "Unless you have something else going on?" I ask him.

"No. You're coming with me."

Well, all right, then. "Thanks anyway," I tell Corey. He looks disappointed but doesn't comment otherwise. Corey and Case decide to stay for another round, so we say our goodbyes and head out. Landon is quiet, giving all new meaning to the strong, silent type. His body is still as he walks beside me with his hand on the small of my back. He opens the passenger door of his SUV for me and waits until I'm strapped in to shut the door. I watch him as he jogs around the front of the SUV and slides in behind the wheel. His hands grip the wheel but he makes no move to start the car.

"Landon?"

He turns to look at me, his cerulean blue eyes dark with an emotion I can't name. "Don't go."

"Don't go where?" I ask, confused.

His jaw clenches. "Don't go out with Corey."

"What are you talking about?"

"Corey," he says through gritted teeth. "You agreed to have dinner with him tomorrow night. You're not going."

My hackles rise. "The hell I'm not." I don't know why I say it. I have no interest in going anywhere with Corey. But I'll be damned if he thinks he can boss me around.

"I mean it, Tessa. You're not going. Call him and tell him no."

"You're being crazy. You can't tell me what to do." I'm seething now, and for no reason really. I'm overreacting, but so is he. I also know that if I just came out and told him he's the one I want, this wouldn't be happening. At least, I don't think it would be.

"That's because I am crazy!" he yells and then goes silent. He's breathing heavily, and when he speaks again, his tone is softer, yet still firm. "I'm fucking crazy about you, Tessa. You're mine. My girl, not his, and I can't stand the thought of you going out with him."

I sit here in the passenger seat, my heart aflutter because he said the words. Not just in jest but with sincerity, and I know there is no way I can resist him. Hell, at this point, I don't even want to. I just want him.

"Okay."

"Please, I—" He stops as my acceptance registers with him. "Okay?"

"Yeah. I won't go out with him. To be honest, I wasn't sure what I was agreeing to. I was too nervous about asking you inside when we got to my place to tell you I'm ready for that date. The real one."

"Tessa." He leans over the console and engulfs my face with his big hands. "Say it again."

"Landon Barker, will you go on a date with me? A real one?"

He doesn't answer, but instead, his lips press against mine. His tongue glides across my bottom lip, and I open for him. He kisses me without reservation, and suddenly, our argument is no more. The only thing between us now is passion and some pent-up sexual frustration, at least on my end.

My hands grip his shirt as I try to pull him closer. I groan when his lips fall away and he rests his forehead against mine. "We can't do this here. I won't risk someone seeing you."

"What is it you think we're going to do, Barker?" I ask. I'm breathless from his kiss and giddy from this new development, so the teasing aspect of my question is seriously lacking. Not that either one of us minds.

"I'd rather show you." Sitting back in his seat, he buckles himself in and backs out of the parking lot. As soon as we're on the road, he reaches over and laces his fingers through mine, placing our combined hands on his thigh while he drives. His grip is firm yet comforting. Outside, I'm cool, calm, and collected now that I've caught my breath from his kisses. On the inside, I'm giddy like the sixteen-year-old me. I'm glad I let Autumn talk some sense into me. After only one kiss, I know that any time spent with him, even if it ends in a broken heart, is going to be worth it.

CHAPTER 14

Landon

I'M SUPPOSED TO BE TAKING HER HOME, BUT I'M CALLING AN
audible. I want her at my place, in my bed. That's all I've been able
to think about, and now it's going to happen. I don't ask her if it's
okay. It's easier to ask for forgiveness than for permission. Besides, the
way she returned that kiss told me all I needed to know. She's in this.

We're in this.

Finally.

Pulling into my place, I hit the button for the garage, and it slowly
opens. I pull in, turn off the engine, and shut the door. Lifting her hand
to my lips, I kiss her knuckles before pulling away and climbing out of the
SUV. I race to her side, and this time, she waits for me. Tugging open the
door, I offer her my hand as she steps out. As soon as the door is closed,
I'm on her. I push her back against the car, and my mouth claims hers.
Tessa's hands find their way to the nape of my neck, and her fingers glide
through my hair. She's so tiny, and I need better access. Bending, I lift

her into my arms. With my hands on the backs of her thighs, I take her mouth once again.

"Landon," she breathes as my lips trail down her neck.

I want to fucking devour her, every delectable inch. Instead, I force myself to slow down and pull away. Her green eyes are glassy as she gives me a half smile. I realize that I could be moving a little fast for her, and I don't want that. I want her to be in charge, which is a new concept for me when it comes to the opposite sex. I'm learning that everything with Tessa is different.

"I know I said I would take you home, but then you said you wanted the date, and we kissed, and well, I just wanted you here. In my home, in my space. I don't expect anything, just your company," I ramble. Looks like the asking for forgiveness part of the evening has come around. I've done nothing wrong, but I don't want her to get the wrong impression either. If she asks me to take her home, I will. In fact… "If you'd rather I take you home, we can do that. I just… I really needed you here, in my arms."

"I was kinda hoping to get more kisses." She bats her eyelashes, and I can't stop the deep, throaty chuckle that escapes my chest if I tried.

"Done." And since it's kisses she wants, I press my lips to hers for the third time tonight and take my time tasting her. By the time I'm done, we're both breathless.

"That'll do, Number Eighteen. That'll do," she says, her head now resting back against my SUV.

"Come on, you." I tighten my grip on her and carry her inside. Once we're in the kitchen, I position her on the island. My hands rest on either side of her, caging her in. "You thirsty?"

"No, thank you."

I'm trying really hard not to drag her off to my room to ravish her. Instead, I stand here, stock still, staring into her big green eyes.

"How about a movie?"

"Movie?" She nods. "That, I can do." Snaking my arms around her,

I whisper, "Hold on tight," as I lift her into my arms and carry her into the living room.

"My feet work. The ankle healed weeks ago," she teases.

I sit down on the couch with her straddling my lap. "I like you close," I admit.

"How close?"

Her words are barely a whisper as she leans in and kisses my neck. "That works," I say, gripping her hips to keep her close. I like her right here where she is.

"You know, we've never tried the cuddling thing here at your place. Maybe you won't like it on your home turf."

"Did I not tell you? I'm a professional cuddler now."

"Really? Giving up the starting QB spot for cuddling. I didn't see that one coming." She grins down at me, and my lips ache to kiss her. So I do. Just a quick peck to her lips.

"Nah, but there's this girl, she's pretty much knocked me on my ass."

"Aw, poor baby." She juts out her bottom lip, so I nip at it with my teeth, soothing the ache with my tongue.

"She's got this long, dark curly hair, and her eyes… they're this green I've never seen before. She's open and honest and not afraid to call me out on my shit. She's pretty much my dream girl."

"Have you told her?" Her eyes soften because we both know the answer.

"Yeah." My hands slide behind her neck, bringing her closer. "I've told her, but maybe I should remind her, you know? In case she's forgotten, or maybe she thought I wasn't being serious?" I raise my brows at her, daring her to challenge me.

"Oh, I'm sure she believed you, but maybe she might like to hear it again, you know, just to seal the deal."

I nod. "Tessa Deaton, you're everything."

She bites down on her bottom lip, stealing my attention. "I'm worried about a broken heart, but Autumn helped me see the light. I don't want to wonder what-if."

"What-if what?"

"What if I let this pass me by? Would I always regret it?"

"I don't give up that easily, Tessa."

"I'm glad."

One hand still behind her neck, the other wrapping around her waist, I pull her into a hug. "I don't know what all this means. The things you make me feel. The breathless, fluttering, romantic sap that I've never been, but I want to know more. When it comes to you, I find I want it all."

"It?"

"You. Us. The future. Cuddles on the couch, kisses, laughs, meals, dates, you coming to my games. You name it, I want it. As long as it's with you."

"Well, I say we start with that movie." She slides off my lap, and I let her. When she bends over to grab the remote from the coffee table, I don't even hide the fact that I'm ogling her ass. After tonight's declaration, I have that right.

She takes a seat next to me, and I put my arm around her, pulling her close while she starts to surf the channels. Her phone rings, and she hands me the remote while she pulls it out of her back pocket. "I'm sure it's Autumn checking on me." She glances at the screen, then nervously back to me. "Unknown number. I'm always worried it's going to be about my mom or something, and it's always a telemarketer, but I still answer." She sits up and slides her finger across the screen. "Hello." She pauses and glances nervously at me over her shoulder. "Hey, Corey."

Motherfucker.

She's here with me, so I have no right to be pissed off, but damn it, can he not see that she's all mine? She left with me. She chose to let me take her home, well, my home, but it's the same thing. We're together.

I give up on finding anything to watch and unashamedly listen to her conversation.

"Oh, about that. Listen, I was a little distracted tonight, and I didn't realize what I had agreed to. I'm seeing someone. It's new, but I'm excited to see where it goes." She pauses. "Landon." Again, she's quiet, and I want to beat on my chest that she's just told him she's my girl. Well, close enough anyway. "Thanks, Corey. Sure, I'll see you around." She ends the call and places her phone on the table before taking her spot and curling back into my chest.

I pull her impossibly close and hand her the remote. I don't care what we watch. Chances are, I'm only going to be watching her. She flips through the channels for several minutes before yawning. "Can't find anything," she says, tossing the remote beside her on the couch.

I'm not ready to take her home. We just got here. I just got her. She peers up at me, and I know what's coming. She's ready to go. "Can we go to bed?"

"You're staying?"

"Unless that's not okay? I can have Autumn come and pick me up." She moves to sit up, but my hold is strong, keeping her next to me.

"No. I want you here."

"Okay. I'm exhausted. It's been a long day."

"Yeah," I agree. Game days always take a lot out of me. I stand from the couch, lace our fingers together, and bring her with me as I lock up the house and turn off the lights. I lead her to my room and give her some boxers and a T-shirt to sleep in. "There's the bathroom. Take all the time you need. I'm going to go down the hall to the guest room to shower."

"Okay." Nothing but easy acceptance from my girl tonight.

She disappears behind the bathroom door, and I just stand here and stare after her. I meant what I said when I told her I just wanted her here in my space. For weeks, I've lain in bed at night, wishing she were here, lying next to me. I'm letting her take us where she wants this to go, but at the same time, I'm a man. A man who only has to hear her voice for my cock to take note. It's going to be a long night, but I already know it's going to be the best night I've ever had. Just because it's her, Tessa. Just her presence alone makes it so.

Shaking out of my thoughts, I grab some clothes and head down the hall to grab another quick shower. Sure, I showered after the game, but I have to take care of business if I'm going to survive sleeping next to her tonight. Turning the water as hot as it will go, I strip out of my clothes and step in. The water massages my tense muscles. I'm not sure if it's from the game or from knowing Tessa is staying with me tonight. Either way, the hot water does wonders. Grabbing the bottle of body wash, I squirt a handful into my hand and wrap it around my already hard cock.

It's not hard to imagine her here with me, knowing she's just down the hall. I close my eyes and remember what it felt like to have her in my arms. I remember the first taste of her on my tongue as we kissed.

My hand pumps faster.

Over and over again, I work my cock. My balls tighten, and I have to brace myself with my free hand on the shower wall to keep from losing my balance. My eyes are still closed as I let my mind wander to what it would feel like to be inside her. To hear her soft moans of pleasure. That's all it takes. My back stiffens as my release pours out of me, and I call out for her. I should be worried she might hear me, but I couldn't care less. I want her to know what she does to me. That just the mere thought of her brings me to my knees. I don't play games, not when it comes to someone as important as Tessa. There's never been anyone like her, not for me.

By the time I make it back to my room, Tessa is sitting on the side of my bed. She's wearing a Cougars T-shirt with my name on the back. The jersey she wore today was similar, but this is different. This time, it's my shirt against her skin, and sure, my name was on her back earlier today, but this feels… more.

"All set?" I ask, making my way to the opposite side of the bed. I don't really have a side living alone. I can take the entire thing if I want, and most nights I end up in the middle. Tonight, though, that will be different. Tessa will have her side. I like that. I like it a lot.

"Yes. Thank you. I wasn't sure if you prefer a side." She nods toward the bed.

"No. It's always just me, so I never have to choose."

"Well, what side do you take when people sleep over?" she asks, like the words taste bitter in her mouth.

"No one stays here. At least not here in this room with me."

"Come on, Landon. Be straight with me. I'm not a gentle flower. I can take it."

"I don't bring women here, Tessa. Just my mother. That's me being straight with you. Look, I know we've skirted around this, but just because I was photographed at an event with a woman doesn't mean I slept with her. Now, don't get me wrong, I'm not a saint and have never claimed to be. This is my home, Tess. My place to just be me. I don't bring random women into my sanctuary."

"You brought me here."

I walk back around the bed, and her eyes follow me as I stop to stand in front of her. Bending down, I cradle either side of her face in my hands. "You're different, Tessa. I want you here."

"Only me, huh?" A slow smile crosses her face. "So I get to pick my side of the bed?"

I can't help it. I have to kiss her. Leaning in, I place a loud, smacking kiss on her lips. "Yeah, baby. You can pick your side of the bed."

She nods. "Okay. Get in." She stands and gives me a pointed look, telling me she means business.

Never in my wildest dreams did I ever imagine a spitfire of a beautiful woman would be bossing me around, but here we are. Shaking my head at her antics, I head back to the other side of the bed and climb under the covers.

"You settled?"

"Yes."

I watch her as she turns out the lamp on her side—well, the side she's standing on—and the room is bathed in darkness. I feel the bed dip and the covers ruffle as she climbs beneath them. I exhale with the knowledge that she's just claimed her side when I feel her moving, and then her body is right next to mine.

"Change your mind?" I ask her. I can't see her face, but I know she's close.

"No." She lifts my arm and slides under, resting her head on my chest. "I just want to be where you are. We can share a side."

I'm not sure how to explain it, but it feels a lot like my heart's tripping over itself in my chest at her words. This gorgeous, kind, sexy, thoughtful woman has managed to turn me into a romantic fool when it comes to her. In no other situation, with any other woman, could I ever imagine myself having this kind of reaction to those words. In fact, I would be running for the hills. Not with Tessa.

"I like this plan."

"Me, too."

We lie in total darkness for what seems like hours when in reality it's a matter of minutes. "Landon," she whispers.

"Hmm," I ask as I run my fingers through her thick locks.

"I really want to kiss you."

"Are you asking for permission?"

"Maybe? I'm not sure what this is or how this works."

"This is us in a relationship. This is whatever you want it to be. You don't have to ask for permission to kiss me or touch me. You're welcome in my home and on any side of this bed that you want. This isn't just something to pass the time, Tessa. I want to see where things lead with us. You are the first woman I've ever felt this way about. I'm not letting you go anytime soon." *If ever.* I keep that thought to myself.

"Just us, right? I mean, we're exclusive? I know that sounds crazy, and I feel stupid even asking, but I want us on the same page. I won't do this if I don't have all of you."

"We're exclusive, and you already have all of me."

"In that case…" I feel her weight lift off my chest, and her hands roam from my chest, up my neck, until their softness cups my cheek. "Kiss me."

Not needing to be told twice, I flip her over on her back, causing her to squeal. Even in the dark of the room, my lips find hers easily. I devour her. Her taste is so new yet familiar as I explore her mouth.

Rolling to my side, I continue to kiss her. My hands roam over her body, but I don't take it any further than that. There's something to be said about making out like teenagers as an adult with a woman who consumes your thoughts. It's exciting and innocent, and we need this. This time to just be together. I'm showing her that this is more, that *she's* more.

I don't know how much time passes us by, minutes, hours, even; we have no concept of time as we get lost in one another's kiss. I never knew a night like this would be so… rewarding. Tessa, here, in my bed, in my arms, her kisses branding me and mine her. This is definitely a night for the history books as one I will never forget.

CHAPTER 15

Tessa

I'VE BEEN STARING AT THE WALL FOR OVER AN HOUR. MY BODY'S in the same position as I think about where I am and last night. Landon was a complete gentleman, and while my body screamed for him to take me, it was perfect. I wouldn't change a thing about our time together. Hence the reason I'm lying as still as I can, not wanting to leave this bed or his embrace. His body is aligned with mine, his arms wrapped around me, and it's a comfort like I've never known.

"I can hear you thinking," his deep, sexy voice says from behind me. I can't hold the giggle from escaping. "That is a sound a man can get used to waking up to."

I roll over so that we're face-to-face. "Good morning."

"Morning. How long have you been up?" He leans in for a kiss, and I turn my head. "What's up with that?"

"Morning breath."

"Fuck morning breath. Waking up with you in my arms deserves to be celebrated with a kiss, morning breath be damned." He leans in again, and this time, I let him kiss me, keeping my mouth closed. "Tessa," he growls, making me laugh. As soon as my mouth is open, he takes full advantage and slips his tongue past my lips. Suddenly, I couldn't care less about morning breath either.

"What are we doing today?" he asks when he finally pulls away.

"I'm not sure what you're doing, but I have to work. Speaking of, I should get up and get moving. I still need to go home and change. Can you take me home?"

"No, no, no. Call in sick. Tell Autumn that your lips are sore from kissing. Tell her that you're stuck in a warm bed for the day and that I forbid you to leave it."

"I'd love to, but I can't. Autumn depends on me, and the animals, too. Besides, don't you have practice today?"

"No. We get the day after a game off."

"Really? I would think that you would get right back to it."

"Nah, some teams do. Coach says we need a day to rest and let our bodies heal."

"I hardly think that one day is long enough for that. I've seen those hits some of the guys take and even you when you're getting sacked." I grin.

"Always busting my balls." He shakes his head, but a smile tilts his lips.

"It's a tough job, but somebody has to do it." I peck his lips and then roll away from him.

"Get back here," he demands playfully.

"Can't. Now get moving, Number Eighteen." I grab my clothes from the chair in the corner of the room and disappear into the bathroom. By the time I'm dressed and have brushed my teeth with my index finger and some toothpaste, I find Landon sitting on the edge of the bed, his hair mussed and a sleepy, sexy smile on his face.

"Ready?"

"Yes."

He stands from the bed, offers me his hand, and links our fingers together. Hand in hand, we head out to the garage. He offers to stop for breakfast, but I'm cutting it close on time, so I decline.

"I should be home around five or a little after."

He leans over the console and kisses me sweetly. "Have a good day, baby."

Butterflies swarm my belly. "You, too." I wave awkwardly and climb out of his SUV. He doesn't move until I'm in the house. Not able to resist, I peek out the blinds and watch him drive away. I pinch my leg and jump from the pain. I had to make sure I wasn't dreaming that this is real, that this is really my life. With a smile on my face, I rush to the shower and get ready for work.

$$\begin{matrix} \times & \times & \text{\textbardbl} \\ \circ & \circ & \text{d} \end{matrix}$$

I've just released the dogs so they can run as my stomach grumbles. Pulling my phone out of my pocket, I see it's just after ten. I should have taken the time to at least grab a granola bar this morning. Oh, well, I'll just have to deal until I can run out for lunch. I rushed out of the house this morning without packing anything. Being hungry is worth not running late. I usually hate to have to rush, and it puts my entire day off-kilter, but somehow, that's not the case today. Well, unless you count my stomach's angry growl. I guess waking up with Landon makes all the difference.

Heading back inside, I find Autumn in our shared office. "Hey, what are you looking at so hard?" I ask, watching her stare at her laptop.

"Just going over the details for the adoption fair this weekend."

"What can I do? We're all set, right?"

"Yes. We have plenty of volunteers, but I'm just worried about the attendance. Our fairs here at the shelter don't do nearly as well as the ones we hold at the mall or other shopping centers. We're at capacity, and I'm hoping we can find some of our animals forever homes."

"Okay. So what do we do? We've got social media ads going. We've passed out over five hundred flyers. We have posters hanging all around town. What are we missing?" Before she can answer, the chime sounds, letting us know we have a visitor. There are no volunteers on the schedule until this afternoon. Standing from my desk, I start for the door, but before I can make it to the threshold, Landon is there.

"Hey." He leans in for a quick kiss. "I assumed you didn't take the time to eat. I know how much you hate to run late, so I stopped at the Cup of Joe Café and bought you your favorite." He holds up the bag from the café as his proof.

"Best bo— guy ever," I stumble over my words.

He leans in close, placing his lips next to my ear. "Boyfriend, Tess. You had it right the first time." His lips press against mine, and that's all it takes for me to get lost in him.

"This is new." Autumn chuckles, pulling us out of our trance.

Landon smiles down at me, hands me the bag from the café, and turns his attention to Autumn. "Landon Barker, boyfriend to Tessa Deaton." He smirks, holding his hand out for Autumn to shake.

"Stop." I pull on his arm, bringing it back to his side. He takes that as an opportunity to lace his fingers with mine.

"Looks like I missed a lot last night from Henry's until now."

"You could say that," I confess.

"What I want to know is why I'm just now hearing about it?" Her smile is wide as her eyes give me a knowing look.

"I was running late and came in and got straight to work. I was going to tell you, but you looked like someone just kicked your puppy, and we started talking about the adoption event on Saturday, and well, this guy decided to show up and started throwing around titles." I bump my shoulder into Landon's.

"Hey, I earned that title. I'm all about throwing it around."

Autumn sighs. "Sorry, I'm just worried about this event."

"What event?" Landon asks.

"We schedule several adoption events each year. Keeps the public informed and reminds them we're here. We're at capacity for the animals, and Autumn's concerned we're not going to have a good turnout. Usually, we go to a shopping mall or a pet store, something like that, and transport a few of the dogs and cats, but since we have Buckwheat and we're so full, we thought we would schedule the event here. We won't have the same traffic as the shopping centers."

"When is the event?"

"Saturday."

He nods. "What time?"

"One o'clock."

"I was hoping you might say that." We stand by and watch as he pulls his phone out of his back pocket, and his fingers fly across the screen. "There." He looks proud of himself as he turns his phone to show me the screen.

@LandonBarkerOfficial Come help me support the Safe Haven Animal Shelter this Saturday at 1 PM. #AdoptAPet #Cougars

"I have twenty-four million followers." He winks. I read the post for a third time, processing what this could mean for the shelter.

"Landon, that's amazing. Wait, don't you have practice on Saturday?"

"We do, but just in the morning. We're reviewing game film. I'll be out of there by noon. I'll get Case and a few of the guys to come, too. They can Tweet it out to their followers, as well."

"Jeremy can, too. I don't know why I didn't think of that," Autumn says. "Thank you, Landon."

"I usually have PR send over pictures and things to sign, but I'm not going to do that this time. I want to get the public here, and I can sign anything they bring with them, but I want to make this day about the shelter."

"Thank you." I rise on my tiptoes and kiss him.

"If that's what I get for doing something nice, I need to step up my game." He grins, and I can't help but playfully roll my eyes.

"You two are so cute together. I love this." Autumn waves her hands at us.

"Yeah, I love it, too," Landon says softly, his eyes holding mine. "You need any help around here today?" He tucks a loose strand of hair behind my ear.

"No, we have a roster of volunteers this afternoon. Thank you for what you did."

"Anything for you." He leans down for another kiss, and I have to force myself not to take it too far, knowing that Autumn is in the room with us. "I'll see you tonight?" he asks when we finally pull apart.

"Yes."

"Pack a bag. I'll pick you up, and we'll go back to my place."

"Okay." A slow grin crosses his face. I don't know if he thought I was going to fight him on it or what, but I'm not. I'm putting myself out there, my heart, too, and letting the chips fall where they may. "Thank you for breakfast."

"You're welcome," he says, giving me another chaste kiss. "Autumn, it was good to see you." He releases his hold on me and steps back. "Later, Freckles."

"Damn." Autumn pretends to fan herself with her hands. "That was hot."

"Yeah, he is," I agree, making her laugh.

"So, you took my advice, I see."

"I did, and we talked last night. We're dating exclusively. I stayed at his place last night."

"Give me all the juicy details."

"Nothing much to tell, really. We made out like teenagers and then fell asleep."

"Huh."

"What? Huh? What's that for?"

"Seems I was right. He's not the playboy you think he is."

"Maybe. He says you can't believe everything you read, and I trust him. He's given me no reason not to. He's picking me up at my place after work, and he just told me to pack a bag, so I guess I'm staying over again. Not that I mind. His bed is like sleeping on fluffy clouds. It's insane."

"The man in it isn't so bad either, right?" She waggles her eyebrows.

"Not bad at all." I laugh as her phone rings.

"Hey, babe," she greets her husband.

I tune her out, not wanting to listen to their conversation, and dig into the bag from the café. Sure enough, he got me my cinnamon coffee cake muffin and Autumn the banana nut. "He's observant, I'll give him that," I murmur to myself.

"That was Jeremy. I told him about Landon, and he's going to send out a Tweet, as well. Hopefully, there are a lot of locals who follow him."

"That's great. Sounds like this event is going to turn around after all." As soon as the words are out of my mouth, the phone rings. Autumn answers, and I take the moment to bite into my muffin.

"That was someone who saw Landon's tweet. They wanted to know what time the event started. Holy shit, Tessa. Maybe we're not ready for this type of exposure."

"Meh," I say, waving her off. "That's good press for the shelter. Hell, maybe we'll even get some new volunteers because of it, too."

"Wouldn't that be nice? Just think of all the things that we could finally do. That ever-growing to-do list we could mark off if we had more help."

The phone rings again, and I answer this time. More of the same… What time does the event start, and what time will Landon Barker be here? Autumn and I scarf down bites of muffin between fielding calls. By the time the volunteers arrive for the day, we've managed to do nothing but answer the phone. Maybe Autumn's right—we might not be ready for a crowd of this magnitude.

"You know, maybe we should have a sheriff here. You know, crowd control and all that. I know it comes out of the budget, but with the way the phone's been ringing, it's probably a safe bet that having someone here would be beneficial."

"I agree. I'll call the sheriff's department now and see if they have anyone willing to pick up a shift."

I quickly give a rundown of what needs to be done to the volunteers and field more calls while Autumn arranges security. In a matter of minutes, Landon has turned this from an "I don't know how it's going to turn out" into "This is bigger than we ever could have imagined."

By the time I pull into my driveway at ten minutes after five, I'm exhausted. It's been a long day of fielding calls. While it's not the physical work I'm used to, mentally I'm drained. In a good way. I never could have dreamed that one simple Tweet from Landon could bring this kind of publicity to the shelter.

Before I even get my car in Park, Landon is pulling in behind me. His long legs carry him to my door, and he's pulling it open before I can even get the chance. "Hey, Freckles."

"Hi." I smile up at him. He offers me his hand and helps me out of the car. "Sorry, I still need to pack, and I could use a shower."

"You can shower at my place. Rough day?"

"Mentally, yes. Your Tweet created a stir. The phone has been ringing off the hook all day long. I can't thank you enough."

"Don't mention it. I got Case and a few of the other guys on board, as well. Trent is going to bring his wife, Luna."

"Seriously? You're amazing."

"Amazing enough for a kiss? It's been way too long." He leans in and presses a soft kiss to the corner of my mouth. "I missed you today."

"It's been like six hours since you saw me last." I'm going for nonchalant like I didn't miss him, too.

He nods, and the expression on his face is serious. "That's too long, Tess."

"Get used to it, pal. What do you think is going to happen next week when you have an away game?"

"You know my schedule?" He grins.

"Is that creepy?"

He chuckles. "Not creepy at all. Come on. Let's get you packed, and we'll pick up some food on the way home. I was going to make dinner, but I do believe my time is better spent holding you." He wraps an arm around my shoulders and guides me into the house.

As I'm tossing items into an overnight bag, I wonder if this is all too soon. Am I rushing this? It feels right, though, and that's what matters. I can only imagine what Autumn would be telling me right now. She and Jeremy fell in love in a week. Not that I love Landon, but I do really like him. We're both adults, and as long as we're both on the same page with where this is going, I'm not going to let my fear get in the way.

"You ready?" Landon asks when I enter the living room.

"Yes. I think I have what I need."

"You know, I've never asked you, why don't you have any animals?"

"The landlord doesn't allow it. Doesn't mean I haven't brought a few home from time to time." I shrug. "One day, I'll buy my own place so I can have a pet."

"Dog or cat?"

"Dogs."

He nods. "Yeah, man's best friend. I had a golden retriever as a kid. His name was Ace. If I wasn't at football practice, I was out in the backyard with him. He died during my senior year of high school. I swear he was a member of the family. Hit me and my parents hard."

"Landon Barker, you're nothing but a big ole softy."

"Shh," he says dramatically. "Don't let that get out. It will ruin my street cred."

I throw my head back in laughter. "Sorry to break it to you, Number Eighteen, you don't have any street cred. Your skill and your number get you respect."

"As long as it gets me yours." He stands from his spot on the couch and reaches for my bag. "What sounds good to eat?"

"Honestly, a burger from Henry's."

"That's my girl," he says, guiding me outside with his hand on the small of my back. He stops and makes sure the door is locked. "I was thinking I could drop you off at work in the morning on my way to the field and then pick you up. That way we're not taking two cars."

"You don't have to do that."

"It's selfish, really. It gives me more time with you."

"Well, when you put it like that." I smile, and he returns it. His is just as wide as he leads me to the passenger side of his SUV.

"You want me to call it in?" he asks, reaching for his phone.

"Nah, we can go in and eat."

He reaches across the console and links his fingers with mine, and we're on our way to dinner. Just like that. He's so seamlessly slipped his way into my life, and I realize I wasn't really living before Landon.

CHAPTER 16

Landon

"Hey, Henry." I wave to him at his spot behind the counter. With Tessa's fingers laced with mine, I lead her to a table in the back corner. It's hard to tell when any of my teammates will show up, and I want her all to myself. They've yet to meet her officially as mine, and part of me wants to shout it so the entire world can hear, but the other part of me wants to keep her for myself. There has only been one incident where the press got a photo of us, but you can't see her face. I want the world to know, but at the same time, I don't want that intrusion into our lives. They print complete shit, and I have no doubt there will be something printed that will threaten what we have. It's not a risk I want to take.

Not with her.

So, for now, I'm going to keep her all to myself. Well, until this weekend, that is. My Tweet is getting national attention. They're going to want to know my connection to the shelter, and I'll tell them. That gives us time before the world thinks they have a right to invade our privacy and meddle in our lives. I hate it, but I love football. It's the price I pay to play a sport I love for a living.

"Tessa, nice to see you again," Henry greets her. "This guy treating you right?"

She smiles and nods. What she doesn't know is that he'd ream my ass if there was any other answer than yes. "Perfect gentleman," she replies with a kind smile.

"Now I know you're pulling my leg. This guy?" He points at me.

"Right?" she agrees with him. "I was surprised myself."

I should give them a hard time, but the smile on her face makes any amount of ribbing worth it.

"All right, here's a menu. What can I get you to drink?"

"Water for me, please," Tessa says.

"Same for me, Henry, thanks."

"I want to try something different. Any suggestions?" Tessa asks, her eyes scanning the menu.

"It's all good. I've never had anything that came from Henry's kitchen that wasn't."

"Really? Okay." She scans the menu again. "I think I'm going to go with chicken tenders and onion rings."

"Excellent choice," Henry says, placing our drinks and straws in front of us. "What about you, Landon?"

"I'll have the same. Barbecue sauce, please." I hand him my menu.

"Tessa? Barbecue?"

"Yes, please." She opens her straw and places it in her drink, taking a long pull. "How was your day?"

It's a question I've come to expect from her; she actually cares about how my day went, not the money or the fame, but how it affected me. "Good. I didn't do a lot. I went to the gym and worked out, then did a little cleaning."

"Cleaning? I thought you had someone who cleaned for you?"

"I do, but this kind of cleaning is all on me. I just went through some of my clothes, moved some things around." What I don't tell her is that I cleared out a couple of drawers for her and made some space in my closet and in the bathroom for her things. I want her to feel comfortable at my place, and this is just another way of me showing her. I want her. I want her in my house, in my bed, in my life, and by my side.

"Look at you being all domestic," she teases.

I just shake my head and smile. "What about you? The phones were crazy?"

"Almost as soon as your Tweet went out, the lines were lit up, and it was like that all day. Turns out, the quarterback for the Cougars has a pretty big fan base."

"There's only one fan I'm interested in."

"JJ's loyalty lies with his daddy's team, so you're safe."

Reaching across the table, I take her hand in mine. "Just you, Tess. You're the only one who matters."

"Barker!" I hear yelled across the quiet room.

Turning, I see Trent and his wife, Luna, making their way toward us. "Trent, Luna, this is my girlfriend, Tessa," I introduce as soon as they reach the table. Trent raises his eyebrows in surprise but otherwise keeps his cool. "Tess, this is Trent Caudill, our right tackle, and his wife, Luna."

"Nice to meet you." Luna offers Tessa her hand, and they shake.

"And this little one?" Tessa points to Luna's pregnant belly.

"Baby Caudill. We're not finding out until delivery."

"Oh my gosh, I'm not sure I could do that." Tessa smiles kindly.

"It's been tough, trust me. I've almost caved a few times, but this one"—she points over her shoulder at Trent—"keeps me on course."

"It's exciting to find out the day he or she's born. There are too many things in life that are instant gratification. There's something to be said for the waiting… and the suspense." Trent pulls Luna in close, and I happen to agree with him.

"I guess I never put much thought into it," Tessa states. "When are you due?"

"Five days before Thanksgiving. It's bad timing with it being mid-season, but you can't exactly make these things happen on a timeline. We tried for months. The plan was for the off-season, but life had other plans."

"Do you want to join us?" Tessa offers.

"Sure," Luna agrees.

Just like that, the women have hijacked whatever plans Trent or I had for the evening, but from the way he's looking at his wife, he doesn't seem to mind. I don't either. Trent is a good guy, and his wife is his world. I don't have to worry about him hitting on Tessa or telling her any wild stories. I'm not one to hop from bed to bed, but I'm not a saint either.

Tessa scoots her drinks across the table and climbs out of the booth. I stand, letting her inside to where she pushed her drink, and then slide in next to her. Luna sits across from her, and Trent from me.

"So, how long have the two of you been together?" Luna asks, her eyes flashing to me, and then her focus turns back to Tessa.

"We've been talking for a while, but officially, me getting to call her mine, this weekend." I lean over and kiss Tess's temple.

"Aw," Luna sings. "You two look so cute together."

"Welcome, how's my favorite mom-to-be?" Henry asks Luna.

"Hanging in there."

"Here's your water and glass of milk," he says, placing them in front of Luna. "What can I get you, Trent?"

"Just water, thanks, Henry."

"You two know what you want to eat?"

"Cheeseburger and fries. Run the burgers through the garden," Trent orders for them.

"Coming right up." Henry turns and walks away, only to come right back with a tall glass of water for Trent before he disappears again.

The ladies fall into conversation, as do Trent and I. We spend the next hour chatting about anything and everything, and with each second that passes, I want more of it. I want more of being a unit, a couple with her. I want more nights like tonight with Tessa by my side.

× × ♪
o o

"They were really nice," Tessa says in my SUV on the way to my place. "Luna's got that pregnancy glow."

"That's a real thing?" I ask her.

"Yeah, couldn't you tell?"

"No, but I'm a man. I'm not meant to notice those kinds of things, unless it's my woman," I add.

"Oh, I see, so there's still hope for you." I hear the humor in her voice.

Hitting the button to open the garage door, I pull in and turn off the engine. As if she's stayed with me hundreds of times, Tessa climbs out, reaching into the back for her bag. She doesn't wait for me as she heads for the door that leads to the utility room. I take my time shutting the garage door and grabbing my bag from the back, as well. I stop off in the laundry room and empty the contents into the hamper.

"Tess," I call out when I don't see her in the kitchen.

"In here," she calls back, and I follow her voice down the hall and into my bedroom. Her bag is on the bed, and she's pulling items out of it. "I'm overdue for that shower," she explains, not bothering to look at me.

In a way, that makes this easier. "Hey, so I cleaned out a couple of drawers, you know, in case you wanted to keep anything here."

She stops messing with her clothes and turns to face me. "Mr.

Domestic." Her tone is teasing, and I don't know what I expected, but it's not that.

"There might be some closet space, too."

"Might be?" A grin tilts her full, kissable lips.

"There is. I told you I moved some things around today."

"For me?"

"Only for you." I reach out and pull her close, kissing her soft and slow.

"Hold that thought, QB. I need a shower." She grabs what she needs and heads to the bathroom.

"Wait," I call out just before she disappears behind the door. Reaching into my dresser drawer, I pull out the same shirt she slept in last time and toss it to her. Her only reply is to smile and continue on into the bathroom, closing the door behind her.

I'm tempted to put her clothes away, but I want her to do it. I want her to feel comfortable here. I know I'm moving us right along in this relationship, but I can't seem to help myself. The more time I spend with her, the more I want. It's like she's an addiction. One I don't want to break.

Ignoring the nagging feeling to put her things away, I strip down to my boxer briefs and T-shirt, tossing my dirty clothes into the basket in the closet. I turn off the overhead light and turn on the TV instead. It gives off just the amount of light she'll need to put her things away.

The bathroom door opens and, even with the low glow of the TV, I can see she's beautiful in my T-shirt, her wet curls piled on top of her head. I don't take my eyes off her as she makes her way to the bed and finishes unpacking her clothes for tomorrow.

"Where should I put these?" she asks.

Realizing I told her but never showed her, I climb out of bed and meet her at the dresser that the TV sits on. "This side is yours. All four of them."

She peers up at me under long, wet lashes, and I swear my fucking heart stutters in my chest. "You're beautiful."

"Thank you, Landon." She quickly turns away and makes quick work of placing her clothes in the top drawer and tossing her bag on the floor beside the dresser. When she turns back around, I step forward and wrap my arms around her.

"I'm glad you're here, Tess."

Tilting her head back, she gazes up at me. We're stuck in this silent stare. My cock twitches as my ache for her increases with her this close. She's wearing my shirt and, by the looks of it, no bra, and I would assume panties. She's practically naked, and I want to explore her body. I want to savor every inch of her, but I promised her she would have the power when it comes to us and sex. I wish I had taken a shower to help soften my need for her—no pun intended.

"Landon," she whispers, swiping her tongue across her full lips.

I take a step closer and align my body with hers. My erection brushes her belly, and she inhales a breath. I don't say a word, keeping my eyes locked on hers. I hope she can see it. That I won't hurt her and that this isn't just about winning a date or winning her. It's so much more.

She's so much more.

My chest rapidly rises and falls just from being this close to her. When her small, soft hands land against my chest, I feel as though I can't breathe. I stand stock-still, letting her do her thing while her hands roam over my chest. I swallow hard when she reaches the waistband of my boxer briefs. The same boxer briefs that my hard-as-steel cock is peeking out of. Her eyes never leave mine as she slowly rakes her index finger over the tip.

"Tessa," I warn.

She bats those lashes at me, her deep green eyes shining. "What's it going to take, Landon?"

"W-What?" My voice cracks; I'm barely maintaining my control.

"To break this calm you have. It's like nothing fazes you." Her voice is soft, almost a whisper.

"Trust me, Tess, my control is hanging on by a thread."

"Yeah?" she asks, hopeful. "So what's it going to take?" She swipes her index finger over the head of my cock again, making me fist my hands at my sides. "What if I did this?" She cups me, her small hands gripping me through my boxer briefs.

"Tessa," I growl. It's supposed to be a warning, but it sounds more like a mating call, which is pretty accurate at this point.

"What if I did this?" She slides her hands under the waistband of my underwear, and I snap.

Hands on her hips, I grip them firmly and lift her in the air so we're eye level. "I want you, Tessa. Any fool can see that, but I need to hear you say it. Tell me you want this. I promised you we would go at your pace, and if you're fucking with me right now—" I pause and swallow hard. "I'm going to need a cold shower. A long one."

"Your eyes, they're such a deep blue right now." Her hands that are resting on my shoulders cradle my face. "I want you, too."

The words are barely spoken before I'm crashing my lips to hers. In three long strides, I'm peeling my lips from her mouth and tossing her back onto the bed. "Strip." She climbs to her knees with her eyes locked on mine and pulls my shirt over her head. My mouth drops open as I stare at her naked body. "No panties?" I grit out.

She shrugs. "An unnecessary barrier." Crawling to the edge of the bed, she reaches for me, but I take a step back. I can't let her touch me, not like this. I'm ready to blow as it is.

"Top drawer." I nod toward the nightstand. Understanding crosses her face, and she moves to grab protection. With both hands, I strip out of my underwear, kicking them out of the way. Tessa places a strip of condoms on the pillow, tearing one off and handing it to me.

I shake my head. "Too soon. Lie back on the bed."

She does as I ask, and I wish her hair were down. I've imagined her dark locks splayed across my pillow a hundred times. That's all right, though. We've got plenty of time. My eyes rake over her, and I can't decide where I want to start first.

"Landon." My name is a whispered plea. "I need you."

Something happens. I don't know what this feeling is. My heart races, my palms sweat, and my stomach flutters at her confession. I've never wanted anyone to need me. I've even had women say those same three words to me in the past, but none of them made me feel this way. None of them made me feel… breathless.

"I'm a lucky bastard," I murmur before climbing onto the bed and settling between her thighs. She wraps her legs around me, causing me to fall into her. I'm worried I'm going to crush her, but her laughter tells me that's not the case. "I'm supposed to be taking my time with you," I say, pressing my hands flat on the bed on either side of her head.

"I'm ready now."

"You sure about that?" Needing to be sure, I balance my weight on one arm and slide a hand between us. Painfully slow, my fingers find their way to her clit and lower as I guide one, then two inside her.

"Told you," she breathes. Her eyes are shut, and her head is tilted back.

"Open your eyes, Tess." I wait until she's looking at me. "This for me?" I ask, slowly pumping my fingers in and out of her.

"You know it is," she sasses.

"You're making this very difficult for me to worship you."

"Next time," she states as she locks her knees around me, not letting me go.

My cock brushes against her pussy, and a shiver races down my spine. "Condom." My voice is gravelly. She reaches beside her and hands me one. I pull away from her, and she whimpers when the connection between us is broken. "I had plans," I tell her as I rip open the little foil packet and slide it over my length. "I wanted to take my time with you. I wanted our first time together to be magical, a night we would both always remember."

Her eyes soften. "Anytime with you is magical, Landon. We're in this, right? The two of us? We'll have time to go slow and explore later. Right now, I need you. I feel like we've had weeks of foreplay and then last night… I want this. I want you," she confirms.

I hover over her, and her legs are once again fastened behind my back. Her eyes are locked with mine. "You're beautiful." She is. I've never seen a more beautiful woman. Her face is void of makeup, and her freckles are on display. Just a light dusting, but I love them and plan to trace them with my tongue later. She's real. She's here for the right reasons. I can feel it deep in my soul. As I stare into her eyes, I know I'm falling in love with her. Hell, I might already love her. There has never been anyone like Tessa Deaton in my life.

Reaching between us, I guide my cock into her entrance, and her back arches off the bed. I freeze, giving her time to adjust to me, but she lifts her hips, seeking more.

More of me.

More of us.

"Landon." Her voice is a half plea, half moan.

"Tell me what you need, Tess. You're in control here." She has no idea how true those words are. I would do anything for her.

"All of you."

With a nod, I give her my acceptance. I give her all of me. Not just my cock, but my heart. Nothing has ever felt like this before. Like being inside her is being home. Like nothing else in this entire world matters. Football is the closest I've ever come to feeling like this, and it doesn't hold a candle to Tessa.

"Is that the best you've got, Number Eighteen?" She smirks up at me.

That's when I realize I've just been holding myself still inside her while my mind wanders, thinking about what she means to me. She has no idea what I'm thinking, but I appreciate her eagerness and playfulness. That, too, is something new. Maybe because I've never known any other woman like I know Tessa. Maybe it's because my heart is involved, but my guess is it's just her, just Tessa. Everything I feel is because she is who she is.

And she's all mine.

CHAPTER 17

Tessa

HE WINKS AND ROCKS HIS HIPS FORWARD, ELICITING A MOAN from deep inside my chest. He looked all too serious there for a minute and, if it had not been for the fact that he was buried deep inside me, I might have wondered if he was regretting this. However, I know that's not the case. Not now that he's moving—pulling out and pushing back in, taking his time teasing me.

"Now's not the time for games, Barker. Let's leave that out on the field, 'kay?" I tap my hands against his rock-hard chest, which is vibrating with laughter.

"I never knew sex could be fun."

"Oh, it's fun all right. Once we get to the good stuff." I lift my hips, seeking more of him.

"We have all night."

I nod. "Okay, and we have an entire box of condoms, so let's move this along, shall we?"

"I suddenly feel used." He pulls almost all the way out, and I groan as he pushes back in. There is humor in his voice, so I don't bother to comment.

"That, more of that," I urge him instead. I wasn't kidding when I said it feels as though we've had weeks of foreplay and then last night... last night was something off the charts. Sexy and comforting. He kept his word; he never tried to move things past kissing and roaming hands. Part of me hates to admit it, but I was testing him. He didn't seem upset or aggravated; he didn't even mention sex. He was perfectly content.

He tilts his head and presses his lips to mine. It's sloppy and filled with an urgency I've never felt before. His thrusts increase in speed, and all I can do is hang on. Sliding my hands under his arms, I grip his back. My nails bite into his skin, but he doesn't seem to mind. In fact, it seems to spur him on.

My entire body is on fire, and I have electricity coursing through my veins. My release starts to build, the ache growing with each thrust of his hips. "Don't stop," I manage to force the words out.

"You wanted fast. That's what you're getting. I'm so fucking close. Your pussy is squeezing the fuck out of my cock," he pants.

I don't know if I'm supposed to respond, but I can't because when he swivels his hips and hits that spot—you know the one that makes your legs quiver and has you feeling as though you're free-falling off a cliff? Yeah, that spot—and all I can do is bite down on my lip and hold on for the fall.

"Fuck, Tess," he grits out, slamming into me hard, and the fall that was on the horizon is here. My nails dig deeper, my back arches off the bed, and my legs hold tight as my release washes through me. On and on, tremors rock my body until there's nothing left. I want to fall back into the mattress and revel in it, but he's not done. Landon breaks free, pushing my legs backward, holding on to the backs of my calves, and hammers into me. A few quick thrusts and he's clenching his jaw, calling out my name as he releases inside me.

When he finally stills and lowers my legs, he bends to kiss my lips. I feel him start to pull away, so I lock my arms and legs around him, holding him close. I'm not ready to lose this connection. This feeling of being his. It's more than just intimacy, more than just sex. It's... everything. He's *everything,* and it's this moment I know I'm in deep. There is no chance of me keeping my heart out of this. I'm already too invested. I was only kidding myself thinking that keeping him at arm's length would prevent a broken heart.

Maybe we'll live happily ever after?

Not that I believe in fairy tales. I grew up without a father and with a mother who was still in love with a man she had only known for a week. That's not very fairy tale-ish. It's real, and in a way, I'm glad. I didn't grow up with some unrealistic expectations of love and relationships. Life is hard; relationships are just as difficult, and it takes work. I'm willing to put in the work.

"I gotta take care of this." He drops a kiss to my forehead and slowly disentangles his body from mine.

I immediately miss the connection. Grabbing the blanket, I pull it up over my naked body to ward off the cold. It's a poor excuse for a replacement, but it will have to do. Closing my eyes, I replay what we just shared, trying to catalog every movement to my memory.

"Hey." Landon's soft voice has me opening my eyes. "Let's shower." He pulls the covers back, stands, and lifts me into his arms.

"What is it with you carrying me around all the time?"

"I like you in my arms, Freckles."

When he says it like that, I can't be annoyed he's packing me around like a caveman would, and the nickname... well, that's growing on me, too. When we enter the bathroom, it's already steamed up from the hot water. Landon steps inside, taking full advantage of the open walk-in space with me still in his arms.

"How are you going to shower while holding me?"

He chuckles, a deep sound that vibrates through his chest. "You think I can play football while holding you?" he asks, kissing the tip of my nose.

"Nope. I think the team and your coach might have something to say about that."

"But everything is better—life is better when you're in my arms."

Who needs hot water? I melt from his words. "Sweet talker." I pinch his side, and he wiggles, finally relenting and setting me on my feet.

"Not fair." He pouts, and I have to admit, it's adorable. He reaches for me, but I step back before he can make contact.

"Shower," I remind him. "We're never getting out of here if you don't keep your hands to yourself."

"Is that such a bad thing?"

"Yes." I laugh, dodging his advances again. "I have to work tomorrow, and you have practice."

"Let's call in sick."

"Are you even allowed to do that?" I ask, reaching for the body wash.

"Sure, it happens, but not very often. Most of us play through it."

"We're not calling in sick. We're going to shower and then go to bed."

"So bossy," he taunts. I turn to rinse, and he smacks my ass.

"Hey." I whip around to stare at him over my shoulder. He doesn't look the least bit apologetic. "You better watch your back, Barker," I tease.

"Bring it, baby." He quirks his brow at me in challenge.

Turning back to face the wall, I finish rinsing off before stepping out of the shower. I managed not to get my hair wet. Not that it really matters, as it's still mostly wet from my earlier shower. After quickly drying off, I make my way back to the bedroom and find his T-shirt on the floor. Sliding it over my head, I slip under the covers. It's hard to believe tonight was our first time together. He feels so familiar, like we've been intimate with one another for years.

"You good?" he asks from the doorway of the bathroom.

"Yes."

He turns off the lights and, in a few long strides, is standing on what is now his side of the bed. He reaches for the lamp, clicking the knob and bathing the room in darkness. The covers rustle, the bed dips, and I'm being pulled into his embrace. His arms wrap around me, and I let my body relax into his. "Night, baby," he says softly.

"Night." As soon as I close my eyes, I feel sleep start to take over. I've never felt more content than I do when I'm in his arms.

× × ♪
○ ○ ♩

This week has been magical and exciting and too damn fast. My days have been filled with fielding phone calls, taking care of the animals, and making sure we have everything we need for Saturday's adoption event. My nights have been filled with Landon. We've stayed at my place twice and at his the rest of the week. Our lives are so different, yet we've still managed to intertwine them. At least for now. It's only been a week.

"Are you ready for tomorrow?" he asks me.

We're at his place. I'm perched on the island, watching him put toppings on our homemade pizza he just whipped up. He's gorgeous, kind, loving, sexy, has a good career, and he cooks. I hit the boyfriend jackpot.

"Yeah, I think so. We're hoping it's a huge success."

"What happens if all the animals are adopted?"

"That gives us room for more. We get calls daily that we have to turn away because we're out of room."

"I don't know why that surprises me. I guess out of sight, out of mind. I never really gave much thought to so many animals needing homes."

"Few people do. But, Landon, with one simple Tweet, you've brought the awareness to an entirely different level. Then Jeremy tweeted and your teammates. I'm a little worried we're not going to be able to handle the crowds."

"Nah, it's going to be great. There's something I want to talk to you about, though."

"Uh-oh, that doesn't sound good. We've barely started this boyfriend-girlfriend thing."

"No." He reaches for a dish towel and wipes off his hands, then places them on my thighs. "It's nothing like that. You're stuck with me. But it does involve us. You see, I'm sure the press is going to be there with all of this publicity. They've been calling the main office, asking for quotes all week. They're going to ask me why the sudden interest, and I want to be honest with them."

"Okay. That doesn't seem so bad."

"They're going to know who you are, Tess. You're no longer going to be the 'rumored' new girl seen sliding into my SUV. They're going to know where you work, your name, and that you're my girlfriend. With that comes the tabloids; some are good, most are not. They like to start shit and spread rumors, anything to sell a paper. I don't want to lose you over this."

"What? That's crazy. You're not going to lose me over some stupid tabloid."

"They can be ruthless, Tessa. Trust me, I've lived it. I don't want that to touch you, but at the same time, I want to shout to the fucking world that you're my girl. But I need you to do something for me."

"Anything."

"Come to me. If you read or hear something, come to me and ask. I'll always be honest with you, and 99 percent of the time, it's going to be a lie you read or hear about. Just... give me the chance to tell you what really happened. They like to throw a spin on the most innocent of acts and make them seem scandalous."

"I can do that."

"I mean it, Tessa. I wanted more time with you." He runs his fingers through his hair. "I wanted more time to show you I'm a good man, one you can count on, one who will be faithful to you. I wanted time to prove that to you before they came barging into our lives, but I would rather they hear it from me."

"Okay, then we wait."

"You see, that's just it. I can't be near you and not show how much you mean to me. I can't avoid you all day. I won't. I refuse to. So, it's now. I just have mixed emotions. I want it out there... that I'm off the market. That this beautiful green-eyed girl has captured my attention, but I want to keep you safe. Safe from the rumors, just... safe from the vultures that are the media."

"You've never given me a reason not to trust you. I don't think you're asking too much. If I hear something, I'll come to you. In fact, I like that you're being open and we're talking about things. I want us to be about more than just sex." Not that the sex isn't fantastic. This has been a really, really good week.

"We are more, Tess. We're so much more, baby." He leans in for a kiss.

"Now," I say, our mouths barely a breath apart, "feed me."

He chuckles, presses his lips to my forehead, and backs away. "As you wish, milady." He adds the final layer of cheese to our pizza and pops it in the oven. "Practice ends at noon, so I'll be there right after."

"That's perfect. The event starts at one, so you won't miss much. You sure you don't mind hanging around? You can just make an appearance and jet. Isn't that what most of you big-time celebrities do?"

"Maybe, but I'm not just some big-time celebrity. I'm your boyfriend before anything else, and a supportive boyfriend stays to help."

"Yeah, but most boyfriends aren't the starting quarterback for the Los Angeles Cougars."

"Right? You're lucky."

"Oh, you think so?"

He leans in close. "I know so." His lips hover over mine but never connect as a knock sounds at the door.

"Expecting company?" I ask.

"Nope. Be right back." He pushes off the counter and disappears into the living room to answer the door.

Deciding to make myself useful, I hop off the counter and begin cleaning up, putting the extra toppings away and washing the few dishes he used to make the dough. I hear voices but don't pay too much attention until Landon is standing in the doorway of the kitchen wearing a grin.

"Tessa."

"Landon," I mock him.

"There are a couple of people I'd like you to meet." He takes a step forward and then another, and my eyes stray from him to the doorway. Landon reaches me and slides his arm around my waist. "Tessa Deaton, these are my parents, Carly and Bryan Barker. Mom, Dad, this is my girlfriend, Tessa."

"It's so nice to finally meet you. Landon has told us so much about you." His mom, Carly, steps forward and wraps her arms around both of us, hugging us tightly.

"Let the girl breathe, honey," his dad, Bryan, says. When his mom steps back, he comes in for a hug, as well, just not as tight or nearly as long as his wife's. "Nice to meet you." He steps back and turns his attention to his son. He gives him a subtle nod. Had I not been watching, I might have missed it.

"What brings you two to town?" Landon asks. He's all calm and cool, standing with his arm around my waist, while I'm freaking out. My hair is piled on my head in a knot, I'm still wearing my work clothes, and I probably smell like wet dog. It was bath day today as we got the animals ready for tomorrow's event. Not exactly the best way to meet the parents.

"Can we not just drop in on our only son?" his mom asks, smiling.

"You can, but you rarely do," Landon counters.

"Well, you're all over the news and social media, talking about this adoption event at the shelter. We wanted to come by and support the cause. Turns out, we're killing two birds with one stone and catching your game on Sunday."

"That's so nice of you, thank you," I speak up, and then realize maybe I shouldn't have.

"Well, you made quite the impression on our son, although we didn't know that you two were official. Congratulations," Carly says, then she leans in and whispers, "He left that part out." Her whisper is more of a quiet voice so that Landon can hear her.

"It's new, and between work and spending time with Tess and getting the shelter ready for tomorrow, we've been pretty busy."

"I forgive you," she teases. "So, what are you two doing for dinner?"

"Pizza. You're welcome to stay," Landon offers.

"Oh, no." His mom waves him off. "We have a room and want to take a stroll on the beach. Tonight is the perfect night to do that."

"Why did you get a room when I have all this space?" Landon waves his hand around his condo.

"We didn't want to intrude," his dad speaks up.

"You're not intruding. How many times have we gone over this?" Landon asks, exasperated.

"Well, now that you've settled down..." His dad winks at me, and Landon groans.

"Damn it, Dad, how many times do I have to tell you not to believe everything you read?"

His dad throws his head back and laughs. "You're too easy, son. We know those trash mags are just trying to sell papers. But in all seriousness, we didn't want to cramp your style."

Landon looks down at me and playfully rolls his eyes. "See what I have to deal with?"

"Stop." I push my elbow into his side, causing him to act like I actually hurt him. His body is made of steel; I doubt he even felt it.

"You kids have a good night. We'll see you tomorrow at the shelter. Tessa," his mom addresses me, "if you need any additional volunteers, we're happy to help."

"That's so sweet of you. Thank you. I hope we have it covered, but at this point, I'm not sure. Landon has really caused a media frenzy, and we're not sure what to expect."

"Well, count us in. We're going to go to the hotel and change, then take a walk on the beach. Love you." She leans in for another hug, and with a wave, they're gone as fast as they came.

"I cannot believe I just met your parents for the first time looking like this. I'm a mess."

"What? No, you're not. You're perfect."

"We said honesty," I remind him.

"Well, if I'm being honest, you're beautiful." I roll my eyes playfully. "Didn't your mother ever tell you your eyes will get stuck like that?" he teases.

"She did, and I chose not to believe her." I stick my tongue out, making him laugh. The buzzer sounds on the oven, and he gets to work, taking the pizza out of the oven and slicing it up. "What do you want to drink?"

"Just water for me. I got some of that bottled root beer you like if you want to switch it up. It's on the top shelf."

"You know, you keep spoiling me like this, I might not ever go home. Making me dinner, bringing me lunch and breakfast, picking me up from work, whispered confessions of beauty, and now my favorite root beer. A girl could get used to this," I say, grabbing some napkins and following him into the living room. Setting our drinks on the table in front of us, I take the plate that Landon offers me.

"Good."

"I don't know. I haven't tried it yet."

"No, I meant good that you could get used to this. If that's all it takes for you to be here all the time, challenge accepted. I'm going to be stepping up my game."

"I was kidding."

"I'm not. I like you here. This place feels like home when you're here."

"This is your home, and I've only been here consistently for a week."

"Don't care. Everything feels different, better when I'm with you."

"You don't have to sweet-talk me to get lucky, Lucky. I'm a sure thing."

"Autumn and her nicknames." He's grinning as he shakes his head.

"What? It fits. Jeremy was Cocky; you're Lucky."

"How you figure?"

"You got me, didn't you?" I have to bite down on my bottom lip to keep from laughing.

"You know what? You're right. Lady luck was on my side."

CHAPTER 18

Landon

WE FINISH WITH GAME FILM EARLY, SO I RUSH THROUGH MY shower and head to the shelter. Case and some of the guys are stopping to eat before joining us. I called ahead and had pizza delivered to the shelter. I know there will be popcorn and things like that served, but a man's gotta eat and see his woman, so delivery was the best option. Anything that gets me to Tessa faster is always the way to go.

It's just a little past eleven when I get here, and already, the news stations are set up. I don't see much in the way of guests, maybe a few lingering around. Most of the people I see are wearing Safe Haven Animal Shelter shirts, so I know they're volunteers.

Pulling my SUV around back, like Tessa told me to this morning, I lock it up and head inside using the back door. From the sounds of their voices, Tessa and Autumn are in their office.

"So, how are things?" Autumn asks.

"Good."

"Good. All I get is good? Come on now, I want the dirt."

"We've got work to do. Not to mention, there are people lingering everywhere. That's the last thing Landon and I need is our sex life plastered all over the papers."

"Oooh, so there is a sex life. Tell me more," Autumn quips, and I hear them both chuckle.

"Yes, and it's amazing and he's... I don't know. He's everything I never knew I wanted. I'm just trying to go with the flow and not worry about the what-ifs."

"Pfft, there are no what-ifs. I'm telling you, that man's in love with you."

She's not wrong. I should feel guilty for eavesdropping, but I remain where I am just outside their office door.

"He is not."

"Keep telling yourself that," Autumn tells her. "Tell me this. If he were to tell you that he loves you, what would you say?"

"Honestly? I'm not sure. I would be in shock. But if that day ever comes, I'd tell him I love him, too."

"I knew it!" Autumn cheers, and if she says anything else, I miss it.

My feet carry me into their office and take me straight to Tessa. She's standing with her hands on a box of flyers, but she drops them and turns to face me. I take her face in the palm of my hands and hold her stare. Her green eyes are filled with worry when they should only ever be filled with love.

"Let's try it," I say, keeping my voice low. It doesn't matter. I know that Autumn is hanging on every word.

"Try what?" she asks softly.

"Oh, Tess." I smile down at her. "I'm in love with you." Her green eyes widen and grow wet with tears. She opens her mouth, then closes it.

"This is the shock," Autumn says, helpful as ever.

"I love you," I say again, and this time, a lone tear trickles down her cheek.

"I-I love you, too. But it's soon. We're crazy, right?"

"No," Autumn and I say at the same time.

"When you know, you know," Autumn adds. "Trust me on this. Cocky and I fell in love on a road trip with Pinky, and we were complete strangers. It happens when you least expect it. Embrace it. Enjoy it. Live it. You never know when that chance might be taken away from you. In my case, it was my Jeremy, but I got him back, and you can bet your ass I'm holding on tight."

"What do you say, Tess? You want to hold on tight?" I ask her.

"Only with you."

"There's my girl." I lean in and kiss her, swiping at her bottom lip with my tongue, begging her to open for me.

"As much as I love this, we have work to do. Come on, love birds," Autumn says as she leaves the room. She's acting as though we have to go, but I know she's giving us privacy, hence the reason she shuts the door behind her.

"Did that just really happen?" Tessa asks.

"Yeah, it did."

"I-I didn't expect that."

"I know, but I heard you two talking, and it felt right. It might not have been the most romantic admission of love, but I promise you, it's with all my heart."

"I love that it was spontaneous. It's real. Not that practiced or planned isn't real, but that's not life, not really. Very rarely do things go as planned, and it's definitely a moment I will always remember."

"A story for the grandkids."

"Come on, you two." Autumn knocks on the door.

"I need to get out there."

"Where do you need me?"

"There are three news stations waiting for you to give them an interview."

"Do it with me?"

"Landon, I—" I hold up my hand to stop her.

"You are the woman I love, and if I'm going to tell the world we're together, I want you by my side."

"Like this?" She looks down at her work polo shirt and khaki shorts.

"Just like this. Come on." With a quick and final kiss to her lips, I link her fingers with mine and lead us outside to the main entrance of the shelter, where the news reporters and camera crews are ready and waiting.

"Landon, why the interest in Safe Haven Animal Shelter?"

"Landon, any thoughts on tomorrow's game?"

"Landon, who's the woman?"

Question after question is fired off. I pull Tess up next to me, wrapping an arm around her shoulders. "One at a time, please." I hold up my free hand, and the crowd quiets down. "First of all, I want to thank you all for being here. For giving the Safe Haven Animal Shelter some screen time. I can answer two questions at once. "Why Safe Haven and who this beautiful woman is. This is Tessa Deaton, the love of my life." Girlfriend makes it sound like we're in high school. It's freeing now that I've told her I love her. I can shout it to the world. "She assists Autumn Baldwin, and before you ask, yes, Jeremy Baldwin's wife."

"The love of *my* life," Jeremy repeats as he and Autumn join us.

"What about tomorrow's game? Coach Baldwin, any insight?"

"I'm sorry, but that's a question I'm afraid I'm not willing to answer. The team looks good, and that's all I'm going to say. Today is about the shelter, about these two amazing women who pour their hearts and souls into this place, and the animals who will hopefully find new homes today."

A few more rounds of questions that Autumn and Tessa field and we're free to go. The reporters stick around to get some footage of the animals and the guests arriving, but they leave us alone.

"Hey, you two," I hear from behind us. I turn to see my parents wearing huge smiles. "Tessa, this place is amazing. What a great turn-out," Mom praises.

"Carly, Bryan, this is Autumn, my best friend and boss, and this is her husband, Jeremy. Guys, this is Landon's parents." Handshakes and "nice to meet yous" are exchanged.

"Put us to work," Dad speaks up. "We're happy to help."

"That's so kind of you. I think we have it under control right now, but I might have to look you up later," Autumn replies.

"Well, we're going to go walk around. Let us know if you need us," Mom says, linking her arm through Dad's and walking toward where the animals are.

"Your parents are great," Tessa says, smiling up at me.

"They are," I agree. "Back to business. What do you need?"

"Well, that tent over there"—she points to a white tent with tables underneath—"is for you and your teammates."

"Yo, Barker!" I hear yelled, and I don't have to look to know it's Case.

"Speaking of..." I say with a chuckle.

"Oh, it's the lovely Tessa. So nice to see you again." Case doesn't give a single fuck that I'm standing next to her with my arm around her shoulders. He swoops in, lifting her off her feet and giving her a hug.

"Release my girl," I tell him. My voice is gruff, but he knows I'm kidding. *Mostly.* By the time he puts her back on her feet, Thomas, Kaden, and Jack all step in and do the same thing. They know it's going to irritate the fuck out of me, which is why I bite my tongue. It's not until Case mentions Corey that my hackles truly rise.

"My brother's been asking about you," he tells Tessa.

"Nope. Not happening." I pull Tessa into my chest, her back to my front, and rest my chin on top of her head. "She's taken."

Case grins. He knows she's taken. Fucker wanted to get me riled up. Payback's a bitch, though. I'll remember this.

"Now that the pissing contest is over, I'll show you where you're all going to be." Autumn steps in and takes charge. I'm sure she thinks she's diffusing the situation. It's not like I'm going to start a fight with my teammates. Although if they were serious, I wouldn't hesitate. Not when it comes to Tessa. I know they're razzing me to try and ruffle my feathers. It worked.

Bending my head and placing my lips next to her ear, I whisper, "I love you." I follow it with a kiss to her neck before releasing her and following after Autumn, Jeremy, and my teammates.

× × ♪
o o

It's been over three hours since I've talked to Tessa. I've seen her, my eyes scanning the crowds looking for her, but as far as getting any time with her, that's been nil. Bad for me, good for the shelter. The turnout has been incredible, and from the looks on the smiling kids' faces as they pack animals into their cars, it's been a huge success.

"So, Tessa." Case grins when there's finally a break in the action. We've been signing autographs for three solid hours.

I nod. "Tessa."

"I told you we should have put bets on it," Jack grumbles.

"What are you talking about?"

"You see, QB, we knew you were toast the minute you laid eyes on her. We could all see it. It was just a matter of time before she wore you down."

I throw my head back and laugh. "You think she wore me down? I wish it were that easy. She fought me every step of the way. As far as me being toast, I'll admit that. At first, I was blowing it off that she turned me down, but I was persistent, and the more time I spent with her…"

My eyes scan until I find her. She's kneeling next to a little girl who has a kitten in her hands.

"He's a goner," Kaden chimes in.

"Yeah," I agree. No point in denying it. There's not a damn thing wrong with me being in love. I'm not embarrassed by it. If anything, I want to show her off. *She's incredible.*

"Hey, guys," Jeremy says, walking up to the tent. "Thanks for being here today. I appreciate your support of Autumn and Tessa."

"Does this mean you're going to take it easy on me at practice next week?" Thomas asks.

"Nope." Jeremy chuckles. "Really, though, I know we have a game tomorrow, and I'm sure this is the last place you want to be today, but we really appreciate you being here. Autumn and Tessa bust their asses for this place. It's nice to see they're getting the word out."

"Like your status didn't bring any of these people in," Jack tells him.

"Maybe, but it's not my name on the backs of all these jerseys." He nods toward the crowd. "I'm new to the team, and I haven't played in a long time. Unless they're a collector of my ass photographs, it's all you."

"W-What?" Case sputters with laughter.

"Oh, let me tell you about the ass photographs," Autumn says, stepping up behind her husband. He wraps her in his arms as she tells us all about it. She has us all rolling with laughter by the time she's finished. "Anyway." She grins, clearly proud of herself. "Things are winding down. You guys can head out. Thank you for being here."

"Wanna grab a beer at Henry's?" Case asks our group. Thomas, Kaden, and Jack immediately agree. "Landon?"

"We might catch up with you. I'm going to stick around and see if Tessa needs anything."

Thomas begins to sing "Another One Bites the Dust," making everyone laugh. "Next thing you know, he's going to be walking down the aisle and having babies like Trent."

He's joking, but what he doesn't realize is the thought of that... it's not scary. Not even in the slightest. That's... unexpected, but then again, everything with Tessa is new and unexpected. I'm a greedy bastard because I want more of it.

More of her.

Any way I can have her. If that means with a ring on her finger and growing round with my child, I'll take it. In fact, now that the thought is in my head, I can see it clearly. Our future flashes before my eyes. I can see it playing out, plain as day, and it's not fear I feel, it's excitement. I want to spend every day of forever with her by my side.

CHAPTER 19

Tessa

THE CROWD IS ELECTRIC AS WE WALK INTO THE COUGARS' stadium. It's as if the entire building is lit up with the excitement of the fans.

"Damn, I'm glad I left JJ with his aunt Alice. This place is crazy." Autumn links her arms through mine as we filter our way through the crowd. "Maybe we should start taking them up on sitting in the box," she says once we find our seats.

"What? And miss all the action. Pfft." I wave her off. "This is where it lives." I give her a cheesy grin.

"Yeah, *it* meaning the madness."

"Exactly. It's exciting and electric. Besides, I like to cheer and scream, and I don't think that would be allowed in the box. Then again, I wouldn't really know, as I've never been in there."

"Fine, we can try it once." I hold up my index finger for emphasis, making her laugh.

"Excuse me, are you Tessa Deaton?" a woman asks from next to me.

"Uh." I look over my shoulder at Autumn, then turn back to the woman. "Yes, do I know you?"

"No, but I'm a huge fan of Landon Barker. You're his girlfriend, right?"

I nod. I didn't expect this. "That's what I thought. He can do so much better than you," she sasses, then turns and marches up the steps. Turning to face forward, I try to wrap my head around what just happened.

"Did she say what I think she said?" Autumn asks.

"She did. Those box seats are looking better and better," I admit.

"Oh, hell no." Autumn stands, but my hand on her arm stops her.

"Don't. She's entitled to her opinion. I'm different from any woman in his past."

"Yeah, since you have a title that none of the others had."

"That, too. Let's just watch the game." Luckily, kickoff is a few minutes later and I'm able to push the woman to the back of my mind. Mostly. I mean, who isn't going to be affected by a comment like that? The first half of the game flies by, and before I know it, it's halftime.

"You want anything?" Autumn asks.

"No, thanks."

"You want to come with?"

I could use the restroom, but I don't want to run into any other disgruntled so-called fans, so I opt to stay here. "I'm good. Thank you."

She leaves, and I pull my phone out of my pocket to not seem like the loner girl sitting alone. I'm scrolling through my social media when I feel a tap on my shoulder. Turning, I see a guy who's about my age, mid to late twenties. He has a scruffy beard, mustard on his shirt from, I'm assuming, the half-eaten hot dog in his hand, and he has a beer in the other. His eyes are glassy, and it's obvious that he's beyond wasted.

"Yes?" I ask, keeping my voice polite, trying not to let my earlier irritation or my dislike for this guy show.

"I'd do you." He grins, taking another messy bite of his dripping mustard hot dog. His buddies cheer and laugh.

I don't know what to do. What do you say to that? So instead, I don't say anything. I turn back to the field and find Landon's eyes on me. I smile, not wanting him to see I'm irritated, and raise my hand in a wave. Our seats are prime, bottom row on the fifty-yard line, so he's close enough to see that something's wrong. His blue gaze is penetrating as he takes me in. Then, without warning, he spits out his mouthguard, rips off his helmet, jogs to the concrete wall, and propels himself over it. *How did he jump that high?* My man's got skills.

The crowd goes wild, and his coach is glaring at the back of his head. "What are you doing?" I hiss when he's over the wall.

"What's wrong?"

"Nothing. You're going to get in trouble," I say, eyeing his coach.

"What happened?"

"You're really his girlfriend?" the drunk guy behind me asks.

"She's mine." Landon's voice is firm and loud. So loud, in fact, everyone in our section heard him. Hell, I'm not sure the entire stadium didn't hear him.

"Barker!" his coach yells.

"This guy bothering you?"

"No, but that bitch from earlier probably still is," Autumn says, standing at the end of our aisle.

"Explain." His blue eyes bore into mine.

"Nothing. I'm fine, and you're overreacting. You're going to get fined or, worse, benched. Now go." I push at his chest, but he doesn't budge. With all that gear on, he looks even bigger. *Larger than life.*

"We're not done talking about this," he says as Coach Neil yells out for him. Before I can shy away, he wraps one of his big, calloused hands behind my neck and pulls me into a kiss. "Let them talk, Tessa. We know what this is. I love you." He quickly kisses the corner of my mouth, and then he's gone—back over the wall and jogging toward the locker room with Coach Neil beside him.

"Look!" Autumn points to the Jumbotron screen, and they're re-playing the kiss with pink and red hearts.

Well, if people didn't know about us after yesterday, they do now. "I can't believe him," I say, sitting back down in my seat. Autumn elbows me, letting me know the camera is on me. I smile and wave, not letting on that I'm embarrassed and still reeling from my not-so-nice fan inter-actions. I mean, I guess the guy was okay. At least he said he'd do me.

All throughout the game, the cameras keep panning to me. It's usu-ally when I'm on my feet, cheering for Landon and the rest of the Cougars. I can't wait to see what the media has to say about this. I can see the head-lines now. *Cougars' Quarterback Slumming it with Local Girl. First Look as She Acts a Fool, Cheering for Her Man.*

"Another win, baby," the drunk guys behind us say. "Tell your man, good game," they tell me before filtering up the steps.

Autumn grins. "They're fun."

"Oh, yeah, they're fun, but I could have done without the 'I'd do you' comment."

She throws her head back and laughs. "I don't want to be around when you tell Landon about that. I can't believe he climbed the wall to check on you."

"He's crazy. Certifiable."

"Nah, he's in looove," she says dramatically.

We're still sitting in our seats, letting the crowd thin out. We're sup-posed to meet Jeremy and Landon outside the locker room. The passes hanging from our necks guarantee us access. "I think I should just text him and tell him I'll meet him at Henry's."

"Nope. You're not going to run from this. That's part of dating him.

It's not always sunshine and roses, Tess, but he's in this with you. He made that clear at halftime."

"I know. You're right. It's just going to take some getting used to."

"Well, I'd say after his little stunt, there are going to be images of the two of you kissing everywhere, so you need to get used to it. It's out there, and it's happening."

"I can do this." I stand and stretch.

"Damn right, you can. Come on. Let's go find Cocky and Lucky and get one of those juicy burgers from Henry's. It's calling my name."

Thankfully, most of the crowd has thinned as we make our way to the locker rooms. We flash our badges, and sure enough, the big bouncer guy lets us in, no questions asked. There's a long hallway where wives, kids, and, I assume, other family members wait for their players. In our case, player and coach.

"JJ would have loved this," Autumn states.

"You should have Jeremy bring him when there's not a crowd."

"Yeah, we didn't get to explore the locker rooms when we brought him for training camp."

The doors open, and players begin to filter out. None that I know, so we stand and people watch. I'm not much for conversation about me and Landon where everyone can hear us. I've been heard enough today. Or seen, rather. Either way, I've had my fill for the day.

Most of the crowd is gone by the time Jeremy, Case, Trent, Thomas, Jack, and Kaden exit the locker room. Everyone on the team I've met, except for the man I want to see most. "Where's Landon?" I ask Jeremy.

"He's getting his ass chewed by Coach Neil," Case offers.

"Oh, no." I cover my mouth with my hand, my wide eyes staring at Jeremy, waiting for his confirmation.

"I wouldn't say chewed." Jeremy tries to downplay it. "He is in his office."

"He knows better," I say, irritated that he would put his position on the team on the line. Hell, it wasn't even worth a fine I'm sure he's getting right now.

Trent nods. "Yeah, but when it's your girl, the heart always wins. We know we're going to pay for it, but it's worth it."

"This guy"—Kaden points to Trent—"did something similar. Only he stole a mic from a reporter and asked Luna to marry him." Trent's all smiles as his buddy tells the tale.

Before I can comment, the locker door opens, and we all turn to look. Landon grins and holds his hands out at his sides. "I'm feeling the love," he says, his long legs carrying him to me. He wraps me in a hug, lifting me off my feet.

"I'm going up to the box to get my wife," Trent tells us. "She prefers the stands, but since she's pregnant, I like her to be in the box, without crazy fans being able to get to her." With a wave, he's ambling down the hall.

"Yo, meet us at Henry's!" Jack calls out for him. Trent throws his arm in the air, giving him a thumbs-up, but doesn't stop.

"Spill," he says, placing me back on my feet but not letting me out of his hold.

"Nothing to spill. Great game," I say, deflecting.

"Tessa."

"Landon."

"Autumn," he says with a sly grin, his eyes watching for a response from me.

"I'll fill you in at Henry's," she offers, and he smirks.

"Are your parents coming with us?" I ask him.

"No, they're going to head back home. They have an hour drive ahead of them. They said to tell you goodbye. They called me a few minutes ago."

I feel bad that I forgot to look for them. I was too flustered with everything that happened at the game. "Mom said we looked good up on the Jumbotron."

"Ugh," I groan, resting my forehead against his chest. My head bounces from where his chest vibrates with his laughter.

Fifteen minutes later, we're sitting at several tables we pushed together to make a longer one in the middle of the private section of Henry's. The gang's all here, according to Case. Henry takes our drinks and appetizers orders, and holy hell, these guys can eat. I shouldn't be surprised at their size after the exertion a game takes out of them.

"Spill," Landon says, turning in his chair to face me.

"It's nothing."

"Tessa," Autumn says, her tone warning.

"Fine." I roll my eyes dramatically, and she sticks her tongue out at me. Time to rethink this best friend thing. "Just some woman about my age wanted to know if I was your girlfriend. I said yes, and she walked away."

"Tessa!" Autumn scolds.

"Fine. She said you could do better," I mumble.

"Who was she? What did she look like?"

"She was just some woman in a Barker number eighteen jersey like hundreds of others who were at the game today." I pull at the exact jersey from my chest to prove my point.

"You're not like the others," Landon insists.

"To them, I am. I'm just some normal girl, just like them. Nobody knows my name, I don't have famous parents, I don't get paid millions of dollars a year, and I'm wearing the same shirt they're wearing. So, yes, I'm just like them."

"No. You're. Not. You are mine. They are not. You have my heart. They do not. You, Tessa, are everything they're not. Don't let some crazy cleat chaser get in your head. We talked about this."

"We talked about the tabloids. I didn't expect to be confronted at one of your games. Oh, and then there was the drunk guy behind me."

"What about him?" he asks, his voice is steely yet calm.

"Oh, after the woman left, he proceeded to bend over the seat and tell me that, and I quote, 'he would do me.' Can you believe that?"

"I should have punched that fucker while I had the chance."

"Right, and be in even more trouble with your coach?"

"A small fine, and it was worth it." He leans over and presses his lips to my temple.

Thankfully, the conversation moves on from the crazy people I interacted with tonight. Luna invites Autumn and me to her baby shower, and of course, Jeremy and Landon are tagging along. Something about if Trent gets to be there, so do they. But it's Trent's baby. I didn't try to reason with them. Next week is an away game, and the season is in full swing. I'll see less and less of him, so I'll take any time with him that I can get.

"You want to talk about the game?" Landon asks once we're back at my place.

"No. It just shocked me, I guess. I'm fine."

"Are you, Tess? Are you really fine? I won't lose you over this."

"Hey." I reach out and place my hand on his leg, where he sits facing me on the couch. "You're not going to lose me. Where is this coming from?"

"I've seen it, Tessa. I've seen the press tear couples and families apart, and they won't do that to us. Next time, call security, and we'll press charges."

"Do you hear yourself right now? She didn't do anything but give me her opinion, which she's entitled to. It's that pesky little thing called freedom of speech. Sound familiar?"

"I get it, but harassing you… That's out of the question."

"Honestly, Landon, she was actually nice about it. She wasn't mean; she didn't yell. She just said it as if she were asking about the weather. It was strange as hell, but now that I look back on it, I'm glad she didn't cause a scene. It could have been much worse. The drunk guys were just that: drunk and obnoxious. Who's to say they wouldn't have made a comment even without her? They were drunk. That's what you do when you're drunk. Act a fool. They didn't hurt me or touch me. So get this *losing me* stuff out of your head."

"I know it's irrational. Trust me, I get it. But you haven't seen it the way that I have… So many times, the tabloids, the cleat chasers, they tear couples apart, but that's not us, Tess. I won't let that happen to us."

"We're good. I just wasn't prepared for it, that's all. Now I am. Next time, I'll be ready with a comeback."

"Come here." He holds open his arms, and I waste no time going to him, sitting on his lap and snuggling him close. "Much better," he says over a yawn.

"Let's get you to bed, Number Eighteen. You played one hell of a game and even put on a halftime show. You have to be exhausted."

"Ha ha, funny girl." He kisses me softly before I pull away and stand.

"I'm going to lock up; head on to bed. I'm right behind you." He disappears down my small hallway while I check the doors and turn off the lights. I grab his phone and charger out of his bag, and plug it in in the kitchen beside mine before making my way to the bedroom. I strip out of my clothes, not bothering with pajamas, and slide under the covers next to him.

"Love this, Tess. Feeling you like this next to me."

"I love it, too."

"Night, baby."

"Night." In the comfort of his embrace, I drift off to sleep.

CHAPTER 20

Landon

I**T'S THURSDAY MORNING, AND WHEN I SAY MORNING, I MEAN THE** sun isn't even up yet. I've hardly slept at all. We have an away game in New York this weekend. The team flies out at two this afternoon. This is the first time in my career that I don't want to go. Sure, there have been times I've dreaded the flight, but never this. I'm lying here with her in my arms, and the thought of not seeing her for four days is killing me.

I'm going to miss her.

I think back to all the times I gave my teammates shit when they would talk about missing their wives or girlfriends—Trent, especially when he and Luna first got together. It was fun to get him all riled up, but now he just lets it roll. He doesn't give a fuck what we say, and now I get it. I finally understand how he feels leaving her behind. And to add to that, she's pregnant. I don't know how he does it.

I place a kiss on her bare shoulder, and she stirs. "Landon?" Her voice is raspy with sleep.

"Hmm?"

"Why are you awake?"

"Just thinking."

She rolls over to face me. The room is still dark, so I can't see her, but I can feel her gaze.

"Anything you want to talk about?"

"Not unless you want to hear me whine about missing you?"

"You're gonna miss me?" she asks, her voice sugary sweet.

"Hey." I lightly smack her ass. "You could at least pretend you're going to miss me, too."

"I am going to miss you. Who's going to keep me warm at night?" I can hear in her tone of voice that she's teasing me, but the thought of another man getting to be with her like this, like we are in this moment, amps up my worry. Things have been great, but I've been here. Can she do this? Is she really willing to stick with me being gone all the time for my job? I love my job, football is who I am, but Tessa... I love her, too.

"That's my job." I pull her impossibly close. "Fuck, Tess, why'd you have to go there?"

"Hey." She wraps her arm around me and gently strokes my back with her soft hands. "I was just teasing. There's no one but you."

"I know that. It's just even the thought of losing this, losing you to someone who can be here all the time, it guts me."

"I didn't mean to upset you. I was just teasing. Of course, I'm going to miss you. I miss you when you're at practice and I'm at the shelter. I don't know how I'm going to do with not seeing you for four days."

"I'll call you as much as I can." I'm already thinking about staying holed up in my room just so I can talk to her. I requested to room with Trent this time, and he agreed. I don't even want to be around the single guys on the road. It's not the temptation, but the rumors. I want to stay as far away from that shit as I can. I don't need the press posting anything that could shed a bad light on me while I'm on the road. This is going to be hard enough on our relationship without the added drama and rumors that the leeches bring.

"Don't feel like you have to. I'll be here waiting for you, and I'll be watching you on Sunday."

"Come with me."

"You know I can't do that. I can't leave Autumn alone at the shelter. Besides, I can't just call her and ask for time off without notice. We'd need time to schedule volunteers."

"I'll pay for someone to come in and cover for you."

"Thank you, but no."

"I had a feeling you would say that."

"It's sweet, but you're going to be away a lot. It's not just this one weekend. This is our life, and we need to learn to deal with it the best we can. We need to get used to being apart."

"You could quit and travel with me," I offer. She thinks I'm kidding, but I'm dead serious.

"Then I'd be traveling alone. You have all your team stuff you have to do. I won't get to see you much anyway."

"I've never dreaded going away for a game until now."

"Chin up, Number Eighteen," she says playfully. I know she's trying to lighten the mood. "I'll be here, holding down the home front."

Her words spark an idea. A crazy one, but it makes me feel better. "Stay at my place while I'm gone."

"What? That's crazy. Why would I do that when I have a perfectly good home right here, you know, the bed you're sleeping in?"

"I know whose bed I'm in. I just want to know you're there. That you're in my space, in my bed, even if I'm not in it with you."

"Okay. If it means that much to you, I'll do it."

"Thank you." Moving in, I press my lips to hers. Softly, reverently, I try my best to show her what she means to me.

Everything.

My hands roam over her hip and up her side. I palm her breasts, running the pad of my thumb over her nipple. We slept naked last night. I wanted her body next to mine. I wanted to feel her skin, memorize the feeling. Turns out, that was a good idea, because now clothes are not a factor.

My lips travel to her neck, and she tilts her head, giving me the space I need to devour her. "Lie back," I say, moving to hover over her. She's now on her back, and I can feast on her. Take my time showing her what she means to me and how much I'm going to miss her.

Settled between her thighs, my cock throbs as it rests against her belly. Staying on course, I capture a hard nipple in my mouth, nipping, sucking, and licking, driving her crazy, all while tweaking the other with my thumb and forefinger. I don't have enough hands. I want to touch her everywhere.

Her breath hitches when I take her nipple between my teeth. With kisses between the valley of her breasts, my mouth moves to the other, and my hand takes over, gently caressing the one I'm no longer soothing with my tongue.

"Landon," she says breathily. Her hands are buried in my hair, and her chest is rapidly rising and falling.

"Yeah, baby?" My voice is thick with my desire for her.

"S-Stop teasing me," she pants.

Letting her nipple fall from my mouth with an audible pop, my lips head south. "Not teasing. Enjoying you? Yes. Loving you? Hell, yes." I trace a path with my tongue over her quivering stomach, and I don't stop until I reach her pussy. I kiss just above where I know she wants me. Hell, from the grip she has on my hair and the sounds she's making, it might be a need at this point.

"Four days," I say tenderly. "Four days without you, Freckles." I'm done talking. It's time to show her. Moving further down the bed, I position her legs over my shoulders, kissing her inner thigh. My index finger glides through her pussy. She's wet and ready, but I need more time.

"Please," she begs, her hand grappling for my hair to hold on as my mouth hovers over her clit. "Oh, God," she breathes when she feels my hot breath.

With my tongue, I make small circles, causing her hips to rise off the bed, and her grip on my hair tightens. Her need only fuels my desire. Pulling away, I blow gently on her sensitive bud, and she squirms beneath me. I'm salivating. I can't tell if it's her or me that it's coating my chin.

"Mmm," I hum.

"D-Don't stop, please," she pleads.

One hand works up to her breast to play with her nipple, while the other slides one, then two fingers inside her. In tandem, my tongue and my fingers fuck her. She's pulling on my hair. Her grip is firm, and her moans of pleasure have precum leaking from my cock. I need her to come.

Now.

My tongue presses harder, flicking her clit like it's my job while my fingers piston inside her. Her walls begin to quiver, telling me she's close. I'm ready to come with her taste on my tongue and from feeling her body's reaction to me. I fight it as I bring her over the edge. She cries out as her body convulses, and I drink her in. Everything she gives me, I take.

When her body finally relaxes into the mattress and her hands fall beside her on the bed, I slowly slide my fingers out of her, licking them clean. Carefully, I remove her legs from over my shoulders and resume the same path I took earlier—trailing kisses up her body until I reach her lips. She kisses me back without abandon, her tongue battling with mine.

Ripping my mouth away, she whimpers. I reach over into the nightstand and grab a condom, tearing it open with my teeth and sliding it over my cock.

"Hurry," she murmurs.

Not needing to be told twice, I position myself at her entrance and slide home. Nothing has ever felt more like home than being connected with her like this. Nothing ever will. Lowering my weight onto her, careful not to crush her, I take my time pushing in and pulling out. Over and over, I slowly make love to her. It's perfect because all I want to do is slow down time. I want this moment to last forever.

"You okay?" she whispers. The room is starting to lighten as day breaks, and I can see her eyes watching me with worry.

"I'm perfect." A few more lazy strokes are all it takes for me to lose my control as I come inside her. I still and then relax, sated. "I'm sorry." I kiss her nose. "That was supposed to last a hell of a lot longer."

She giggles. "It was torture. You teased me. But everything about this moment is faultless. I wouldn't change it for anything. This is how we should always say goodbye."

"Why did you have to mention that?"

"Because I need to get up and get moving to head to work, and you have to pack."

"I don't want to go."

"Of course, you do. It's going to suck, but Landon, you love this game. Football is your life, so you're going to miss me. They say absence makes the heart grow fonder."

"I don't know that I could grow any fonder of you than I already am."

"Come on, you. Let's shower." Tossing off the cover, she climbs out of bed, and I watch her until she disappears into the bathroom.

Fond of her indeed.

X X ⌡
O O ♂

We landed in New York about two hours ago, checked into our rooms, and now here we are in the conference room, eating our catered meal, one that is mandatory. Coach Neil thinks that it promotes team bonding or some shit. He's right. I'm just bitter because I could be in my room, talking to Tessa.

"Arm's looking good," a deep voice rumbles from beside me. Turning, I see the team owner, Joseph Stamper, taking the seat next to mine.

"Thanks." I grab my water and take a long drink. "Team's tight." I'm sure he's about to rip my ass about climbing the wall to get to Tessa. I paid my fine, though, so we should be able to move on.

He nods. "We're off to a great start. Speaking of starts, I didn't realize you were seeing anyone until the press reported it at the pet adoption, and then there was your stunt at the game last week. Lots of good feedback from the shelter adoption."

I can't help it. I grin. "Tessa." Even I can hear the fondness in my voice when it comes to her.

"You know we had to fine you for that, but the team has had a lot of positive press from your little show. I have to ask, what caused you to climb into the stands? What couldn't wait until after the game?"

I shrug. "She looked upset." I'm waiting for his reprimand that never comes.

"You're telling me that because she looked like she was upset, you climbed the wall, ignored your coach when he yelled for you, and knew you were going to be fined, but you did it anyway?"

"Yep."

He surprises me when he clamps a hand on my shoulder. "She's lucky to have you."

"Just the opposite, in fact. I'm lucky to have her."

"She looks familiar."

"Tessa Deaton." I give him her full name. Everyone already knows at this point.

He shakes his head. "Let's keep the wall climbing to a minimum the rest of the season, huh?" He says the words, but there is no heat or reprimand in them. In fact, he looks amused and something else I can't quite put my finger on. As long as it's not his anger, I don't care. Not that it would stop me. My contract is solid for the next four years. Besides, this is Tessa we're talking about. If she needs me, well, I'm going to be there. Climbing a wall or not.

"I'm not making any promises."

He shakes his head, smiling, but instead of replying, he takes a long pull of the glass of amber liquid he's drinking. Alcohol is off-limits to the players, but I guess if you own the team and it's not your ass getting tossed around on the field, you can afford that luxury.

The rest of the night passes in a blur. Food, laughter, jokes, and the entire time, I'm always thinking about her. When we're finally free to go, Trent and I bust ass back to our rooms, both of us already with our phones to our ears.

"Hey, you," Tessa answers.

"I miss you."

Her soft laugh washes over me. "I miss you, too. How was the team dinner?"

"Good. The owner, Joseph Stamper, stopped to talk to me. I thought for sure I was going to get an ass ripping, but he seemed more amused than anything about my wall climb."

"The local news did a piece tonight. They're questioning if I'm going to be at the away game, and if I am, if you'll be climbing every wall at every stadium to get to me."

"I would."

"I know you would, but you can't afford all those fines."

"I can, actually."

"I assumed you were paid well, being a professional athlete and all, but that's insane. Do you realize how much money that is? Ten thousand dollars per game?"

"Tess, I know we don't talk about money, and that's one of the things

I love most about you. You're not with me because of my bank account balance, but, babe, do you know how much my last contract was for?"

"No."

"Google it."

"Can't you just tell me? I don't like to Google you. I'd rather you tell me anything and everything that you want me to know."

"I love you. I want you to know that."

Her voice softens. "I love you, too."

"I signed a five-year deal last year with the Cougars."

"Okay."

"For one hundred and sixty million."

"Dollars?" she asks, choking on her words.

Her shock has a sense of pride washing over me. Not because of the bank balance or that I've managed to shock her, but because she *is* shocked. I finally found a woman who's interested in me, Landon Barker, not the quarterback, not the one-hundred-and-sixty-million-dollar contract. Just me.

"Dollars," I confirm.

"Wow. Okay, then."

"You're amazing. Have I ever told you that?"

"A few times."

"Well, I'm saying it again."

"Thank you," she says over a yawn.

"I'll let you go. I know you have to work tomorrow."

"What about you? What's your day look like?"

"We'll do a short practice, some walk-through drills, and some game tape."

"Exciting." She yawns again.

"It beats a nine-to-five."

"Don't downplay it. You love it, and you know it."

"I do. Get some sleep."

"Night, Lucky."

I chuckle at her use of the nickname she and Autumn cooked up. "Night, Freckles." I've barely ended the call when my phone lights up with a message. I grin when I see it's one of my best friends and former roommates from college, Reid Montgomery.

Reid: Jumped any walls lately?

I can't stop the laugh that bubbles out of me.

Me: As a matter of fact, I have.

Reid: You getting all domesticated on me, Barker?

Me: Damn right.

Reid: Happy for you, man. Give a guy a heads-up next time, so I don't find out on Sports Central.

Me: It's been crazy. You're right. One day soon, we're going to have to get together so you can meet my girlfriend, Tessa.

Reid: You'd better lock her down before I get there. You know the ladies love me.

I know that he's teasing, but it still grates on my nerves.

Me: Not this one. She's mine. Keep your ass in Nashville.

Reid: Damn, another one bites the dust.

Me: You'll understand one day.

Reid: That's what they tell me. Beckett and Reynolds are both in the same boat.

Me: Good for them.

Reid: Yeah, yeah.

His message is followed by a string of laughing emojis.

Me: I'm hitting the hay. Good luck tomorrow against Georgia.

Reid: Give Dallas some hell, will ya?

Me: You know we will. Talk soon.

I smile as I plug my phone in to charge and close my eyes, drifting off to sleep.

CHAPTER 21

Tessa

I
T'S WEEK THREE OF THE REGULAR FOOTBALL SEASON, AND
Autumn and I are traveling to our first away game. The bonus is that
it's in Georgia, and my mom is coming with us. Landon insisted that
he get her a ticket, as well. We're actually in a private Cougars box. It's the
first time we've sat in one, but Landon was adamant that he didn't need
some crazy fan spouting anything off while my mom was with me. He's
worried about making a good impression. For the record, he has nothing
to worry about. He makes me happy; that's all Mom cares about. Besides,
if he flashes her those dimples and blinks those baby blues, there's no way
she can't like him. I'm so excited to see her and for her to meet Landon.

"There she is." I point out my mom to Autumn and take off running toward her. She's ready for my hug when I reach her. "I missed you
so much."

"It's good to have you home." She steps back and rakes her eyes over
me. It's been six months since I've seen her. Far too long, but life tends to

get in the way. Plus, it's a long-ass drive, and flights are not cheap enough to visit more often.

"Autumn," Mom says fondly. "How are you?" She releases me and pulls Autumn into a hug just as fierce as the one she gave me.

"Good. I love your hair."

"Me, too," I tell her. "I love the highlights."

"I thought it was time for something different. You don't think it's too much?"

"No," Autumn and I say at the same time.

"Come on. Let's get you ladies home."

"Thank you for letting me stay with you," Autumn says.

"How did you convince Jeremy?"

"He convinced me to have another baby."

"What?" I stop and look at her. "You didn't tell me that!"

She shrugs. "We've been tossing around the idea, and that was his concession. I can stay with you and Caroline instead of at the team hotel, but we start trying."

"That's amazing."

"It is." She waggles her eyebrows, and we all laugh.

"What about Landon?" Mom asks once we're in the car and headed toward her place. "When do I get to meet him?"

"This afternoon, they're having a team dinner that immediate family gets to attend at the hotel. We have to be there at three. It's early to bed for the boys tonight, and game day's tomorrow."

"Boys," Mom scoffs. "Have you seen them? I can only imagine they're even larger in person."

"They are some big boys," Autumn agrees.

We spend the rest of the ride catching up. Autumn tells Mom stories of JJ and Pinky, and I fill her in on how things are going with Landon. I leave out the more intimate details. Mom and I are close, but not that close.

"Home sweet home," Mom says, pulling into the driveway of her small ranch home. "You girls get settled in. Grab a nap. Whatever you need. We have about three hours before we need to head to the hotel. It's about thirty minutes from here."

"Thanks, Mom. I'm going to freshen up, then I'll be back down. I never get to see you. I'm not going to nap away the time we do have."

Her eyes glisten with unshed tears. "I'd like that."

Lugging my bag down the hall, I point Autumn in the direction of her room and then disappear into mine. Pulling my phone out of my pocket, I text Landon.

> Me: Hey, just made it to Mom's. Are we still on for this afternoon?
>
> Landon: Yes!
>
> Me: Good. See you soon.
>
> Landon: I miss you.

His message is followed by an image of him pouting. He's pretending to be sad, but the happiness in his blue eyes gives him away.

> Me: Miss you, too.

Tossing my phone onto the bed, I grab some clothes to change into and head to the bathroom to freshen up before making my way downstairs to spend some time with Mom. Walking past Autumn's door, I hear her on the phone with JJ. He's staying with Jeremy's sister, Alice, this weekend, and he's rambling on about all the fun stuff they've been doing. Autumn and Jeremy are great parents, and I can't wait to watch their family grow.

X X ♪
O O ♪

My palms are sweating as we walk into the hotel. I don't know why I'm suddenly so nervous for Landon and my mom to meet. Maybe it's because it was high school the last time I introduced her to anyone. Maybe it's because I'm afraid he'll see the house I grew up in and it hits him that I'm just some common girl and that our lives are too different. Maybe it's because I love him with my entire being, and I'm afraid that by letting him into my past and developing a connection with my mom, the pain is going to be even more striking if this ends.

"Tess!" I hear him call out for me. My eyes scan the crowd until I see him. Suddenly, all my worries fade away. His cerulean blue eyes are shining, and his dimples are on full display when he reaches us. He doesn't care who's around. He pulls me into his arms and buries his face in my neck. "Missed you," he murmurs.

Lifting his head but keeping me in his arms, I embrace him and cuddle into his chest. "Landon Barker. So nice to meet you, Caroline." He takes the initiative and introduces himself to my mother.

"Nice to meet you, as well. I'd ask if you're taking good care of her, but I think I have my answer." Mom's smile is broad as she takes in the two of us cuddled together.

I know I should pull away from him, but I can't seem to make myself do it. Not to mention, I don't think he would let me if I tried.

"I've got us a table. Autumn, Jeremy is with us, as well. He's talking with Coach Neil and the team owner. He'll join us in a few." He looks down at me and kisses my forehead. "Let's get seated." He finally drops his arms, links his fingers through mine, and guides us through the masses. Players and their families linger everywhere in the large room. "This is us." He pulls the chair out for me and then tries to for my mom, but she and Autumn are already sitting.

The four of us make small talk over the appetizers, and by the time the salads are served, it feels like we've all been friends for years. There's no awkward silence or lull in conversation. Landon is at ease, as is my mother. Her smile tells me she really likes him. Autumn has met my mom a few times since I've known her, so she fits into the conversation just as smoothly. Jeremy joins us, and Mom tells him she loves his accent, so he lays on the charm, hamming it up for her. Autumn just smiles and rolls her eyes.

"This was amazing," Mom says, pushing her plate back. "Landon, thank you for inviting me. I know this is a family event, but it was nice to get to meet you and see the two of you together."

"And me," Jeremy chimes in, making us all laugh.

"It was my pleasure. Besides," he turns and looks at me, his eyes softening, "we're family now." The look in his eyes tells me he means what he says, and by the audible "Awes" coming from Mom and Autumn, they know it, too.

"Bugger had to steal my thunder," Jeremy says, but it's his exaggerated *thunda* that has us all laughing again. I swear he forces his Australian accent to be thicker, more pronounced just for Mom.

"Sounds like this is the table to be at," a man, probably in his early fifties, says, stopping to stand next to our table. There's a woman on his arm, and although she's beautiful, her resting bitch face takes away from her natural beauty.

"Mr. Stamper, this is my wife, Autumn," Jeremy introduces.

"And this is my girlfriend, Tessa, and her mother, Caroline. Ladies, this is the team owner, Joseph Stamper."

Joseph's smile seems to falter as he looks at me and then my mom. I hope he's not angry that we're here. His eyes float to Autumn. "Nice to meet you, Autumn. Welcome to the Cougars family," he says politely before his gaze turns back to me. "Tessa." His voice is softer, almost reverent. "You seem to be getting our team some positive PR." He gives me a kind smile.

"Oh, no, that's all Landon," I say with a nervous laugh. "There's no controlling him."

"Not when it comes to you," Landon says, not caring who hears him.

"Caroline, was it?" Mr. Stamper says, glancing at my mom. His eyes are locked on her. "It's good to see you… here supporting Landon. You all enjoy your dinner," he says, walking away.

"His wife is an odd one," Autumn says, and I nod my agreement.

"Goodness, I'm worn out. I didn't sleep well last night, too excited for your visit. I think I'm going to call a cab." Mom reaches into her purse to hand me her keys. "You two keep the car and come home when you're ready."

Concern has me dipping my brows. She's edgy. "Are you okay?" I ask.

"Oh, yes, I'm fine. Just tired, and you kids need some time without your momma hanging around. Landon, thank you for inviting me. It was a pleasure to meet you."

"I'll have the team car drive you. We have one for emergency purposes." Mom tries to stop him, but he has his phone out and arrangements made, not bothering to listen to her protests.

Landon and I walk Mom outside and wave goodbye as the car pulls away. "You think she was acting funny?"

"I don't know her well enough to tell. It's a plausible story. I wouldn't sleep well either, knowing I was getting to see you after six long months."

"Six months is way too long."

"Agreed. Has your mom ever thought about moving to California?"

"Nah, she loves where she lives. I've tried to convince her to move a few times, but she always says she has a life in Georgia. I get it, but I miss her. Sometimes I wonder if I should move back home to be closer to her."

"We need to start working on her. I can't lose you to Georgia. I'd never get to see you during the season, and that is not something I could live with."

"I'm not moving."

"I know. She is. We're going to convince her. How about we fly her out for the holidays and have a couple of places for her to look at? Maybe sell the luxury of Los Angeles and the idea of seeing you more? Think that will work?"

"She's visited before, Landon."

"Yeah, but the stakes are higher this time around. You're in a committed relationship, and soon, there will be grandkids involved, and she's not going to want to miss that. We need to play that angle."

"Grandkids?" I ask. We're standing outside the hotel at the private back entrance, having this conversation. Anyone could be lurking and hear us, but he doesn't seem to care.

"We both want kids, right? We talked about this."

I nod slowly. "I do, and we did, but you're thinking about us having kids?"

"That's part of the progression of two people who love each other."

Again, I nod. "It is. I guess I'm just surprised."

"Tess." He bends his knees so we're eye to eye. "I love you. Not just for today or the present. I love you for the yesterdays, the todays, and the tomorrows. All of them—past, present, and future. That's not going to change."

"I love you, too."

"Come on. Let's go back inside and mingle. I want you to meet more of the team."

Hand in hand, we make our way back into the hotel and spend the next two hours laughing and talking with his teammates. Luna and I talk for a long time, and she reminds me about her baby shower. It's in a few weeks when the guys have a bye week. I can't imagine having to work your life around a professional football team, but then again, that's exactly what I'm doing. In my mind, Landon and I have two very different lives, but the reality is that we've made it work. Because we want it to work. It's an enlightening revelation, and it makes our earlier talk hit home even more so. I want that with him. The future, house, kids. All of it. I've been afraid to voice it, but the want is deep-rooted in my soul.

"I guess we should get going." I look across the room to where Autumn and Jeremy are talking to Thomas.

"I was planning on sneaking you up to my room."

"You sound like a teenager." I chuckle.

"Not that they'd actually check," he says with a smile.

"No, you need your rest, and we're not doing that to Trent."

"Fine," he grumbles good-naturedly. "Thanks for being here, baby. Thanks for letting me meet your mom."

"No place I'd rather be."

"I can think of one place," he whispers huskily as his lips press to mine.

"Barker, keep it PG," the deep voice from earlier says from behind us.

I can feel my face heat with embarrassment. "No promises," Landon replies, cocky as ever.

"Landon," I scold him under my breath.

"Tessa, it was nice to meet you."

"You, too, Mr. Stamper."

"Please." He swallows hard. "Call me Joseph."

I nod. "Landon, walk me out?"

"If I have to." He sighs dramatically, and I can't hide my smile.

"Come on, Number Eighteen, you need your beauty sleep."

"Hey!" He pretends to be offended. We both know he doesn't need beauty sleep. He was gifted with damn good genes, and he's nowhere near offended.

"I was just coming to find you," Autumn says as we approach. "I'm going to stay here tonight." She snuggles into Jeremy's chest.

"Shoulda been a fucking coach," Landon grumbles, and we all laugh.

"Come on, you big baby. Walk me to the car. Autumn, if you need a ride tomorrow, just call me."

"The team car will bring her home," Jeremy replies confidently.

After a round of hugs and goodbyes, we head outside to Mom's car. "You going to be okay driving back on your own?"

"I grew up here," I remind him. "I'll be fine."

"Lock your doors, and text me. No… call me as soon as you make it back to your mom's."

"Landon, I'll be fine."

"Humor me, Freckles."

"Yes, I will call you when I get to Mom's."

"Good." He nods, liking that he got his way. It's a small concession really, and we talk every night before bed that we don't spend together, so I would have called him anyway, or he me.

We reach Mom's car, and he wraps his arms around me, holding me close. "I love you, Tessa. Drive safe."

"Love you, too," I mumble against his chest. "I'm kinda sad I won't be in the stands, cheering you on at the game. It feels like I'm going to miss all the action."

"Nah, you'll have the best seats in the house. We have several boxes so I'm not sure who's going to be in the booth with you, but they're all Cougars, so the three of you will be in good company."

"We'll be fine."

"I know you will." One more kiss that curls my toes and he pulls back to open the car door for me. "Drive safe." He waits until I'm buckled in before closing the door and taking a step back. I force myself to start the car and pull away.

I've never wanted to be near someone like I do Landon. It's as if his soul calls to mine; it's unlike anything I've ever known. As I drive back to Mom's, I think about what our future might look like, and excitement bubbles in my chest. Landon and I, we've got this. Our future is what we make it, and I see great things headed our way.

CHAPTER 22

Landon

PRACTICE ENDED TWO HOURS AGO. THE REST OF THE GUYS rushed to get out of there, but I stuck around and ran a few more routes with Kaden. The season is halfway through, and we're undefeated. The team is tight. We're connecting and meshing, and it shows on and off the field.

"You headed home?" Kaden asks as we enter the locker room.

"I have to run up to the office before I go. Apparently, there was some fan mail, a little boy who's in the hospital. I'm going to sign some things to send to him, then pay him a visit as soon as I get the chance."

"Careful, your good guy is showing," he jokes.

"Must be Tess," I reply.

He chuckles. "Lucky Bastard, I still don't know how you got her. You and Trent both hit the significant other lottery."

"What's up? You getting the urge to settle down?"

"Nah, but if I happen to stumble upon a Tessa or a Luna, then I don't plan on letting them go."

"Wise decision."

"All right, I'll see you at practice tomorrow." He waves, and then it's just me. I take my time with my shower and getting dressed. I have nowhere to be. Tess is at work, and my house feels empty without her there. Shoving my practice clothes into my bag, making sure I have my keys, wallet, and phone, I make my way up to the offices.

"Hey, Landon," Sally, the receptionist, says. "I have everything laid out for you in the small conference room. There's some extra stuff just so we have it on hand. Head on back."

"Thanks, Sally." I head down the long hallway and see the framed pictures of past players and coaches. It never ceases to hit home with me when I walk down this hallway that I'm one of the lucky ones. My talent and hard work have me living my dream. I get to play the game I love for a hell of a lot of money, and I get to do things like sign jerseys for sick kids. I get to bring smiles to their faces, just for being me. It's humbling.

Tossing my bag on the floor in the corner, I grab one of the many Sharpies that Sally has laid out for me and get to work. I sign ten or so jerseys and at least double that in T-shirts before I sign a few balls. I'm just getting ready to start signing the stack of posters, at least a hundred if not more, when the door opens. I'm surprised to see Mrs. Stamper, the team owner's wife, standing in the doorway.

"Landon," she greets, gliding into the room like her shit doesn't stink.

I don't think I've ever seen her smile, not a truly genuine smile, not like the ones I get from Tessa. "Mrs. Stamper."

"A word?" she asks, closing the door.

This is the smaller conference room, so there are no windows, and I'm suddenly on edge. Bridgett Stamper is not the kind of woman who likes to be told no. "What can I do for you?" I ask her.

"I'm going to cut right to the chase. You need to end things with your girl toy."

What. The. Fuck? "Excuse me?"

"You heard me. End it."

"No." I drop the Sharpie and cross my arms over my chest. "You can't control what I do in my personal life."

"Oh, but I can. You see. I don't like her. I don't want her around. I can make your life hell, even trade you."

"Bullshit. You don't run this team; Joseph does." I stay rooted in my seat, even though I want to get the fuck out of this room with her. This is so out of left field, I never could have seen this coming.

"Are you willing to risk your career for some piece of ass?" she sneers.

"That piece of ass is the love of my life. You can threaten me with whatever the fuck you want. I don't give a flying fuck."

"Oh, but you should. You see, my husband likes to make me happy." Her index finger, with a nail that seems even longer and painted blood red, draws a line on the table as she inches closer. I'm out of my seat and moving to the other side of the room before she reaches me. I don't want to be anywhere near her.

"You don't even know Tessa. How could you possibly hate her?" Hell, how could anyone? She's the kindest and most real person I've ever met.

"I don't like the way she looks at my husband."

"Enlighten me. How exactly does she look at him?" I was with Tessa when she met Joseph and Bridgett, and most of that time, she was looking at me.

"Like she can take him away from me." Something passes in her eyes, but I can't explain it.

"That's crazy."

"I know what I saw. You have until the end of the weekend to end it and announce it publicly, or you'll regret it."

"Fuck you."

Her eyes rake over my body, making me feel filthy and ready for another shower. "We could arrange that, too. I could show you what being with a real woman is like." She licks her lips, and I want to puke.

"Not a chance in hell."

"Pity, we'd be good together. Regardless, you know my terms. Make it happen, or you will be traded. As for your little girlfriend, I'll make sure she wants nothing to do with you."

"Fuck. You," I say again, because who in the fuck does this woman think she is?

She cackles, a sound so high-pitched it feels as though it could make your ears bleed. "I've bent over backward to be where I am, and I'm not letting you and that little mouse of yours ruin it for me. Do it or else. You have until Saturday night at midnight." She turns and walks out the door. She's gone just as quickly as she arrived, and I'm left standing here with my mouth hanging open at her audacity, with anger coursing through me. I don't give a fuck what she says. I'm not losing Tessa. Not for her, not for her husband, not for the team, or football. Tessa comes first.

It's a startling revelation for me. I knew I loved her, but the depth of my feelings had never really struck until this moment. I love Tessa more than I love the game of football. I meant it when I said I don't give a fuck what she does to me or my career. Tessa is the one thing in my life I won't give up. Ever.

Taking a few minutes to calm the hell down, I go back to the stack of posters and quickly work my way through scribbling my name and number on each of them. When the last poster is signed, I grab my bag and storm out of the room. Sally is still at her desk and waves at me, but she doesn't say anything. I'm sure the expression on my face says it all.

As soon as I'm in my SUV, I call Tessa. "Hey, how was practice?" she greets me.

Closing my eyes, I let my head rest against the headrest in my SUV, letting her voice wash over me. "It was good. Stayed back and ran a few routes with Kaden. I had to sign a few things for some fan mail after that." I'm going to tell her about Bridgett's little visit, just not over the phone. I need her in my arms when I tell her so she knows, so she can feel that I'm not worried. I need her to see that as long as I have her, my life with be complete.

"You sound tired," she comments.

"A long day. How's work?"

"It's going. Buckwheat is sick, so we're waiting for the vet to get here to take a look at him. I might not get out of here on time tonight. JJ is sick, too, so I told Autumn that I would stay."

"Is JJ okay?"

"Yeah, just a cold, but he wants his momma. I'll just come by your place when I'm done if that's okay."

"You staying with me?" I fly out in the morning to Ohio for an away game. I need her in my arms tonight. I feel like a caged animal after my conversation with Bridgett, and as bad as I hate to, I need to tell Tessa. I don't want to keep anything from her.

"Yeah. I'll just have to stop by my place and get some clothes."

"You don't have what you need here?"

"Not for work."

"Send me a message about what you need. I'll stop by and get your key and go pick it up."

"You don't have to do that."

"Tessa, it gets you in my arms that much faster. I'll be by in about half an hour. Need anything? You got lunch?"

"No, I'm good. Thanks, babe."

I smile at the endearment. She doesn't use it often, but when she does, it makes my heart race.

"Love you," I say, ending the call. It's amazing how just hearing her voice and knowing that I'm on my way to see her can brighten the shittiest day.

I'm sitting on the couch, waiting for Tessa to get here. My house smells like the baked spaghetti that's in the oven, staying warm, and my mind is racing. The more I think about that little scene with Bridgett today, the more pissed off I get. Who does she think she is? Telling me who I can and can't date. I abide by the terms of my contract. I'm a damn good football player. She doesn't have the right to tell me what I can and can't do in my personal life.

My phone rings, and I see Case's smiling mug on my screen. "Hey, man," I answer.

"You want to grab a beer?"

"Nah, thanks, though. Tessa should be getting here soon. She had to work late. They have a sick horse at the shelter."

"Sucks. What's up with you? Missing your girl?"

"Always, but that's not what's wrong."

"Care to fill me in?"

I release everything about this morning on him, including my rant about how Bridgett has no right. By the time I'm finished, I'm breathing heavy, and my fists are clenched at my sides.

"Fuck her," Case seethes. "She can't do that. You need to go to Coach Neil and tell him what's up. You don't want this shit backfiring on you."

"I know. I need to tell Tessa, too."

"Fuck, maybe go straight to Stamper himself. Wait, maybe take Coach with you as backup. I can't believe her. That bitch is shady as fuck. You can see it in her eyes. Stamper seems like a solid dude. I haven't spent much time with him, but they don't seem anything alike."

"I agree. I haven't really thought much past telling Tessa."

"She's going to freak on you, isn't she? Try to push you away and shit to save your career. She's that kind of woman, putting those she loves first."

"You think she will?"

"Yes." There is no hesitation in his answer.

"Fuck, now I really don't want to tell her. I know she'll be worried about my position, she'll be angry for me, but I never once considered she would end us over this."

"She's one of the good ones, Barker. Kind, selfless. I don't really know her well, but I can see that in her. I'm not saying it would be forever or even that she would be successful, but I know she would try."

"Fuck me. I'm telling you right now, Case, if I lose Tessa over this, fucking heads are going to roll."

"Calm down, Incredible Hulk. Talk to Coach." As he says it, I hear the front door open.

"Hey, Tess just got home. I'll see you tomorrow."

"Talk to Coach," he says before hanging up.

"Hey, how's Buckwheat?" I ask, meeting Tessa in the hall. She looks exhausted. Taking her hand, I lead her into the dining room and pull out a chair for her.

"He has equine protozoal myeloencephalitis."

"Dumb that down for me, Freckles." She laughs, which is what I was hoping for.

"It's also called opossum's disease. It's where horses come in contact with opossum feces, and it affects their neurological system."

"Sounds serious."

"It is. If caught early enough, most horses recover, or so the vet tells us. However, Buckwheat is old. He's twenty, so that will play a factor in it, as well."

"When will you know if he's out of the woods?"

She sighs heavily. "Hopefully, we will see an improvement in the morning. The vet is coming back out for another injection."

"Anything I can do?"

"No, but I appreciate your willingness to help. What smells so good?"

"I made baked spaghetti."

"I'm starving."

"Perfect. You sit tight, and I'll make you a plate."

"I can do it," she says as her phone rings. She pulls it out of her pocket. "It's Autumn."

"Take it. I'll be right back." I kiss the corner of her mouth and make my way to the kitchen to grab us both a plate. After setting a plate for her and one for me on the table, I head back to the kitchen. I grab a bottle of water for myself and pour Tessa a glass of her favorite wine; she looks like she could use it. When I make it back to the dining room, she's still on the phone, but she's eating her spaghetti. She mouths "Thank you" when I set her wine in front of her.

"Yeah, the vet said it's a fifty-fifty chance of recovery at this point. We caught it soon, which is good. It's just a wait-and-see kind of thing," she explains to Autumn. "Oh, and before I forget, he wanted me to tell you he'd be back next week for the other animals' checkups and that if you want to bring Pinky, plan on Thursday."

I still can't believe that Autumn and Jeremy have a pet pig in their house. A farting pig, apparently, from the stories I've heard. It's odd, but to each their own. Hell, if Tessa wanted a pet pig, I'd move heaven and earth to get her one. I can only imagine that was Jeremy's exact reasoning when it came to Autumn. There's not much a man won't do for the woman he loves.

Including giving up his career. I hope that it doesn't come to that. I don't think that Bridgett has that kind of pull. Case is right, talking to Coach is the right step. I'm going to hold off on mentioning it to Tessa until I talk to him. I don't want to worry her, and frankly, I want to have more information on what she can and can't do. I don't want to give her a chance to push me away.

"Okay. Give JJ a hug from Aunt Tessa. See you in the morning." She lays her phone on the table and reaches for her glass of wine. "Thank you for this." She holds it up before taking a drink. "Sorry about that. She wanted an update on Buckwheat."

"I get it. I hope he's okay."

There is sadness in her eyes. "Me, too. If this doesn't work, if he doesn't respond to treatments, we'll have to have him put down." Her voice cracks.

"Think positive."

She nods. "This is amazing, by the way."

"Good. Eat up. We have plans after dinner."

"Landon, I really just want to chill." Her shoulders slump as if she's disappointed she has something else added to her plans tonight.

"Good. That's exactly what we're doing. So, eat up."

A slow smile tilts her lips. "I love you." Her words are soft, but the meaning is no less powerful.

Leaning over the table, I kiss her. "I love you, too."

CHAPTER 23

Tessa

"GO RELAX ON THE COUCH WHILE I CLEAN UP."

"I can help." I stand from the table to gather my plate, but his hand over mine stops me.

"I've got this, baby. Now, go sit."

I do as he says because I'm mentally exhausted, and I know Landon. He's not going to let me help. Wasting time arguing about it is not going to do either of us any good. A few minutes later, he's holding out his hand for me.

"The leftovers are in the fridge. You're staying here while I'm gone, right?"

"Yeah, unless you don't want me to?"

"I want you here." His voice is firm, his decision final. Not that I expected anything different. "You can have the leftovers while I'm gone. I made a small bowl for you to take in your lunch tomorrow."

"Landon Barker, if your fans could see you now. Being all domesticated, making my lunch."

"Yeah? You think that would help my image?"

"I don't think you need any help in that department, Number Eighteen."

"Hey, you did dub me Lucky Player after all," he taunts.

"Well, aren't you? You are here with me right now," I tease.

"Damn right, I am," he agrees. He pushes open his bedroom door and doesn't stop until we're in the bathroom. "Strip, baby." His voice is soft yet husky. He reaches down into the huge clawfoot tub and turns on the water.

"You're running me a bath?" I ask, my heart melting into a puddle at my feet.

"I'm running *us* a bath," he corrects, pulling his T-shirt over his head and letting it fall to the floor.

Before I know it, we're both stripped naked, and Landon steps into the tub, holding his hand out for me. I step in after him. He settles himself, resting against the back of the tub. "Sit," he says, opening his legs for me to join him. I waste no time sitting down and leaning against his chest. The hot water lulls over us, and his arms wrap around me.

"How did you know this is what I needed?"

"A bath?"

"No. You."

"Because I need this time with you, too. I hate leaving you when we have away games."

"I know, but the season is halfway over. We've almost made it."

"Yeah, can you get time off work? Maybe we can take a trip once the season is over? Somewhere tropical, where I get to see you in tiny scraps of material all day long."

"I don't really do that out in public."

"Hell no, I'm talking private beach. No way am I letting another man ogle you. Hell, to be honest, we don't even need swimwear. Let's just lie naked in bed all day."

"You really think you could do that? Spend a week just lying in bed."

"Ah, but you missed a key point. Two of them, in fact."

"What's that?"

"I said *naked* with *you*."

I laugh. "So, do you think you and I could be naked in bed for a week?"

"Yes." No hesitation in his answer.

"Really? You wouldn't get bored?"

"Not if I'm with you."

"Aw, you're such a sweet talker tonight." Come to think of it, he's acting kind of strange. I turn to look at him. "You okay?"

"Yeah, just dreading leaving you. It gets harder with every trip."

"You sure that's all it is?"

He nods. "Some stuff I need to talk to Coach about, about my contract, but nothing to be worried about. Just a lot on my mind."

"What time does your flight leave tomorrow?"

"Nine. So I'll be up and gone before you leave for work."

"Why so soon?"

"Not sure. The time we fly out always varies. It just depends on the chartered plane and the pilots' schedules."

"Makes sense, I guess. I couldn't imagine having to coordinate all those schedules."

"What are you going to do while I'm gone?"

"Work. I need to do some laundry, so I'll go to my place for a while. Depending on what's going on with Buckwheat…" My voice trails off. I can't imagine having to put him down. I pray that this medication does what it's supposed to do.

His hands move to cup my breasts. "You going to miss me?" he asks huskily.

"Always."

Tilting my head back against his chest, I close my eyes and enjoy his hands roaming my body. When his touch moves south, and his fingers slide through my folds, my back arches, causing me to push my ass into his hard cock.

"I need you, Tessa."

His words are full of grit and raw need. It's a side of him I've never seen before. He almost sounds desperate to have me.

"I'm yours. Take what you need."

"Stand up," he growls.

I do as I'm told and stand. He steps out and holds his hand out for me. I take it, letting him help me out of the tub. I expect him to hand me a towel, but instead, we both stand, dripping water all over the floor, our chests heaving with the desire surging between us.

He takes one step, then another until he's next to me. Reaching over, he pulls open the vanity drawer and grabs a condom. Within seconds, he's sheathed his hard length.

"Tess," he says, moving to stand in front of me.

"Take me, Landon." That's all I needed to say for his control to break.

"Arms around my neck," he says, his voice gravelly. Doing as I'm told, I lock my hands behind his neck, and with his hands on my hips, he lifts me. I wrap my legs around him and hold on tight. "Tell me to stop if I go too fast. If I hurt you, tell me to stop."

"Delay of game." I smirk, and he chuckles, a sound that rattles from deep inside his chest.

"I'm going long and deep," he says as he pushes inside me. He stills, giving me time to adjust to him. He kisses me; it's soft and sweet. Nothing like the fire that's staring back at me in his blue eyes, or his warnings that if it's too much, he'll stop. When he breaks the kiss, he slowly pulls out and thrusts back in. Only this time, he doesn't stop. Over and over and over again, his feet planted on the floor, he thrusts into me. All I can do is hold on for the ride as my body takes him deeper than ever before.

My head tilts back as an orgasm tears through me. My body shakes, my legs squeeze him tight, and my nails dig into his scalp. "Landon!" I cry out his name as the spark he's ignited in my core spreads throughout my entire body.

"Fuck, you're squeezing me," he says with a grunt, and he stills with a roar as he releases inside me.

I wrap my arms around him, burying my face in his neck. It's as if I've had an out-of-body experience. My body is still spasming around him. I've never felt anything as intense as that.

Never.

"You okay, baby?" he whispers.

"I think you killed me. In the best way," I add, because I know he's going to worry he hurt me. "I'm not sure what that was, but we can do more of that soon. 'Kay?" I ask, tapping his shoulder.

He throws his head back and laughs, causing me to lift mine. His baby blues are bright, and whatever was plaguing him is gone. At least for now.

"Now I need a shower."

"Me, too." Without putting me down, he moves to the walk-in shower and turns on the water. "You're beautiful like this," he says, staring into my eyes. "I love that I'm the only one who gets to see you this way. Sweaty and sated, eyes glazed over from my cock."

"Modest much?" I tease.

"Bringing you pleasure makes me feel ten feet tall."

"You're on a roll tonight with all the sweetness."

"Just making sure you know what you mean to me. Leaving you messes with my head," he admits. "I hate not being here with you, and I don't ever want you to question how far my love runs. It's deep, baby. Deep in my soul, and it's all for you."

"I love you, too." I kiss his cheek, and he moves us into the shower and under the hot spray. He carefully sets me on my feet and disappears to get rid of the condom. He's back in no time, taking the shampoo out of my hands and washing my hair for me. His hands roam my body, and mine his, as we wash away the day and our lovemaking. That's what it was. No matter how hard or fast, no matter how soft or slow, it's nothing but love between us. I can feel it. Just like he said, it's soul-deep, as if he's a part of me. I don't ever see that changing.

After our shower, we climb into bed. Cuddled close to his chest, I drift off into a peaceful sleep.

X X ⌐
o o ∫

The next morning, I wake to an empty bed. There's a note with nothing but *I love you, L* written on it, next to me on his pillow, where his head should be. I miss him already and wish he had woken me up to tell me he was leaving. Climbing out of bed, I make my way to the bathroom. My hair looks like I was ridden hard and put up wet, and in a way, I was. I giggle to myself just as my phone rings. I run back into the bedroom to answer it, hoping it's Landon, and I'm in luck.

"Hey, I miss you already," I greet him.

"Damn, Tess, that's one hell of a greeting. I miss you, too, baby. We're getting ready for wheels up. I just wanted to tell you to have a good day."

"You should have woken me up."

"Nah, you looked like an angel sleeping in my bed. I didn't have the heart to wake you. I don't know when I'll be able to touch base again. I'll text you when we land. Keep me posted on Buckwheat."

"Will do. Safe flight."

"Love you," he replies and ends the call.

I finish getting ready, pop a bagel into the toaster, and pull out the container of spaghetti that Landon made for my lunch today. Fifteen minutes later, I'm in my car and headed to work.

"Morning," Autumn greets me when I arrive at the shelter.

"Buckwheat?" I ask. "I see the vet's truck outside."

"Yeah, he's with him now," she says, taking a huge gulp of coffee.

"Rough night?"

"Something like that." She smirks. "I hate when they're out of town, and JJ was already asking for Daddy first thing this morning. Maybe we would be okay with just the sales from his ass photographs?" she muses.

I just smile and shake my head. "I hear ya. Although I don't have a little boy missing his daddy."

"Not yet."

I smile. "Maybe one day. Things are going great with us."

"That's easy to see. That man is crazy about you, Tessa."

"The feeling is mutual."

"You watching the game on Sunday?" she asks.

"Yep. You?"

"We are. Why don't you come to the house and watch it with me and JJ? He'd love to see you."

"Sure. What are we eating? Snack foods? Want me to pick up some pizza and wings?"

"Pizza and wings. That way, neither of us has to cook. Well, I'll make some cookies or something. Here." She reaches for her purse. "Let me give you some money before I forget."

"Nope. It's on me. Cheese still for JJ?"

"You know it. One day, the kid will eat more than just cheese on his pizza."

"Got it covered."

"Hello," a deep voice calls out. Autumn and I both head to the reception area to greet the vet. "He's responding to the medication, but he's not out of the woods yet. I gave him another dose, and I'll stop by tomorrow to give him another. Will either of you be here?"

"I will be," I tell him.

"Great. I'll stop in before I leave tomorrow to give you an update."

"Thanks, George," Autumn and I say at the same time.

"Oh, and thanks for the heads-up about next week. Pinky could use a checkup." Autumn gives him a wide grin.

He just shakes his head and smiles. "You got it, boss. You ladies have a great rest of your day."

George is in his early sixties, and he's still in disbelief that Autumn and Jeremy have a pet pig. It's not the pig that surprises him. It's that they let the pig live in their house and even take it for walks on a leash.

"He still thinks you're crazy."

"I know. I love it. Sure, Pinky is not a conventional pet, but the way we met and fell in love isn't either."

"Your life is what you make it. Besides, JJ loves Pinky. Now, where are we at for the day?"

"Just cleaning cages and feeding. Thanks to the adoption fair, we're still not at capacity, so it shouldn't take us long." So many of our animals found their forever homes. "I thought we could tag-team it instead of splitting up today."

"Yes! It's been way too long since we've done that." Just as I say the words, the chime sounds on the door. Looking up, my mouth drops open. "Mom? What are you doing here?" I rush around the counter to give her a hug.

"We wanted to surprise you."

I turn to look at Autumn. "You little sneak."

She holds her hands up in the air. "I'd love to take credit for this, but it wasn't me. I didn't know anything about it."

"Landon," Mom says.

"Really?" I ask, and my voice cracks.

"He called me the other day and said, and I quote, 'we need to get you to Los Angeles more often.' I agreed, and here I am."

"I can't believe he did this." I hug her again.

"He said we're staying at his place?" she asks, raising her brow and giving me a look that only a mother can pull off.

My face heats. "Yeah, he likes to know I'm there while he's away."

"That man is whipped," Autumn chimes in with a laugh.

"Oh, I could tell with how adamant he was that I come and visit," Mom agrees. "So," she changes the subject, "what are the plans this weekend?"

"Well, I work all weekend here, and I was going to go over to Autumn's and watch the game on Sunday."

"Tomorrow, you're only here until noon," Autumn corrects.

"Perfect. I'd love to tag along and see what it is my little girl does every day. Most of the time when I visit, you've taken time off. Is that okay?" She turns to look at Autumn. "Do you mind?"

"Of course not."

"Well, ladies. We've got work to do. I'll put your bags in the office." The rest of the day, Mom helps out, and with the third set of hands, the work is done even faster. By the time lunch rolls around, we're finished.

"You two go on home. Spend some time together."

"We're fine to stay," Mom tells her.

"No. I insist. You'll be back here tomorrow. I would volunteer, but I'll have JJ, and it's hard to get anything done when I'm here by myself with him."

"No worries, it's fine," I assure her.

"Go, catch up."

"Call if you need me. I can come back."

"It will be fine. Now go." With a round of hugs, Mom and I grab her luggage and head out the door. I haven't heard from Landon, and I thought I would have by now. I send him a text, thanking him for bringing Mom here. It will be there for him when he lands. As Mom and I drive to his place, my heart is full. Overflowing with love for my number eighteen.

CHAPTER 24

Landon

THE ENTIRE FLIGHT, I HAD MY HEADPHONES ON AND PRETENDED to sleep. I'm exhausted, yet sleep never came. I keep thinking about Bridgett and her threats, and I get even more pissed off. Case is right that I should talk to Coach Neil, and I've already texted him, telling him that as soon as he has a free minute, I need to speak to him. I just hope it's as soon as we land. This shit is festering inside me, and I'm about to blow. No way can I focus on the game when all I have is anger inside of me for what she thinks she can do. That's the worst part. I don't really know if she has that kind of pull. If she does, and Tessa can't go with me, I guess I'm retiring early. Just the thought has me clenching my fists. Why does she get to dictate when I'm done playing? Fuck me, then there's Tessa and my conversation with Case. I won't let her push me away. I need to tell her about this. I told her I would always be honest, but damn, she had such a bad day, and I didn't want to pile this unnecessary drama on top of it all.

What a fucking mess.

I take a seat in the front of one of the shuttle buses that take us from the airport to the hotel. I don't feel like being social. Case plops down in the seat beside me, making me groan. "You talk to him?" he says, keeping his voice low.

"No. But he knows I want to talk the first chance he gets."

Just then, Coach Neil climbs on the bus and takes the seat across from us. "When we get to the hotel and get everyone their keys, we'll talk," he says softly. I nod and sit back in my seat.

"You want me to go with you?"

"Nah, thanks, though." Case and I played in college together, along with our other best friend, Reid, who plays for the Nashville Rampage. The three of us have been thick as thieves ever since. I know they've always got my back, but with this, I have a feeling the fewer people involved, the better it will be. Sure, he knows, but I don't want him heavily involved and have his contract compromised, as well. I don't want Bridgett to take him down with me, if that's how this plays out.

Forty-five minutes later, I'm pacing the floor in Coach Neil's hotel suite. I've just told him everything, and he's just sitting on the couch, watching me. "Say something," I say, running my hands through my hair.

"It's bullshit. Joseph doesn't let her have anything to do with the team. I can almost guarantee that he knows nothing about this."

"Why the fuck is she after me? And Tessa? You've met her. She's the kindest, sweetest person out there. I don't fucking get it."

"Landon, your contract is solid. You have a no-trade clause."

"I know that, but damn it, they have the Cougars' legal team behind them. Who knows what kind of fucking contract violation she'll try to pin on me." He pulls his phone out of his pocket and taps the screen, placing it to his ear. "What are you doing?" I ask, and he raises his index finger, indicating I need to give him a minute.

"Hey, Stamper." He greets Mr. Stamper by his last name. "Coach

Neil, when you get here, I'd like a word with you. In private. Call me." He hangs up the phone. "He'll call," he assures me. "Joseph's a good man."

"I thought so, too, I still do, but his wife is the Wicked fucking Witch of the West. What does he see in her?"

"I'm not sure, but they're total opposites. We'll get to the bottom of this, Landon. I assure you."

I nod. "Okay. I guess all we can do is wait. I'm going back to my room. She said by Sunday, so the clock is ticking. I'm not worried about me. It's the threat that she'll make Tessa hate me. I couldn't live with that. I can handle giving up the game, but I won't give her up."

He nods. "I'll take care of it."

I don't have much choice other than to believe him. "Thank you." I leave without another word and slip into my shared room with Trent. He's on the phone with Luna, and it's then that I remember I didn't let Tessa know we landed. Pulling out my phone, I see a message I missed from her. I've been so wrapped up in my anger that I didn't even notice.

Tessa: I love you, Lucky. Thank you so much for bringing my mom here. I can't tell you what that means to me. You're incredible.

My heart expands reading her words. There is nothing that I wouldn't do to make her happy. Nothing. I start to text her back and decide I need to hear her voice. Dialing the phone, she picks up on the first ring.

"Landon." She sounds happy, and for the first time today, I feel some of the anger slip away.

"Hey, Freckles. Good surprise?"

"You knew it would be. I can't believe you did this."

"I told you we need to get her in the habit of visiting more often. Maybe we can even get her to love it and move closer."

"I wish. How was your flight?"

"Uneventful."

She chuckles. "Well, that's always good, I guess. You sound tired."

"Yeah, I didn't sleep much last night. I never do when I have to leave you."

"There you go again," she says softly. "Saying all those sweet words that make me melt."

"I mean them, baby. Every single one of them. You're the love of my life." I feel like I'm laying it on a little thick right now, but damn it, I want her to understand. She needs to understand this is real for me. I should tell her. The words are on the tip of my tongue. I need to tell her, but not like this. Not over the phone, and not until we talk to Stamper. When I get home Monday, I'll tell her everything while she's in my arms, where she can't run or push me away. Fucking Case, I hope he's wrong.

"Is that Landon?" I hear Caroline ask. "Tell him I said hello."

"Mom says hi."

"Tell her I said hello. What are the two of you getting into today?"

"We're going to go to the beach. Grab some dinner. Just hang out."

"You're staying at my place, right?"

"Yeah, we're here now."

"Good. I need to get down to a team meeting. I'll call before bed. Love you, Tess." I almost choke on the words.

"Love you." Her voice is cheery as the line goes dead.

I need this ended. I hate this feeling of not knowing what's going to happen. I hate that I'm so far away from her. Most of all, I really fucking hate Bridgett Stamper. I just can't figure out why she hates Tessa. One meeting that was mere minutes and they simply said hello.... What's her endgame with this? I just can't seem to figure it out.

As if things couldn't get any worse, Joseph's flight was delayed. He chartered a plane, and apparently, there was something going on with the engine, so he didn't get here until today. Saturday. Saturday, as in the deadline that Bridgett gave me to publicly announce that it's over between me and my girl. Something I refuse to do. Consequences be damned.

The entire team is in the private dining area, eating dinner. Today has been a lazy day, as Coach calls it. We ran through tapes this morning, but other than that, it's a chill day at the hotel, getting rested up for tomorrow's game. I scarf down some grilled chicken and vegetables, but I don't taste them.

My time is running out. She said midnight, and it's already pushing eight. I don't know if she was bluffing or telling the truth. Something tells me it was a bluff, but it's risky not to take her seriously. I just hope Mr. Stamper can handle this quietly.

"Landon." Coach Neil appears beside me. "Got a minute?" he asks.

"Sure, Coach." I catch Case's eye from across the table, and he gives me a subtle nod. Trent does the same. I broke down and told him last night. It was driving me insane, and since we're rooming together, he knew something was up. I know they have my back, but at the end of the day, it's Joseph Stamper I need in my corner. I just hope Coach Neil is right, and he's going to be.

Silently, Coach Neil and I get in the elevator. Neither one of us speaks as it takes us to the top floor of the hotel. I follow behind him and wait as he knocks on the door. "Come on in," Joseph says. "Have a seat." I want to tell him that I'll stand, but I don't need to piss him off, too. I want him on my side. "What's going on, Neil?" he asks.

"I'll let Landon tell you."

So, I tell the story again. I make sure to keep my anger in check, knowing I'm speaking about his wife. I look him in the eye as I recount her visit with me. By the time I'm finished, my hands are fisted at my sides, and he's looking... guilty?

"I don't care what she threatens to do, I'm not ending my relationship with Tessa. If I have to give up my career, then so be it."

"Wait, hold up." He holds his hand in the air and stands from where he was sitting on the couch. We're now standing eye-to-eye. "You're not giving up your career, and you're not letting go of Tessa." Her name is spoken with reverence. "I know why she's targeting you, and I'm afraid it's my fault."

"Explain," I say through gritted teeth. If he made a pass at her, I'll kill him. Why didn't she tell me? There are a million scenarios racing through my mind.

"Have a seat."

"I'm good." I cross my arms over my chest and square my feet. I'm not backing down to him. I don't give a fuck who he is. "Explain," I say again.

"After I saw you climb the wall, and the pictures of you and Tessa were everywhere, I realized that she looked familiar to me."

"You said that," I say, remembering our conversation.

He nods. "You see, there was this woman. Beautiful dark hair, big green eyes, looked a lot like Tessa back then. We met for a week when we were on spring break. We were inseparable that week, and I was going to ask her to try long-distance until we could work it out. She was amazing, vibrant, and full of life. In just six short days, I fell hard. I knew she was the love of my life. I wanted to fight to make it work. Our last night together was… one I relive every single day of my life. The morning after, she was gone. Nothing but a note thanking me for the amazing week and that she would never forget me. It wasn't until that moment that I realized I didn't know her last name. I never gave her mine either. My father was the owner of the Los Angeles Cougars, and I was sick and tired of women coming onto me for what they thought they could get. I just wanted to be Joseph. That's who I was with her. Just me."

"What does this have to do with Tessa? Other than the resemblance? Does Bridgett think you want to be with my girlfriend?"

"No." He shakes his head. "Seeing Tessa brought back all those feelings, but even more so. I mean it when I say not a single day has gone by that I didn't think of her and our time together. I was crushed. When I got home, Dad informed me he was ill and it was time for me to take over running the team. He wanted me to be settled, a family man, and all I wanted was my beach girl. Bridgett was a family friend. We grew up together. Her parents and mine were best friends. One night, while getting piss-ass drunk, thinking about my life, Bridgett showed up. We made a pact. A marriage of convenience. She'd be my wife and, in turn, would get to live a life of luxury that being married to a Stamper brings. As for me, I didn't have to worry about falling in love again, something I knew would never happen. I knew there wouldn't be anyone else for me."

"So your marriage is one of convenience?"

"Yes. I care about Bridgett, but I don't love her, not like a man should love his wife. Not like you love Tessa."

"I still don't understand," Coach Neil speaks up. "How does this involve Landon and Tessa?"

"When I saw Tessa, everything came flooding back. I decided I wanted to try and find her. The love of my life. I hired a private investigator. I didn't have much to go on, but I did have Tessa's picture and one from a photo booth from all those years ago." He reaches into his wallet and pulls out a small strip that contains two images. "She has the other two," he says, handing them to me.

My mouth drops open. "Oh, my God. She looks just like her." I study the image that's worn from, my guess, years of carrying it in his wallet.

"I found her, Landon." I look up to see him watching me closely. "I found my Caroline."

It takes me a minute to register what he's saying, and then it clicks. "Holy shit, Tessa's mom?"

He nods. "Yes. Caroline Deaton." He says her name with so much reverence that even I can feel what she means to him. "I can only assume Bridgett has found my file and put two and two together. I didn't try to hide it. Our marriage is one of friendship. Why do you think we've never had any kids?"

"You've been married for what? Twenty years?"

"Twenty-five."

"And you've been… celibate all that time?"

"No, but I had a vasectomy, which pissed her off."

"Holy shit. So she wants Tessa gone, thinking that if she's around, her mom will be, too, and that you'll divorce her?"

"Yes. She signed a prenup, so she'll be well taken care of. But I'm afraid there's more."

"What's that?"

"Landon, I have reason to believe that Tessa… that she's my daughter."

I sit on the couch, my legs not able to hold me up any longer.

"The timeline fits."

"Fuck. I get it. It all makes sense to me now." I close my eyes and take a deep breath. "Is it safe to say I'm not getting traded?"

"No. You're not."

Relief washes over me, but there is still one issue that I need to take care of. "She gave me until midnight tonight."

He nods. I watch as he pulls out his phone and tries to call her. "Voice mail," he mumbles before sending her a text.

"I have to warn Tessa."

"Wait." There's panic in his voice. "I don't want them finding out like this. I don't know if I'm her father, but I want to be, and this isn't how I want that to go down."

"Fine. But I'm still warning her." Pulling my phone out of my pocket, I call Tessa.

"Hey, Lucky, I was just thinking about you."

"Yeah?" I ask, my heart slowing just from the sound of her voice.

"Yes. I bought some pillows for your living room today to liven this place up a little." She laughs. "I hope you don't mind. If you don't like them, I can take them to my place."

"No, baby. I don't mind. Do whatever you want. As long as you're there, that's all that I care about."

"Aw." I hear Caroline in the background.

"I should have told you that I have you on speaker."

"I don't care who knows how much I love you, Tessa. Your mom included. I'm glad the two of you are enjoying your time together. Listen, there's something going on. I don't want you to worry, but a crazy fan is starting rumors of a trade and who knows what else. It's not true."

"O-kay," she says slowly.

"I'll explain everything when I get home. I just wanted to give you a heads-up in case the media gets a hold of this. Also, would it be possible for you and your mom to just stay at my place for the rest of the weekend? I don't know where this chick is, and I'd feel better knowing that you're safe."

"Yeah, I mean, we were supposed to go to Autumn's to watch the game with her and JJ."

"Have them come to my place. In fact, you can all just stay there. The building has excellent security."

"Landon, are we in danger?" I can hear the worry in her voice.

"No, you're not in danger, but I would feel better knowing you're at my place, safe away from the crazy fans."

"Okay. You sure there's nothing for us to worry about?"

"I'm positive. You think I'd let you be there on your own if there was? I just wanted to give you a warning. Oh, and ask your mom if she can stay a few extra days. I have some things I would like to talk to both of you about." I catch Joseph's eye as I say this, and he looks like he's holding his breath, afraid to breathe.

"I can do that," Caroline chimes in. "I'll call the office and let them know I'm taking a few days of vacation."

"Thank you. I'll see you girls late tomorrow night."

"Love you, Landon."

"Love you, too, baby."

I end the call.

"She's there? Caroline is in Los Angeles?" Joseph sounds half excited and half panicked.

"Yeah, I flew her in to spend the weekend with Tess. I hate leaving her for away games."

"The team flies out Monday morning," Coach Neil speaks up.

"Don't care. I'm flying home to my girl. Fine me, bench me, I don't care."

"You have a family emergency," Coach Neil says with authority.

"However you want to spin it, you can. I'm on the first flight back to Los Angeles as soon as the game's over."

"Tom, hi, Joseph Stamper," Joseph says, his phone to his ear. "I need you to contact my wife. Remind her of the terms of her prenup and let her know that I'll be filing for divorce. Oh, and while you're at it, let her know that anything she says in regard to any of my players and their families will be prosecuted in court. Thanks, Tom." He hangs up and exhales loudly. "If I know Bridgett, that will stop her, and if not"—he shrugs—"I'll take care of it."

"You flying back with me?" I ask him.

"You're damn right, I am." He makes another call to charter a plane for the two of us.

I thought I would come to his suite and he was going to tell me that he made a pass at Tessa or that his wife was a lunatic and thought he wanted something—anything other than what he actually told me. He could be Tessa's dad? How crazy is that? It's such a small world. In a way, I want him to be. I want Tessa to have her father, and I want her mom to stay in Los Angeles. I know that would make my girl happy. Besides, she's not going to miss what comes next.

CHAPTER 25

Tessa

I T'S 1:00 A.M., AND LANDON SHOULD BE HERE ANY MINUTE. HE called just before midnight, telling me that his plane landed and he was on his way here. Mom and I are both up waiting for him. He asked us to be, which is odd, and I'm trying hard not to worry. As far as I know, the media hasn't picked up on any trade rumors involving him. I've been scouring the internet, searching, and nothing. That's a good thing, but I can't help but feel as though there's something he's not telling me. There's something I'm missing in all of this.

The front door opens, and I stand from the couch. I hear his bag fall to the floor and his heavy footfalls as he enters the living room. His eyes are locked on mine as he stalks toward me. When he reaches me, he crushes me in his embrace and buries his face in my neck.

"Oh my God." My mom breathes the words, and her reaction has me pulling away.

Standing in Landon's living room is the team owner, Joseph Stamper,

He's staring at my mom like she's a cool drink of water after being stranded in the desert. "Caroline," he says wistfully.

"I can't believe it's you. After all these years." A tear rolls down her cheek as she stands and takes a hesitant step toward him. "At the dinner, I thought maybe I was hallucinating. You acted as if you'd never met me. I assumed you had forgotten. That our week was a long-lost memory for you."

Landon moves to stand behind me, his arms keeping me held close to his chest. "Just watch," he whispers.

"You're more beautiful today than all those years ago," Joseph tells her. "I was shocked to see you, and I didn't want to cause a scene. But I remember you, my Caroline. I remember everything about you."

She blushes. My mom blushes! "You found me," she says, looking over her shoulder at us, as if remembering we're here in the room with them. There is something in her eyes. Is she worried? She's turned back to face him before I can get a good read on her.

"I did. I should have fought to find you years ago."

"Wow," she murmurs.

I watch as her shoulders grow stiff, and she peers over at me. "Mom?"

"I'm fine." She shakes it off.

"I think the two of you should talk," Landon says.

Joseph's eyes flash to where we're standing, then back to my mom. "Mine?" he asks her.

A sob breaks free from her chest, but she nods. I try to break out of Landon's hold, but he's not having it. "Just keep watching, baby," he whispers soothingly.

"You left," Joseph says, his voice somber.

"I didn't want to say goodbye."

"I never planned to," he says, taking a step toward her.

"No?"

"Never. I wanted you, for as long as you would have had me." He takes another step and then another until they're standing toe-to-toe. His hand shakes as he reaches up and cradles her face. "I loved you, Caroline. I still do."

Mom is bawling, not even trying to hide her tears. He pulls her into his chest and holds her while she cries. I can do nothing but stand here and watch as it all happens. It's as if we're watching a well-rehearsed play.

"Mom?" I ask when her sobs weaken.

She lifts her head and smiles, then looks back at Joseph, who nods. "Tessa, you might want to sit down for this."

Landon takes her warning and, with my hand in his, takes a seat on the couch, pulling me into his lap. Across from us on the loveseat, Mom and Joseph sit, as well, their hands tightly entwined.

"Spring break, my last year of college," Mom starts. She tells me how she and Joseph met, how they spent a magical week together, and how she slipped out of his room at dawn with nothing but a note left behind. "I didn't know his last name, and he didn't know mine. We had no way to reach one another."

"That's why I wasn't there," Joseph chimes in.

"I don't understand. Why you weren't where?"

Mom takes a deep breath. "Tessa, Joseph is your father."

My breath stalls in my chest. "W-What?" I couldn't have possibly heard her correctly.

"I didn't know about you, Tessa. I didn't know how to reach your mom. When I met you, you looked just like her, and I decided it was time to find her. I assumed she would be married, and I told myself if she was happy, I'd step back, but she's here, and she's not married, and now there's you. I never could have imagined that I'd find her and my daughter, too."

She lied to me. "You told me he left us. You lied."

240

"I did, and I'm sorry. Honey, I didn't know how to explain it to you when you were younger so that you would understand. I didn't know how to tell you I met a man and fell in love in a week, and in that love, we made you. You were so young, and I needed you to understand."

"Why didn't you tell me when I got older?"

"I never thought we'd be here. I never thought I'd see him again. By the time you were old enough to understand, I didn't think it mattered. He wasn't in our lives, and I couldn't think of a scenario where he ever would be again."

"You're married," I say to Joseph, and he nods.

"That's where I come in," Landon explains. He goes on to tell me about the threats and how Bridgett found the file on my mother and, as a result, about me.

"Oh my God. I can't believe this is happening." Everything I thought I knew about my life is wrong. How could she have lied to me all these years? "You should have told me, both of you." I pull out of Landon's embrace and stand. "You both should have had enough respect for me to tell me the truth."

"I wanted to. I just wanted to find out what was going on first. You had such a bad day at work with Buckwheat, and I didn't want to make it worse when I had no idea what her endgame was. I called you to warn you after talking to Joseph in case she went through with her threats. Thankfully, his team of attorneys was able to stop her."

"And serve her with divorce papers," Joseph adds.

"There's a lot that we need to talk about. It's late. Why don't you get some sleep, and we can get back to all of this in the morning?"

"I— I can't be here."

"Tessa," Landon says, reaching for me. "Please, let's just get some rest."

"Fine." I march off down the hall without a second glance at any of them. I climb under the covers and settle myself on the edge of my side of the bed. I squeeze my eyes closed, trying to block it all out. It doesn't work because I hear Landon come into the room, shutting the door behind him, and climb into bed. I don't fight him when he snuggles up next to me, wrapping me in his arms.

"I'm sorry, Tessa. I never meant to hurt you. It was the opposite of my intention. I didn't want to lose you. I didn't know what was going on or why she would want you out of my life. I had to know so I could give you the facts. You're my life, Tessa. If you believe nothing else, believe that."

I don't reply as tears silently roll down my cheeks. I love him, and I feel his love for me, but we promised to always be open and honest. Then again, he did call me and let me know something was going on. I guess I can understand him not wanting to tell me any of this over the phone, but if he had told me before he left, that would have been a non-issue. "We're supposed to be a team."

"We are a team. I was going to give it up, Tessa. I was going to walk away from my career if the trade was real. No way was I leaving you."

"That's crazy."

"I know how much you love your job at the shelter, and I would never ask you to give that up."

"Do you hear yourself? You're a professional football player with a multi-million-dollar contract. You can't just walk away from that."

"Yes, I can. What I can't walk away from is you. I'll never walk away from you, Tessa."

I think about what he's saying and let the meaning sink in. He was willing to give up his career for me. I might be upset with him for not including me from the beginning, but I have no doubt his heart was in the right place. Slowly, I roll over to face him. He immediately hugs me tight and places a tender kiss on my forehead.

"I would have come with you," I whisper into the darkness. "I'd follow you anywhere, Landon Barker."

"Tess," he says, his voice cracking. "I'd never ask you to do that."

"You wouldn't have to. Relationships are give and take. Yes, I love my job at the shelter, and I would miss Autumn, Jeremy, and JJ, but I'd miss my heart even more."

"I'm sorry. I should have told you as soon as it happened. Lesson learned, I can promise you that."

"Hopefully, nothing like this ever happens again."

"If it does, we're in it together," he assures me.

"Together," I repeat. We talk well into the morning hours. He helps me see Mom's perspective, and although I'm hurt, I understand why she did it. I can't imagine telling my young, impressionable daughter that I met a man, slept with him in the first week, fell in love, and didn't even know his last name. I get it. I still think she should have told me when I was old enough to understand, but like Landon says, it's not my story to tell. Not really. It doesn't change the fact that Joseph didn't know about me. We can only look toward the future, leaving the past where it lies and focusing on what's yet to come.

$$\times \times \int$$

The next morning, Landon and I find Mom and Joseph in the living room, drinking coffee and eating bagels.

"Morning," I say, taking a seat on the couch.

"We went out for bagels," Mom says. "They're in the kitchen."

"I'll get them." Landon leans down, kisses my forehead, and disappears into his kitchen.

"Have you been up all night?"

"We have." Mom smiles at Joseph, and her face lights up. Something I've never seen from her before. Not like this.

Landon comes back, offering me a cup of coffee, but with no bagel in sight. I love how well he knows me. I'm not going to be able to eat until I talk to Mom. "Thank you." He nods and takes a seat next to me.

"I'm sorry," Mom starts. "I should have told you when you got older, but I didn't know how. It hurt too much to think about never seeing him again."

"Is that why you never dated?"

"I dated," she counters.

"You did here and there, but never anyone serious. Never anyone you introduced me to. It's always just been us."

"I would have been there," Joseph's deep voice promises, filled with conviction. "If I had known where she was, I would have been there."

"Why didn't you look for her sooner?"

"I don't know. For fear of what I would find, I guess."

"So, why now?"

"Seeing you. You're the spitting image of your mother, and it made her real again. All these years, that week has been in my mind, almost like a dream, but seeing you... that brought it all right back to reality. One I wanted more of. I knew if I found her and she was happy, I would walk away. I knew my heart would break all over again, but I did it anyway. I was tired of living with what could have been. I needed to know. I never could have imagined I'd find her and you. My d-daughter," he says, choking up.

Landon places his hand on my thigh, giving me the courage I need. "I get it," I tell them. "I understand, but it's going to take me some time. I don't have this... connection that the two of you have. You're a stranger to me," I say, looking at Joseph.

"I want to get to know you, Tessa. I want to be a part of your life. You take all the time that you need. When you're ready, I'd like to add my name to your birth certificate. I know you're an adult, but it's important to me."

"I'm not changing my name." I don't know why I say it. He didn't ask me to. I guess I just need to get that out in the open. Who knows, maybe one day, I might change my mind.

"Not to Stamper," Landon speaks up. He sets his coffee down on the table and drops to his knees in front of me. He takes my coffee and places it on the table, as well, before taking my hands in his. "This isn't how I planned to do this, and I don't have a ring." He grins, giving me a flash of his dimples. I stare down at him, my heart. My breath stalls in my chest when the reality of what's about to happen settles.

"When I thought I might lose you, I felt like my world was spinning out of control. I don't ever want to face that again. I want to know that it's always going to be you that I come home to. You who's sleeping next to me, and you who has my last name. Tessa Deaton, Freckles…" He smirks. "Will you make me the happiest man alive and do me the incredible honor of becoming my wife? Will you marry me?"

Tears are flowing down my cheeks, and emotion clogs my throat. I nod, and he chuckles. "I need your words, baby."

"Y-Yes," I manage to croak out.

He lets out a whoop of excitement and lifts me off the couch and into his arms. His lips press to mine, and suddenly, everything is right in my world. I know it's going to be tough with his career, but we have a great support system surrounding us, and most of all, we have love. Landon Barker is everything I never knew I wanted and everything that I need. He's the love of my life.

"I love you," I say as he sets me back on my feet.

"I love you, too."

"Congratulations, you two." Mom comes to us and wraps her arms around us in a giant hug. "I'm so happy for you both," she says, wiping tears.

"Landon," Joseph says from beside us. It's going to take some time for me to call him Dad. I'm sure I'll get to that point eventually, but right now, first names are the best that I can do. "Take care of her."

"Always," Landon replies.

"You know, you're one lucky baller, right?" Joseph asks him.

"I could say the same for you."

"Yeah." Joseph pulls my mom into his side and kisses the top of her head. "Lucky indeed."

EPILOGUE

Landon

THIS IS MY FIRST BABY SHOWER, BUT CERTAINLY NOT MY LAST. Luna and Trent were showered with gifts from family and friends today. Now, Luna, Autumn, and Tessa are sitting on the couch, eating cake, talking, and laughing. The three-carat diamond ring that Tessa and I picked out together sparkles and shines every time she moves her hand. It's not what I would have picked. I was looking at a six-carat, but she shut me down. I get it. It's not practical when she's working, but I want nothing but the best for her. It also helps that it's a beacon of light, so all the single guys who think they're going to make a move get the hint quickly. At least, I hope they do.

"This going to be you next?" Trent asks, handing me a bottle of water. We try to limit our alcohol during the season.

"I hope so."

"Really? That's not the answer I expected to get."

"No?"

"Not at all, but I can tell you, it's a fucking rush, man, to know that my baby is growing inside her. What's even better is watching her body grow and change and feeling the baby kick. I'm telling you, it's next level." He takes a swig of his own water. "I can still remember the day she told me. I was scared to death. But the minute I heard the baby's heartbeat for the first time, I knew we were going to be fine. How do you love someone you've never met? It's wild as hell, but it's a ride I can't wait to take again."

"Think we're going to go somewhere tropical when the season's over and get married. I hope by then, I've talked her into trying."

He nods toward the living room. I follow his gaze, and Tessa has her hand on Luna's belly, a grin that lights up my life on her face. "Don't think it's going to take much convincing." He walks away, and I watch as he bends to kiss Luna's belly and then places a tender kiss on her lips.

Life is finally starting to settle back down after the media frenzy. As soon as Joseph's divorce went public, it didn't take the vultures long to dig up that Tessa, my fiancée, was his daughter. Bridgett didn't have a leg to stand on in the divorce. The terms of the prenup were clear. Should Joseph decide to end their marriage, she walks away with way more cash than she deserves. She played the victim to the media, but they passed over her play for attention. Surprisingly, the majority of them decided to report on the long-lost love of the Los Angeles Cougars' team owner. Everyone loves a good love story. It helps that Bridgett is not a nice person. She's shown her bitchiness to too many people over the years, and even the media doesn't want anything to do with her. I think they call that karma.

There is one good thing that came out of all of the media attention. Well, two things, actually. One, Caroline moved to Los Angeles. Joseph insisted he get her a place in my building, so we're neighbors for now. I don't see that lasting long. In fact, if he had his way, she would have just moved straight into his place—his new place. However, my future mother-in-law is adamant she won't live with a married man. She's keeping him at arm's length in that aspect of their relationship. Other than a slight peck on the lips and some hand holding, he's in the dark until the ink is on the papers. He has connections and called in some favors. The divorce should be finalized next week.

And the second thing? Tessa moved in with me. It was an easy decision when she came home from work to reporters camped out on her lawn. My building is secure, and she's safer there. Besides, she stays with me most of the time anyway. We have an appointment next week with a realtor to start looking for a home of our own. We need a bigger place for our growing family. The one that I hope we start sooner rather than later. In the meantime, until I convince her, we'll have to settle for bringing home one of the dogs from the shelter. Nothing says committed and domesticated more than buying a house and getting a dog together. Well, you know, unless you count the rock on her finger.

If you'd told me that day at training camp when I first met Tessa that this is where we would be, I would have laughed my ass off. I never could have imagined we'd be engaged and planning our lives together. I never dreamed I'd be standing at a baby shower, wondering how long it's going to take to convince my future wife that this is our next step. Starting a family.

Tessa catches me watching and waves me over. I smile at her and head her way. She's been through a lot these past few weeks, but she's handled it with grace. My girl's heart is huge, and she's already warming up to her dad. It's still going to take some time, but I have no doubt he's going to make damn sure he's a part of her life. I see it when he looks at her or her mom. He loves them both. They say you don't know love until that of your child. Whether or not that's true, I'm not sure, but I know the love of a good woman, and that's something I will cherish for the rest of my life.

EPILOGUE

Tessa

LANDON NEVER TAKES HIS EYES OFF ME. IT DOESN'T MATTER where he is in the room, I can look up and find him watching me. I smile at him, and that's all the invitation he needs to join us. I stand to greet him, telling Trent to take my spot next to Luna.

"Hey," I say when he's close to me.

He bends to give me a kiss. "Hey, Freckles." He nods toward Luna. "You ready for one of those?"

"Are you?" I counter. I'm ready. I want nothing more than to start our life together. That includes having kids.

"Yes."

"Really?" I'm surprised by his answer.

"We can start tonight."

"Hold up, Number Eighteen. I think you're rushing the pass a little."

He throws his head back and laughs. "I love that you know football. Have I told you that?"

"You have." I chuckle. "Although we're going to have to hold off for a bit."

"Why's that?" he asks. His eyes are soft as he stares down at me.

"Well, it just hit me that I'm going to be married to a Cougar. I think I need to take some time and ponder this agreement." I hold up my hand and wiggle my fingers, showing off my engagement ring. "I at least need to let AJ have a—" He cuts me off with a kiss.

"Mine, Tessa. You are mine. You are a Cougar. Our babies will be Cougars."

"I can still cheer for the Mavs, right? You know, some good, healthy competition?"

"As long as you have my last name and you're wearing my jersey, I will concede some cheering for the opposite team. However, not when we play them."

"Deal." I stretch to kiss the corner of his mouth. "You don't think we should be married first?" I ask, going back to our original conversation.

"That's going to happen. But there is no law that states we have to wait until then. Hell, we can get married tonight. I'll charter a plane. We can go to Vegas or Fiji or wherever your heart desires."

"You'd do that?"

"I'd do just about anything to make you my wife, Tessa."

"When the season is over. Your mom and dad and my mom and Joseph. Our closest friends. We'll keep it small."

"Done. I'll make it happen."

"Just like that?"

"Just like that. Looks like you'll be changing your name, after all."

"I don't know. Landon Deaton has a nice ring to it."

"Not as good as Tessa Barker."

"Hmm." I slide my arms around his neck, clamping my hands together. "That does have a nice ring to it." My heart is full. Landon is the man of my dreams, and I could never have imagined we would be here at this moment. What started out as a chase, ended in forever.

"Speaking of ring, yours is shining." He smirks.

"My fiancé insisted I get it. It's obnoxious."

"But you love it."

"I do. I love him, too. Although, I'm not exactly sure he knows how lucky he is."

"You don't think so? Does he kiss these freckles?" he asks, kissing the bridge of my nose.

"Every day."

"Does he get to hold you in his arms each night?"

"He makes sure of it."

"Does he tell you how beautiful you are?"

"Without fail."

"Trust me, he knows he's lucky."

"You think so? Do you think he'd still feel that way if I told him he was going to be a daddy?"

He freezes, his body going stiff. "What did you just say?"

I nod, unable to speak through the tears in my eyes.

"We're having a baby?" he asks reverently.

"Y-Yes." I'm able to croak out.

"Tessa," he breathes as my feet leave the floor. He lifts me, holding my body close to his, his face buried in my neck. I don't know how long we stand this way, but when he finally sets me back on my feet, his blue eyes are misty with tears. "I can't believe we're here right now. That I finally have everything I've ever wanted in my arms."

"Good surprise?"

"Damn good surprise. You're right, Tess. I am one lucky baller."

Thank you so much for reading *Lucky Baller*.

Want to read more about Landon's friend, Reid? You can read his story in Learn the Play, available October 14, 2025.

Never miss a new release: Newsletter Sign-up Be the first to hear about free content, new releases, cover reveals, sales, and more.
www.kayleeryan.com/subscribe

Discover more about Kaylee's books at www.kayleeryan.com

Start the Riggins Brothers Series for FREE.
Download *Play by Play* now.

Start the Kincaid Brothers Series for FREE.
Download *Stay Always* now.

Contact Kaylee Ryan:

Website: www.kayleeryan.com
Facebook: www.facebook.com/KayleeRyanAuthor
Instagram: www.instagram.com/kaylee_ryan_author
Reader Group: www.facebook.com/groups/kayleeryanfans
Goodreads: www.goodreads.com/author/show/7060310.Kaylee_Ryan
BookBub: www.bookbub.com/profile/kaylee-ryan
TikTok: www.tiktok.com/@kayleeryanauthor

OTHER BOOKS

Standalone Titles:
Tempting Tatum | Unwrapping Tatum | Levitate
Just Say When | I Just Want You
Reminding Avery
Hey, Whiskey
Pull You Through
Remedy | The Difference
Trust the Push | Forever After All
Misconception | Never with Me
Merry with Me/ Lucky Baller

Entangled Hearts Duet:
Agony | Bliss

Mason Creek Series:
Perfect Embrace

The Kissing Games Series:
Kissing the Rival

The Everlasting Ink Series:
Does He Know? / Is This Love?
Are You Ready? / What About Now?
Can We Try?

Out of Reach Series:
Beyond the Bases / Beyond the Game
Beyond the Play / Beyond the Team

Kincaid Brothers Series:
Stay Always / Stay Over
Stay Forever / Stay Tonight
Stay Together / Stay Wild
Stay Present / Stay Anyway
Stay Real

Nashville Rampage Series:
Make the Play/Run the Play
Learn the Play/Follow the Play
Change the Play

Co-written with Lacey Black:

Fair Lakes Series:
It's Not Over | Just Getting Started
Can't Fight It

Standalone Titles:
Boy Trouble
Home to You
Tell Me A Story

Never to Far Series
Beneath the Fallen Stars / Beneath the Desert Sun

ACKNOWLEDGMENTS

There are so many people who are involved in the publishing process. I write the words, but I rely on my team of editors, proofreaders, and beta readers to help me make each book the best it can be.

Those mentioned above are not the only members of my team. I have photographers, models, cover designers, formatters, bloggers, graphic designers, author friends, my PA, and so many more. I could not do this without these people.

And then there are my readers. If you're reading this, thank you. Your support means everything. Thank you for spending your hard-earned money on my words and taking the time to read them. I appreciate you more than you know.

Special Thanks: Becky Johnson, Hot Tree Editing.
Julie Deaton, Virginia Carey, Jaime Ryter, Proofreading
Sommer Stein – Cover Design
Wander Aguiar – Photographer
Chasidy Renee – Personal Assistant
Champagne Book Design – Paperback Formatting
Leanne Trn – Content Team
Jamie, Stacy, Lauren, Franci, and Erica
Bloggers, Bookstagrammers, and TikTokers
Lacey Black & Kelly Elliott
Designs by Stacy and Ms. Betty — Graphics
My fellow authors
My amazing readers

www.ingramcontent.com/pod-product-compliance
Lightning Source LLC
Chambersburg PA
CBHW060626260626
47161CB00008B/2814